MW01128622

EVIL ELVES

A COZY CORGI MYSTERY

MILDRED ABBOTT

WINGS OF INK PUBLICATIONS, LLC

EVIL ELVES

Mildred Abbott

for
the Rolling Pin Bakeshop
and
Jay Thomas

Cover, Logo, Chapter Heading Designer: A.J. Corza - SeeingStatic.com

Main Editor: Desi Chapman

2nd Editor: Ann Attwood

3rd Editor: Corrine Harris

Recipe provided by: Rolling Pin Bakery, Denver, Co. - RollingPinBakeshop.com

Fruitcake photo provided by: Samantha Koenig

Visit Mildred's Webpage: MildredAbbott.com

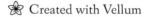 Created with Vellum

The cork exploded from the champagne bottle with an extraordinarily loud pop, causing several of us to flinch and nearly miss the arc of its trajectory across the room to where it collided with the tree topper. Beside me, Mom let out a little squeak as the glass angel shattered and cascaded down the tree.

"I doubt murdering an angel is a very good Christmas omen." Chuckling, Barry pulled Mom to his side, the fuzzy white ball from the end of his tie-dyed Santa hat bumping her forehead. "But it was kind of pretty, like the snow falling outside the window."

Shushing him, Mom and I joined the rest of the crowd turning toward Gentry Farmer, expecting an entirely different type of explosion.

To my surprise, he lifted the champagne bottle in the air, its contents overflowing and splattering over the hardwood floor as he cheered, "Now that's one way to say Merry Christmas!"

With a mixture of relief and holiday spirit, all of us gathered in the main room of the Christmas Cottage joined in with laughter, applause, and echoing the sentiments of *"Merry Christmas."*

Beside Gentry, Susanna and Noelle—his wife and teenage daughter—also appeared relieved and helped pass out champagne flutes to the crowd.

Realizing I hadn't heard a yelp of surprise or bark of anger at the commotion, I peered around Mom and Barry, squinting to see through the feet of the crowd to where Watson remained napping by the roaring fire. From the looks of it, he hadn't so much as budged.

"There's a Christmas card moment if I ever saw one." Katie, my baker best friend and business partner, took in the scene of the two dogs dreaming below the garland-festooned mantle. "I bet I can sneak a Santa hat onto Watson without waking him up. The picture of him and Snoopy snoozing there together in matching Santa hats would get a ton of attention for the Cozy Corgi on Instagram."

I snorted out a laugh and nudged Katie's shoulder. "Oh really? You bet you can sneak a hat onto my grumpy corgi without waking him? Need I remind you of what happened the last time he was forced into an outfit?"

"Technically, a hat doesn't qualify as an outfit." Katie scowled. "But it's not worth the risk. He doesn't love me nearly as much as your Smokey Bear boyfriend, and even *he* wasn't exempt from corgi wrath."

At the mention of Leo, a little ache tightened in my chest. He was visiting his family for the holidays, and I knew that time with them was typically bitter-sweet... on a good day. Plus, it was our first Christmas together as a couple—I was ready to have him home. To curl up together by the fire while the snow fell, the Christmas tree twinkled, and Watson snored happily away.

A shadow began to grow at the edges of that perfect little picture. The questions and fears of what secrets were held about Leo in that manila envelope scratching at the back of my mind, growing ever more insistent.

"Fred?" Mom squeezed my arm. "You okay?"

"Oh, yes. Of course." I mentally shook away the image of that stupid envelope my ex had given me. However, a rush of anger at my equally stupid ex flooded in, followed by another rush of anger at myself. This was why Branson had given me the horrid thing and insinuated its contents held dark secrets of Leo, to throw me off... and I was letting him.

"Are you sure?" Katie studied me. "You... don't look okay."

I refocused on Katie's concerned expression, tempted to tell her all that had been eating at me for the past weeks. I should, Katie *and* my mom. Keeping it in was just making me spin in endless circles. Instead, I forced a smile. "Yeah, I'm good. I was just... thinking about trying to get a picture of Watson, like you said. It would be cute, but I think we should be pleased enough that Watson has decided to nap his way through the evening's party instead of hiding underneath my broomstick skirt and making me stumble my way through the crowd even less gracefully than I already am."

Katie and Mom shared a glance, clearly not buying my excuse, but going along with it. "It helps that he's found another kindred spirit in Gentry and Susanna's beagle. Snoopy isn't grumpy like Watson, but since he's ancient and spends his life napping, they look like mirrored bookends snoring away on either side of the hearth."

"Here you go, Ms. Page. Ms. Pizzolato." Noelle arrived beside us, cutting the tension even further, then moved along to Mom and Barry after Katie and I took one of the champagne flutes.

"Champagne! Fancy." Katie shimmied her shoulders, eliciting a giggle from my mother.

I eyed the golden sparkling liquid with its effervescent bubbles catching the thousands of Christmas lights strung around the Christmas Cottage. "It's pretty. But I'd rather have—"

"A dirty chai." Mom and Katie spoke up in unison, then got lost in giggles once more, allowing the tension to pass, as well as any thoughts of secrets and envelopes and exes.

Barry gave me a wink over their shoulders. "It's times like these I miss Gerald's special kombucha the most. I didn't think I was that big a fan, but now that I can't have it—" His thoughts were cut off, too, when the doors to the Christmas shop opened, letting in a gust of snow as my stepsisters, Verona and Zelda, hurried in, followed by their husbands and four children. Barry gave a second wink. "You're not the only one who's predictable. My daughters, late as always."

The twins and their families joined Mom, Barry, Katie, and me in a flurry of commotion, but with the surrounding chatter, they were barely noticed.

Before we could finish greetings, the tinkling of a glass drew our attention, and the crowd quieted.

Susanna and Noelle had taken their spots directly behind and on either side of Gentry as he lowered the knife he'd clinked against his champagne flute. He tilted his cleft chin in pride as he lifted his voice. "Thank you all for coming out on this snowy night for what I hope will be the beginning of an annual holiday tradition here at the Christmas Cottage, a time for us locals—shop owners and residents alike—to set aside a little time to laugh together, reminisce on the blessings we've had over the past year, and look forward to what lies ahead."

Across the room, I noticed my uncle, Percival, elbow his husband's arm while at the same time making googly eyes to Anna and Carl Hanson. Anna gave a similar smirk, then leaned nearer, having to stand on tiptoe to whisper in Percival's ear. They both chuckled and received shushing motions from their spouses.

Thankfully, Gentry didn't seem to notice their mockery. "More than anything, I wanted this occasion to be a demonstration of my gratitude to each and every one of you for your years of patronage, your unending support of the Christmas Cottage, and your continued loyalty and friendship. We look forward to each of you continuing to make our beloved shop the place you go to fulfill all of your holiday needs."

At that, Anna and Percival nodded toward each other, clearly just having their previous gossip confirmed.

"So, with that—" Gentry lifted his champagne flute in the air once more. "—let us toast to family, festivities, and fealty!" He started to take a sip, but his wife nudged his back, and he lifted the glass once more. "And to Christmas, of course."

"To Christmas!" Everyone lifted their champagne flutes and cheered.

Something about the scene reminded me of *The Christmas Carol*. I couldn't help but glance out the shop windows, almost expecting to see Ebenezer Scrooge with the ghost of Christmas past peering in to watch the merriment of Mr. Fezziwig's party. In many ways, the setting probably wasn't too far off. The Christmas Cottage was in a beautifully refurbished Victorian house. The main space, where most of us were gathered, had probably been a living room at some point, but the rest of the shop continued throughout the smaller rooms of the home, each one having a different theme of Christmas ornaments. Countless Christmas trees and endless lights sheltered between the wooden gingerbread-trimmed doorways, stained glass windows, and rich vintage wallpaper, all of which added to the sensation that we'd magically stumbled back into Christmases of a century or more before.

Katie drained half her glass before grinning up at me. "Did we just cheers to Christmas or pledge our undying loyalty, devotion, and firstborn children to Gentry Farmer?"

"I'm pretty sure the latter." I took a second sip of champagne, once more wishing it was a dirty chai. "I've got to say, he wasn't overly subtle."

She cocked an eyebrow. "Do you think he was trying to be? His and Marty Clark's feud has been anything *but* understated. I'd say this is just one more figurative line drawn in the sand."

"Maybe that means we'll have another Christmas party at Santa's Cause pretty soon," Zelda interrupted cheerfully. "And since they seem to be insistent about outdoing one another, I'll be curious to see how Marty tops champagne and hors d'oeuvres. Of course, they won't come close to the creations Katie will whip up for the Cozy Corgi party."

As if on cue, Verona plucked two toothpick-skewered bacon-wrapped chestnuts off a tray from a server weaving through the crowd and passed one to her twin. "I, for one, am a little over it. The constant bickering and feuding between the two Christmas shops in Estes doesn't exactly infuse the town with holiday cheer, does it?"

"Neither does that." Barry pointed at the hors d'oeuvres his daughters were devouring. "Bacon is murder, dears."

"True. But it's delicious murder." Katie made a show of rubbing her hands together. "I'll be right back. Going to go chase down that little waiter and see if I can snag a tray to myself."

Before I could call after her to ask her to bring me a tray of my own, my uncles and the Hansons scurried over. "Isn't this delicious?" Percival sounded scandalized, and gleefully so. "It's like we're in the middle of our own holiday-themed soap opera. The conflict, the rivalry, the one-upmanship. Why, if we're lucky, the Christmas party Santa's Cause will have to have after this will require caviar and escargot."

The twins both made horrified faces, and I was willing to bet my own expression matched. "Katie was just wondering how you would top champagne. And if fish eggs and snails are the way to do it, I think I'll skip that party."

"Oh, my darling niece." Percival threw a long,

thin arm over my shoulders, his boysenberry faux-fur-trimmed wristwatch brushing my cheek. "I'll make a proper lady of you yet."

"She'll never measure up to you, dear." Gary said the words dryly, but there was a twinkle in his dark eyes.

"Well, of course not." Percival sniffed. "There's only room for one *queen* in town."

Though the rest of us giggled, Anna didn't join in. Her gaze narrowed to Watson before settling on me. "Now, Fred, you know I adore Watson. Utterly and completely and forever. But—"

"Anna, darling, don't start. Please." There was desperation in Carl's voice, but he withered under his wife's glare.

She whipped back toward me. "It's one thing for Snoopy to be present, he's part of the Farmer family, but *Watson*... well. That's just pure favoritism. When Gentry phoned to invite Carl and me, he specifically asked that we leave little Winston at home. I had to hire a babysitter."

"Speaking of which, I should probably call and make sure she's still alive." Carl gave a loud laugh, but it withered quickly again as Anna hissed.

They'd gotten a small, whitish blond, wire-haired terrier mutt a couple of months ago. It was a diaper-wearing, paper-shredding holy terror, one that Anna thought had hung the moon. She looked at me beseechingly. "Did Gentry ask you to leave Watson at home and you just ignored him?"

It was clear what answer she wanted me to give, probably even hoped I'd lie. But I didn't, though I tried to infuse apology in my tone. "No, Gentry said that Watson was welcome."

Anna drew herself up to her full height, her girth swelling in rage. "Well, of all the—"

"Oh, come now, Anna." Percival, who still had one arm around my shoulders, tossed his other over Anna's. "Watson's practically a celebrity in town. Not to mention, your pint-sized demon almost tore that little girl's hand off last week. You can hardly expect—"

"Winston did no such thing." Anna jerked herself free from Percival's embrace. "That evil child was poking at him, and though losing a hand would've served her right, she didn't even get a scratch."

"She was trying to *pet* him," Carl interjected, and though he sounded hesitant, he pressed on under her continued glare. "The only reason she didn't get a scratch was that I grabbed Winston before he could manage. *I'm* the one who got bit instead."

"Well, be that as it may, it's favoritism." Despite the anger in Anna's gaze, it softened somewhat as she looked over at Watson snoring away. "However, I do love that little man. I wish I'd thought to bring his favorite treats."

As we watched, at that very moment, Delilah Johnson, flanked on either side by a couple of her Pink Panther friends, all dressed in sultry Ms. Claus outfits, approached Watson.

He woke, and though he didn't give into happy hysterics, lifted his head and allowed himself to be petted.

Delilah's long red hair fell over her shoulders as her beautiful face glanced around, and she found me. She gave a tight-lipped nod, then refocused on Watson. It'd been weeks since I damaged our friendship, and if anything, the ice she sent my way had only gotten colder.

"That... that... jezebel," Anna hissed again. "I'm going to go rescue Watson from her bad influence." Before I could stop her, Anna shoved her way through the crowd, Carl following several steps behind.

"Here you go."

Katie returned with two small plates filled with an assortment of options, so I didn't bother following. Watson could handle himself with those three. Although he'd be disappointed when Anna and Carl didn't offer one of his favorite all-natural dog bone treats. "I know I always say this around food, but no wonder I love you."

Within ten minutes, Katie left, since she had to get up early to bake the next morning, and the family dispersed as we all made our way through the crowd, chatting with various friends and local acquaintances. Through it all, most of the conversations circled around the highly publicized conflict between the two Christmas shops, though always spoken of in whispers, in case one of the Farmers was near.

After enough time had passed that I felt it wouldn't be rude, I decided I'd follow Katie's example and head home—although not to get up early and cook, but to stay up late and read by the fire as the snow drifted down outside my log cabin. Maybe brew a cup of decaf chai and get Watson one of his dog bone treats, since he'd been such a trouper in this dreaded social situation.

Though I was tempted to simply ghost—gather up Watson and slip away—I decided I should probably tell the Farmers goodbye and thank them for the party. I didn't know them well, but from everything I'd heard and witnessed lately, it seemed like the family was easily offended and held on to a grudge. I didn't know if disappearing from a party would prompt some sort of ill will, but I probably shouldn't take the chance.

However, I couldn't find Susanna anywhere, and Gentry was surrounded by several of his friends—Pete Miller, who had the glassblowing studio next door, Jared Pitts, the manager at Bighorn Brewery, and Joe Singer, the owner of Rocky Mountain Imprints.

At the sight of them, I decided to risk simply leaving. Though I got along splendidly with Jared and frequently did business with Joe, Pete and I had a conflict ages ago when I confronted him about an affair, and things had been tense between us ever since.

Just as I turned to leave, Joe must've felt my attention as his gaze turned on me, and a nervous smile broke over his rather homely features. He always seemed like the odd man out in his group of friends—the others classically good-looking and carrying around the easy grace of those privileged with all that accompanied attractive, financially secure white men. Joe was as large as a giant and timid as a church mouse. With a quick word to his friends, he headed my way, his deep voice so low it could barely be heard over the background chatter. "Are you heading out?"

"I am." Though I was tall, I had to look all the way up to be able to see Joe in the face. "Do you need something?"

He shrugged his massive shoulders. "Well, I got that order of Cozy Corgi merchandise done this afternoon, but the shop was already closed. If you don't mind, I thought I might follow you and drop it off."

I hesitated, thrown off. "There's no need to leave your friends. You can run the stuff down tomorrow. Or I can ask Ben to pick it up."

The hollow of his cheeks flushed under unshaven stubble, and he scuffed his shoes on the floor. "Oh, well... I... suppose..."

He looked so disappointed that I changed directions almost instantly. "But... if it's easier for you now..."

He peered at me hopefully. "I don't want to be a bother."

Feeling like I was comforting an overgrown

puppy, I reached out and touched his thick forearm. "Not a bother at all. Just let me grab Watson."

By the time I told my family goodbye, put on my scarf and jacket, and hooked the leash on a very-unhappy-to-be-disturbed corgi, Joe was waiting for us. He held the door open, and we slipped through, Watson glaring up at the giant suspiciously. Joe merely laughed. "You know, I think I should change the expression on the corgi's face of your logo. He looks entirely too happy."

I pulled my jacket tighter as we stepped out of the shelter of the porch and onto the sidewalk as the snow swirled around us in the breeze. "There's been more than one time I've considered renaming the bookshop and bakery the *Grumpy* Corgi instead of the Cozy Corgi."

Joe laughed again, the sound nearly obliterated by the night wind, but didn't offer further comment.

For his part, Watson paused in his stride long enough to cast a narrowed chocolate gaze on me, letting me know that he might not fully be able to understand what I said but was aware he'd just been made fun of.

Most of the shops in Estes Park lay in a two-block range of Elkhorn Avenue, but a few of the outliers, like the Christmas Cottage, were set a little ways up the curve, farther toward the national park, so the three of us had a bit of a walk. Almost instantly a silence fell, and despite the fact it would have been difficult to speak because of the wind, it felt awkward and uncomfortable.

Even though Joe was typically soft-spoken, I couldn't help but feel like there was some ulterior motive behind his request to pick up the Cozy Corgi merchandise. He'd look my way, then his gaze would dart off quickly, and his nerves buzzed so much they practically generated heat. Clearly there was something, but he didn't hurry to offer it.

"So..." I raced for anything to say, desperate to fill the void. "Any good plans for Christmas? Celebrating with your... um... family?"

At his grimace, I wished I'd kept my mouth shut, or fate had intervened and caused me to slip on the ice to keep me from talking. It had been almost exactly two years ago that Joe's wife had gone to prison. I wasn't sure if he had more family in town, wasn't even sure if they were still married or if Peg was now his *ex*-wife.

Joe shuffled along a few steps before answering. "The guys take care of me. I'll probably spend Christmas morning with Pete and Margie, watch their three kids open presents, and then head over to

Gentry and Susanna's later that night." There were a few more quiet steps, Watson trotting ahead of us, unconcerned about the human awkwardness behind him. "Jared and I hung out last year, but now that he and Sarah Bantam are seeing each other... this being their first Christmas and all..."

I couldn't tell if the wind carried away the last of his thought or if he'd quit speaking. "Well... that's nice. It's always special seeing kids open presents on Christmas." It was the only comment I could come up with, and I counted it a win that I didn't mention him visiting the jail for the holiday.

We'd entered the main section of Elkhorn Avenue and were near Rocky Mountain Imprints before Joe spoke again. "What about you? I imagine you're spending Christmas with your family? With Leo and... ah... Katie?"

"I do. It's a whole big thing." I latched on to the topic, glad for its ease. "Actually took me a little while to get used to. When I was a kid, it was just Christmas with my Mom, Dad, and me. Sometimes my grandparents, but not very often. Now it's like a three-ring circus, but I kind of love it."

"Leo!" We were almost to the front door of Joe's shop when he stiffened and looked behind him. "I wasn't thinking. He must be looking for you. Although... I didn't recall seeing him tonight."

"Oh, no. Leo wasn't there. He's out of town, having an early Christmas with his family." I flinched at the surprise in Joe's eye.

"Oh." He cleared his throat. "I'm sorry. I didn't realize..." More shuffling of feet, and his gaze darted to mine, then away. "I didn't mean to pry."

"You didn't." Suddenly I figured out what he must be assuming, or I thought so. "Everything's okay with Leo and me. It is not quite time for me to meet his family, especially over the holidays." I struggled with knowing how much to say. Leo's relationship with his family was complicated, but it wasn't my place to say so.

"Oh," Joe repeated, yet again, this time sounding skeptical. "I just assumed you'd met them by this time. You and Leo have been together for a bit." He turned toward the door of the shop, shrugged again, and slid in the key. "I'll be right back. Won't take me a minute."

Left out in the cold, Watson looked up at me as if put off by the giant's bad manners.

I couldn't help but laugh as I bent down to scratch his head. "I don't think Joe meant anything by it, buddy. He's just even more socially awkward than your mama."

Watson chuffed and continued on his way, halting at the end of his leash to glare back.

"Hold on, Your Highness. We're stopping to get a whole host of things with your likeness emblazoned on them, after all. The least you could do is—" I flinched, an unwanted thought pushing its way in and making an equally unwanted image of a puzzle snap into place.

Maybe it was more than just being socially awkward. Joe had seemed rather insistent that we get the stuff from his store that night, walking through the snow on our own, and he'd asked about Leo. Surely I was just reading into things. I had to be. Joe and I barely knew each other. And after being part of the reason his wife, or ex-wife, was behind bars, surely romantic notions were the very last thing he had in mind for me. Right?

Before I could decide if the idea of Joe having feelings for me was ludicrous or had merit, Joe was back, his massive arms completely filled with boxes. "Here we go." With an awkward grace, he managed to balance the boxes while fitting in the key once more to lock the door.

"I can carry some of those for you." I reached for one of the boxes.

He sidestepped. "Nah. I've got them. Plus, they're perfectly balanced. Better not tempt fate."

Watson chuffed again as we started off, though happily that time.

Joe and I fell back into silence as we passed store after store. When we crossed the street to the block that held the Cozy Corgi, he spoke again. "Leo and Katie get along, right?"

My heart skipped a beat, and I dared a quick glance up at him, though he kept his gaze fixed straight ahead. "Yeah. They do. They're... good friends." There'd been a time before Leo and I were dating that I had wondered if there was something more between the two of them. Maybe Joe thought so as well. *Hoped* so?

"That's good. It's nice when friends get along with who you're dating." Joe paused midstep to shift the boxes, then continued. "Just like with Jared. The rest of us have only gotten to hang out with Sarah a couple of times, but we all like her. It's nice when friends get along with who you're dating." He repeated the sentiment, fell silent again for a few steps, then spoke once more. "Of course, Jared has always had good taste in women. Melody was wonderful, a little... um... cat crazy, but still. And he's always only had good things to say about you."

I had no idea how to respond to that. And it didn't help me determine if my theory was right or wrong. I was sure Jared had spoken highly of me to Joe, but I doubted Pete had, and I figured Gentry had never mentioned me at all.

As we neared the Cozy Corgi, I decided I should risk sticking my foot in my mouth once more; it wasn't like I wasn't used to the taste. If I was wrong, it would be better to be embarrassed than letting it drag on if my suspicion was correct. Even so, I tried to think of a gentle way to let Joe down. "That is true. I know I love that Katie and Leo get along so well. Leo's never jealous of the time I spend with her, and Katie never feels like a third wheel when the three of us hang out." What I was saying was true, but I decided to oversell it. "That's part of what helps me know that Leo and I are meant to be. The fact that we can—" With the hand looped through Watson's leash, I pulled out my keys, and with my other gripped on the door handle of the bookshop, I froze as it turned in my grasp.

"You forgot to lock up?" Joe didn't miss a beat.

"No. I'm pretty sure I remembered." I pushed

the door for confirmation, and sure enough, it swung open.

Watson growled, his ears instantly folding back on his skull.

I looked down at him, fear slicing through all concerns about Joe's possible interest in me. "Oh no. Watson only does—"

He growled again, and only then did I catch the difference.

I'd been about to say Watson only growled like that when he sensed a dead body, but there was a different tremor to it. Even so, I didn't move forward. "Maybe I should call Susan... er... Detective Green." Memories of Watson and me hiding in the bookshop as we were robbed over a year ago flitted through my mind. If either of us had made a noise or been discovered, we would've been shot.

"This is getting ridiculous." Anger sounded in Joe's voice, surprising me, and he shocked me further by maneuvering around and stepping inside. He laid the boxes on the floor with a crash before smacking his hand against the wall. "Where's the light switch? I think I see what's going on."

Still growling and ears still folded, Watson slinked forward, joining Joe inside the Cozy Corgi.

No chance if someone was midrobbery they

hadn't heard *that* commotion, so I followed, reached to the side, and turned on the light.

I didn't see anything at first, nothing out of place, no books scattered, the cash register wasn't overturned, and there was no dead body.

Maybe in the bakery? Wouldn't be the first time.

"Yep. Just what I thought. *Again.*" Once more, anger sounded in Joe's deep voice, and he stomped over to the main counter, Watson following him and pulling me along with the leash. "This is seriously getting ridiculous. Bunch of moron kids breaking in every night and leaving these stupid elves everywhere like private property is some sort of a joke."

Only then did I see it, sitting on top of the ornate cash register.

A little elf, nothing more than a huge beard, with two green felt shoes poking out from beneath the mass of white fluff and an equally oversized pointed green hat that appeared to be smashed so low it covered the elf's entire face to his tiny pink nose. Beside it, lay a small ribbon-wrapped loaf of fruitcake.

"Santa left you fruitcake? Apparently, you've been a good girl this year." Athena winked her thick false eyelashes at me as she lifted a fishbowl-sized margarita my way. "Although, I'd say it's a little unfair to the rest of us. With all the murders you solve, that kind of stacks the deck in your favor."

"Nah." Paulie had just scooped a huge portion of queso onto a chip, and as he paused with it halfway to his mouth, a large dollop fell and plopped onto the tablecloth. "Fred's good even without solving murders. She's one of the sweetest people in town."

I reached across the table and patted his arm and managed to drag my sleeve through the spilled cheese. "You're always sweet, Paulie."

"Even when you're delusional." Katie leered at me playfully. "You only think she's sweet because of all the pastries she eats."

"And whose fault is that?" Chuckling, I used my napkin to wipe the queso off my sleeve, or at least attempted to. Watson shot up from below my chair, darting his head under the napkin, snuffling and licking, trying to get at the cheese. "Watson! Stop it!" I hissed at him and attempted to push him back down.

He only snorted and darted his tongue out again, managing to snag some cheese that time.

Feeling my cheeks heat, I snatched one of the chips and tossed it under the chair, hoping to distract him.

After a final lick, it worked, and he disappeared once more. I was certain I heard the sound of victory as he chomped away.

I glanced around Habaneros to see if anyone noticed. It didn't seem like they had. "I know Marcus and Hester are always telling me Watson is welcome, and not just on the patio, but still. With the snowy roads, it just seemed simpler to come directly here from the Cozy Corgi instead of going home, dropping him off, and then coming all the way back."

"Nah, nobody minds Watson." Paulie beamed at me, his newly whitened teeth glowing—he might have overdone the bleaching, but it was a vast improvement and made him much more approachable. "He's a local icon, just like you."

"Like that matters." Athena waved Paulie off, grabbed a chip, and without looking, lowered it below her chair. After a second, more crunching could be heard. "Pearl goes with me everywhere, and *she's* not a celebrity. If a place wants my patronage, we're a packaged pair."

"Sure, but your little poodle fits in your handbag and doesn't shed like she's attempting to make a fur rug." Glancing down, I couldn't see the tiny white dog, but as Watson was curled up next to Athena's purse, there was no doubt where Pearl was.

"If I tried to do that, no one would let me go anywhere." Paulie only sounded slightly dejected.

"That's because Flotsam and Jetsam are insane. Sweet, but insane." Katie barked out a laugh. "Although, with them, you're only in danger of getting licked to death. Much different than with Anna and Carl's new dog."

The waitress arrived at that moment, and from the look she cast below Athena's and my chairs, it was clear she wasn't enamored of Watson's celebrity status. "Are you all ready to order, or would you like some more time with the queso?"

Athena lifted her margarita. "As long as you keep these flowing, you can take all the time you need. Besides, it's not like you're in a rush for tables. We'll finish the queso, then order." She gestured around the brightly colored restaurant. Thanks to the snowstorm, the place was only half full. "Oh, but Pearl would like a couple of strips of grilled chicken while we wait."

"Pearl?" The waitress had been turning away, and angled back, confused.

Athena pointed below her chair. "And a few extra strips for her boyfriend."

The protest was easily seen rising to the waitress's lips, but then she closed her mouth, gave a tight nod, and turned away again.

Athena giggled.

Katie did as well. "You're terrible. You just did that to get under her skin."

"And I think you've had enough of these." Paulie attempted to remove Athena's margarita and got his hand smacked.

"You try that again, and I'll contact Santa myself and make sure he leaves you coal." Athena took another sip. "You *and* our waitress."

Paulie rubbed his hand but grinned good-naturedly. "Personally, I don't see the difference. I mean, I understand that getting coal in stockings isn't exactly a compliment, but it's not like fruitcake is any better. Both are about as hard as a—"

Katie sucked in a breath and reached out to smack Paulie's other hand. "Don't you finish that sentence. Fruitcake gets a bad rap. That's only because it's often baked by people who don't know what they're doing." She scowled toward me. "As evidenced by the... thing masquerading as fruitcake Santa left at the Cozy Corgi last night. Nasty." She refocused on Paulie. "When done correctly, it's delicious, and really manages to capture the holiday feel."

Paulie moved both his hands under the table. "Well, that's just because it's you. *You* could even make actual coal taste good."

Katie shrugged in a way that suggested Paulie might be right. "I'll show you. I haven't made it in a few years, but I have a recipe that will knock your socks off."

"They are cute little elves." Athena didn't offer any opinion on fruitcake or coal. "The articles *The Chipmunk Chronicles* ran about them have been a hit."

"I think they're a little creepy, personally. Nothing more than a big old beard wearing hats and shoes, they don't bring to mind elves to me at all." Katie's scowl deepened. "And what Santa's Cause is charging for them is simply ludicrous."

"Nope. You're wrong." Athena giggled and bopped Katie on the nose. "They're cute."

Katie went wide-eyed and rubbed the end of her nose. "Athena Rose, I do believe you're a little drunk."

"More than a little, but not drunk, dear." Athena fluttered her eyelashes, considering. "Let's say *jingled*. It's more festive and in keeping with the season."

All of us laughed before Paulie brought us back to the topic at hand. "I didn't get a chance to come over all day and get the gossip. You found it last night, during the party at the Christmas Cottage?"

I nodded. "Yeah. Joe Singer was delivering some Cozy Corgi merchandise. When we got to the bookshop, the front door was unlocked and there was that little elf and a fruitcake sitting on the cash register."

Paulie grinned toward Athena. "You're kind of right. Even hearing about the elf is a little bit cute." Then his brow creased. "Although, I know nearly everybody was at the Christmas Cottage, but that's hard to believe no one saw Santa Claus walk through the front door of the Cozy Corgi."

"Number one"—Katie lifted a finger—"that's someone *dressed* like Santa Claus, not actually Santa Claus. And maybe they do that every time, maybe they don't. That was just what was on the security feed from when he broke into Delilah's shop. Maybe whoever it is doesn't dress up every time." Katie lowered her voice to an annoyed whisper. "And why Delilah deserves a fruitcake instead of coal, I'll never know." She brought her voice back up to normal volume. "And two, the back door of the Cozy Corgi was also unlocked. So chances are high *the person dressed as Santa* came in through there, and only unlocked the front door from the inside for appearances."

"Still," Paulie said, nonplussed, "there's been an elf left somewhere every night this month, and December's already half over. You would think Santa would be caught by now."

"*Someone—*"

"Fine, Katie." Paulie laughed. "The someone *dressed* like Santa would be caught by now."

"I don't think they're all that worried about it." I helped myself to more queso as I spoke. "Susan didn't come by when I called the station last night. She just sent Officer Cabot to take some photos and make a report."

"Well... no wonder *Santa* hasn't been caught by now." Athena sent Katie a look, daring to be corrected. "From what I've heard about dear little

Officer Campbell Clifton Cabot, he's barely able to find the star on his badge."

"I don't know. Campbell's pretty nice." Paulie's smile softened. "He has a teddy bear hamster named Cujo. He comes in and gets special treats and toys for him nearly every week."

"Here we go." The waitress arrived as if out of nowhere and plopped a small plate of grilled chicken fajita meat on the table. "Would the *humans* like to order now?"

"Absolutely, thank you." I spoke up as it looked like Athena was about to take offense. "I'll do your green chili bowl, and a side of carnitas empanada."

"Oh!" Katie clapped her hands. "That sounds perfect on this snowy night. I'll do the same."

Watson's head popped up again, and with his paws propped on the side of my chair, he was able to strain just enough for his shiny black nose to nudge the plate of chicken.

The waitress sniffed and relocated to the other side of the table, between Katie and Paulie.

Hurrying, before he made a scene, I yanked the plate off the table and laid it on the floor between him and Athena's purse. Proving Athena's assertion that Watson was Pearl's boyfriend, my chubby corgi inhaled three of the six strips of chicken and then sat back as the little poodle popped out of the purse and began to eat slowly. Watson didn't even whine as if refraining from devouring the entire plate cost him anything.

Noticing, Athena wordlessly lowered her hand and scratched Watson's head with her long scarlet nails in way of thanks as she ordered.

As the waitress headed toward the kitchen, the hostess led three young men across the dining room to a table right in front of the large rainforest mural. One of them, a handsome black man, left his friends and headed our way. He smiled down at the dogs and stuck his hand out toward me. "We've only met once, but I'm—"

"Trevor." Smiling, I took his hand. "I remember. You're the artist who makes the elves."

He grinned self-consciously. "I guess with everything going on I should expect everyone to know who I am by this point." With another smile, he looked around the table and greeted each of the others, having to be reminded of their names, before he refocused on me. "I just wanted to apologize. I heard the Cozy Corgi was the latest... um..."

"Santa sighting?" Katie offered.

Trevor grinned, relieved. "Yeah. That's a good way to put it." He stiffened. "Oh, I should be apologizing to you, too. You're the baker in the top portion of the shop, right?"

Katie took his offered hand. "I am. But there's no reason for you to apologize, unless you're Santa?"

"Not hardly." He patted his flat stomach. "Although I can't help but feel responsible. They're my elves being left all over town. It's a little embarrassing, to say the least."

"The only real thing to be embarrassed about is the quality of fruitcake your elves bring." Katie didn't miss a beat. "You might want to talk to Santa about that."

"I'll see what I can do." Trevor laughed good-naturedly and looked back and forth between Katie and me. "Well, I'm sorry again. If you guys decide you want an elf of your own, of course it would be from a different collection, but come on into Santa's Cause. I'm sure Marty will give you a discount." Before he turned away, he knelt to pet the dogs. Watson, true to form, evaded his hand, but Pearl accepted the affection readily enough.

As he walked away, I started to say something, then noticed Paulie's face go pale. Following his gaze, I looked to the two men, a brunet and a ginger, at the table waiting for Trevor to join them. I barely caught one of them leering at Paulie and gesturing at his own teeth, before he realized I was looking and dropped his hand. I turned to Paulie once more. "Isn't that Jake? The new guy at Delilah's shop?"

Paulie nodded, cheeks burning. "Yeah."

"I didn't notice him come in." Athena whirled around in her chair and made a motion like she was going to get up. Paulie shot out a hand and grabbed her arm. She tried to shake him off, but couldn't. "You let me go. I'm going to give that piece of trash a piece of my mind."

"Don't." Paulie kept hold of her until she stilled. "It'll just make it worse."

Katie craned around to look as well, attempting to make the motion nonchalant, and failing utterly. "Why? What's going on?"

For a moment, it looked like Paulie wasn't going to answer, but then he shrugged. "Nothing I haven't experienced a million times before. It's like elementary school all over again." He snorted out a dark laugh. "And junior high, and high school, *and* every phase after." Another shrug. "Jake's just a bully. Nothing new there. He made fun of my teeth before I started whitening them, and now makes even more fun of them."

"Are you serious?" I had half a mind to steal

Athena's idea and stomp over there. "He's gotta be pushing thirty, and he's acting like that to you?"

"Makes sense that he works for Delilah." Katie bit out the words.

I started to contradict her, but didn't. Delilah and I weren't in a good place right then, but she wasn't cruel or mean.

"Who's the redhead?" Athena was still turned around, glaring. "Oh, never mind. I just needed to squint. Finnegan. Marty's nephew."

"Is Finnegan like that to you, too? Or Trevor?" I held Paulie's gaze. "If so, I guarantee it will stop if we talk to Marty. There was enough drama around him opening a second Christmas shop here in town with the conflict between him and Gentry. He doesn't need any more bad press."

"No. I haven't met Trevor before. Finnegan is sometimes there when Jake... does what he does... but he doesn't really join in." He gave me a beseeching look. "Just like I said to Athena, it would only make it worse. Please don't say anything to Marty."

"Well, Jake's an idiot." Katie reached across the table and took Paulie's hand. "Your teeth look wonderful. You're very handsome."

Paulie flinched, but smiled anyway. He was a

long way from handsome, un-stained teeth or not, and we all knew it. "Thanks, Katie." The smile that crossed his face then was genuine and happy. "I never dreamed I'd have friends like you all." He flinched again and looked down at his lap in surprise, and his smile grew. "And you too, little buddy."

Watson had propped his head on Paulie's knee. True to form, though Watson rarely gave Paulie the time of day, he could be relied on to realize when someone was hurting and needed the magic of corgi love.

The rest of dinner never regained the ease that had been there before Trevor, Finnegan, and Jake had entered, but it was pleasant enough. And as I sat in front of the fire reading that night, with Watson snoring at my feet, I made up my mind to go to Madame Delilah's Old Tyme Photography and try to make things better for Paulie, even if Delilah and I hadn't spoken in a couple of months.

Doubtlessly, I had the exact same feeling every season, but as Watson and I walked into the Cozy Corgi Bookshop the following morning and the sensation of *Christmastime is my favorite* washed over me, I believed it was the truest of them all. Though I liked to pretend I should've renamed it the Grumpy Corgi, in truth, *Cozy*, was literally perfect, and never truer than at Christmastime.

My bookshop, like the Christmas Cottage, had been a home at one point, or at least designed that way. However, unlike the Christmas store, which had a large front room and then smaller rooms as you wandered back, the Cozy Corgi was more proportional. A large, long vestibule or cathedral-type room in the center had offshoots at the front, where the large windows looked out over Elkhorn Avenue. Then, arranged symmetrically, were two rooms on either side that led to the back—my favorite, on the left rear, held one of the two fireplaces, and even as I stood captivated at the front door, with Watson staring at me like I'd lost my mind, not for the first time, I could see the fire crackling in front of the antique sofa and purple portobello lamp, surrounded by countless mystery novels. In the center of it all was the long, grand staircase, leading up to the bakery. Behind that, though mostly tucked out of view, was the recently installed elevator, around which Katie had temporarily hung brick-patterned paper over the walls so the rider felt they were going up the Christmas chimney.

Maybe that was it. Katie's bakery was why Christmas was my favorite season. With the lighted garland looping over gleaming bookshelves, a large Christmas tree in the center, sparkling above the hardwood floors, and cut-out paper snowflakes—that Katie, Ben, Nick, and I added to every year—dangling from the ceiling, and topping it off, the aromas of cinnamon, clove, yeast, sugar, and... let's face it, carby, buttery, love, the Cozy Corgi Bookshop and Bakery was quite literally the most perfect place in the world.

The sound of Watson's nails scrambling up the steps brought my attention back to the moment. He cast an accusatory glance over his shoulder right before he disappeared from view. He'd obviously decided I'd gone brain-dead and that it was pointless to wait before he begged Katie for a treat. Well, who was I to disagree?

Following his lead, I crossed the bookshop and started up the stairs. It showed the power of Katie's dirty chais that I merely glanced into the mystery room with longing instead of curling up on the sofa with a book and probably dozing by the fire within a few seconds. But I had only ten minutes or so before we opened, and while it wasn't high tourist season for books, the locals would be pouring in for their daily routine of pastries, coffee, and gossip in Katie's bakery. I needed to get as many dirty chais in me while I had the chance.

Ben must've been in the backroom when we'd come in, because just as I entered the bakery, the sound system clicked on and Amy Grant's "Grown-Up Christmas List" softly filled the Cozy Corgi. Ah... now it truly was holiday perfection.

Sure enough, as I started to greet Katie and Nick, Ben's footsteps sounded up the steps and Watson scrambled away from the bakery counter, forgetting his longed-after treat, completely rushing past me as if I was a ghost, and greeted one of the three humans he treated with deity-like worship. The way Ben instantly fell to his knees and elicited a cloud of corgi fur in greeting confirmed the feeling was mutual.

With a smile their way, I turned back and waved at Nick, who was arranging cinnamon rolls, bear claws, and almond croissants over the marble countertop. "Good morning, you two."

"Morning." Katie slid a steaming mug my way and returned to icing white stripes on candy-cane-shaped cherry danishes.

The heat of the ceramic warmed my hands as the spices did the same to my senses. Taking a sip, I remembered this was the one final detail to truly make the Christmassy morning perfect. With a contented sigh, I leaned against the countertop and took another drink.

"Well...?" Katie looked at me, an eyebrow cocked and one fist on her hip.

I straightened, trying to figure out my faux pas. "Oh, sorry." I tilted the dirty chai her way. "Thank you!"

"No, not that." She rolled her eyes. "You didn't even notice..."

Over her shoulder, I spied Nick's grin, and he looked meaningfully at something as if trying to give me a hint. Unfortunately, I couldn't tell exactly where his stare was pointed. Maybe Katie's hair? I started to comment on that, then didn't. Her chocolate-brown spirals were adorable, but no more so than normal. Then went to the obvious. "Oh! Your shirt, it's new. Very... cute."

"No." Another eye roll. "Well, yes, it is. On both accounts." She gestured down at the green T-shirt emblazoned with the hippo who'd affixed wire wings and a halo to himself and attempted to play the angel on top of the Christmas tree, only to have it bend in half under his weight. "The mug!"

"Oh." I held the mug out to get a better look. "You know me, caffeine first and foremost above all things, except maybe books. I hardly have time to look at what I'm drinking out of before..." I cocked my head and burst out a little laugh. "Oh. My. Lord."

Ben and Watson joined us at the counter, and I held the mug down to him. "Watson, have you seen this? Did you give Katie permission? Are you getting paid in dog treat royalties for your likeness?"

I hadn't been thinking, and at his favorite word, Watson let out a happy bark and hopped on his front paws.

"Here you go." Without needing a second bark, Katie snagged one of the homemade all-natural dog bone treats and handed it to me over the counter.

In turn, I offered it to Watson, who snatched it, gave another hop, and then scurried across the bakery to settle under his favorite table near the window and chomp away. I refocused on the mug, which was emblazoned with a cartoon image of Watson, sitting like a teddy bear, with a Santa hat and a big fuzzy beard that looked suspiciously like the elf figurine that had been left on the cash register beside the fruitcake. It was ridiculous, and if I was being honest, adorable. I looked at Katie, who was offering one of her trademark cocked eyebrows. "Don't you think it's a little soon to rub salt in the wound?"

"What salt? What wound?" Katie sputtered. "There's no wound. No one's been hurt. Sure, there've been break-ins, but Santa hasn't even stolen anything." She caught herself with a shake of her head. "I mean, the *person dressing up as Santa* hasn't even stolen anything. They're just leaving elves, fruitcake, and coal. Really, I think we should be thankful. If it keeps going the rest of the month, I bet tourist season in Estes Park next Christmas will be just as busy as it is in summer. I heard there was a report about it on the Denver news stations the other night. If it keeps going, it might turn national." Katie gestured to the far wall, where some of the bakery items emblazoned with the Cozy Corgi logo were for sale, now complete with an entire shelf of Watson the Elf mugs. "And if so, I'm prepared."

"They are really cute." Ben walked over and picked up a red one. "Since they come in four colors, I might have to get a whole set."

He wasn't wrong. I kind of wanted a whole set as well, though I wasn't going to admit it quite yet. Katie was right, no one had been hurt and nothing had been stolen, but still... Someone was breaking into a different store or home every single night. "When did you even do this?"

"The other evening when I was designing this beauty"—Katie gestured toward her shirt—"with Joe and filling out the next order of Cozy Corgi merchandise. We were throwing around ideas for another T-shirt, and the elf idea came up. But then we decided it would be better to put on mugs and stuff to sell. He drew it and then put in a rush order."

At the mention of Joe, a bit of unease gurgled to the surface. I'd never gotten the chance to clarify to Joe where things stood between Leo and me the other night. Maybe I didn't need to; perhaps I'd been reading into things. Katie had always told me I was oblivious when someone was hitting on me, chances were high I'd misunderstood. I hoped.

"Well…" I took another sip of the dirty chai, letting the spicy warmth soothe my worries. There was no death, and things were good between Leo and me. I didn't need to go looking for trouble. "I agree. They are cute."

"Good, I'm glad you think so." Katie beamed. "The placemats that I ordered with you in the same pose should be in next week, pushing it a little too close to Christmas, I know, but I think they'll be a hit."

I choked, and for the first time the spices and dirty chai betrayed me by trying to go up my nose. "Excuse me?"

Katie nodded, all wide-eyed innocence. "You really do look charming with a beard, Fred. I made it long enough to cover up your broomstick skirt. We can't have mustard hues on Christmas merchandise, after all."

I gaped at her, but when I noticed the twins both covering their mouths to keep from laughing, I caught on. "Oh for crying out loud, Katie Pizzolato! I swear if you didn't keep me well-stocked with caffeine and carbs…"

"You'd what?" She smirked. "Murder me and then solve the case yourself? As I'm sure I've pointed out before, that wouldn't count."

I laughed. "Plus, it would make Susan entirely too happy to arrest me."

"I don't know." Ben considered as he knelt when Watson, apparently finished with his treat, trundled back Ben's way. "I think Detective Green would miss you."

"Miss me?" I laughed again. "She'd stick me in a jail cell and come back every hour on the hour to bonk me on the head with her baton stick."

"Now there's an idea." Katie's tone turned playful again. "Maybe I'll talk to Joe and see if he can design a T-shirt with you behind bars. It can be a Christmas present for Susan."

All four of us laughed at that, but a commotion outside pulled our attention.

I checked the clock. "Goodness, running late, that must be people trying to get in." Although, that didn't make sense. I hadn't heard anyone knocking. Instead of going downstairs, I went to the windows and looked down on the street below. It didn't take long to notice exactly where the fuss was located. Without looking away, I motioned behind me. "You guys will want to see this."

Within a second, the twins, Katie, and I all stared down at the crowd growing in front of Cabin and Hearth. Even Watson propped his front paws on the window ledge, but he only gazed up at Ben instead of trying to see out the window.

Anna, her large gingham dress billowing in the winter morning breeze, clutched a shivering diaper-clad Winston above one breast and shook something black in her other hand as she ranted at George Fletcher—a reporter at *The Chipmunk Chronicles*. Behind her, unable to capture the manufactured rage of his wife, Carl grinned as he held up another elf for the growing crowd to see.

"Looks like your Watson elf mugs are right on time." Nick spoke softly from where his nose pressed against the window.

Katie murmured in agreement, then angled toward me. "Do you think Anna and Carl are going to pretend like they didn't call *The Chipmunk Chronicles* the second they found the elf?"

"Maybe, maybe not." I shook my head but couldn't suppress a grin. "Either way, I guarantee you they phoned the paper before they called the police."

"Are you kidding?" She snorted out a laugh. "They've *still* not called, probably won't until the crowd has dispersed."

. . .

The crowd dispersed around twenty minutes later, and the majority of it stumbled right across the street and through the front door of the Cozy Corgi, past the garland-laden bookshelves, up the stairs—or chimneyfied elevator—and into the bakery. Anna and Carl didn't even bother opening Cabin and Hearth. They simply followed everyone else in and were more than happy to remain the center of attention in the bakery.

"Mark my words, Santa is going to go too far one day." Still holding Winston in one hand as he licked her face in adoration, Anna continued to shake the lump of coal in the other. "I ask you, what cause had he to leave us *this* instead of fruitcake? What have we ever done to Santa? I mean, really... Carl dresses as the man himself every Christmas to visit the kids in the hospital."

Katie let out an annoyed huff before muttering to me, "I don't know why it bothers me so much that they keep talking about this person as if he's actually Santa. It's not like it matters since Santa isn't real, but *Santa isn't real*. I mean, *come on*, we're a bunch of adults who keep referencing Santa breaking into all of our homes and stores."

"If Santa breaks into Scoops, personally, I'd rather him leave me a lump of coal than a fruitcake."

Alex, the typically quiet ice-cream store owner, gave an exaggerated shudder.

"Number one." Katie, apparently having had enough, lifted her voice. "It's someone *dressed* as Santa. And number two, *more importantly*, fruitcake is actually very delightful if done properly."

Poor Alex went scarlet at the admonition.

Anna whirled on me as if I'd been the one who'd spoken, then stomped my way. "And really, just the night before, *you* got fruitcake." Her gaze darted to Katie, then back to me. "Whoever this Santa fiend is, they're clearly playing favorites."

At her absence, Carl stepped into the limelight and started in on an overly dramatic retelling of him and Anna finding the elf.

"You should look into it, Fred." Surprisingly okay with allowing her husband to take the starring role, Anna remained at the counter with Katie and me, her voice lowered to a normal volume. "Really, you owe it to the town. By this point, we depend on you to uncover truths and secrets."

"Anna, please." I couldn't help it, I laughed at the sincerity in her voice.

Winston stopped licking his mama's cheek and snarled at me, then gave a sharp yip.

Anna nodded approvingly, as if thanking him for

his support. "Scoff all you want, but we have a serial... criminal in our midst. Who knows, maybe he's in this bakery this very minute." Obviously the thought had just hit her, as her gaze went wide and she looked around, then lowered her voice as she settled on the owner of the scrapbook shop. "I bet it's that Beulah Gerber. She's always had it in for me."

Katie laughed. "Beulah? What did you do to get on her bad side?"

Anna whipped back around. "*Me*? Why would you assume *I'm* the one who did something? Maybe it was *her*."

That time, Winston turned his growl on Katie. The scraggly little dog truly did have terrifyingly crooked teeth.

Katie whipped out one of the all-natural dog bone treats and held it out to Winston as a peace offering. He just snarled, and attempted to bite Katie's fingers on the other side of the bone.

From below, Watson whimpered plaintively.

Not bothering to make any more of an effort with Winston, Katie tossed the treat down to Watson.

Thrilled, Watson started to head over to his favorite table, but when he realized it was occupied, he returned, sheltered beneath my broomstick skirt, and began to crunch away.

Undeterred, Anna refocused on me. "I'm serious, Winifred. You need to look into it. It's not right for whoever this is to be drawing lines in the sand, dividing us up, labeling some of us good and the others evil."

I smiled at her gently, reminding myself that I often found Anna's overly dramatic manner charming, sometimes, even if this wasn't one of those moments. "I think that might be reading a little too much into it. I imagine it's more random than that, and for sure, not labeling people as good or evil."

"Well, maybe so." Anna nuzzled into the little dog's neck as if seeking comfort. "Otherwise why would that Delilah woman get fruitcake and I got coal?"

"I can't argue with you there." Katie merely shrugged when I gave her a dirty look. "Well, I can't. Even so, I know it's not a pleasant thought—someone breaking into stores and homes. It's still violating, but all they're doing is leaving an elf and some fruitcake or coal. Instead of breaking and entering, think of it as an elfing. They're just... elfifying."

"That's easy for you to say. The *Cozy Corgi* got fruitcake." Nuzzling Winston seemed to have calmed Anna somewhat, and she looked back out at the crowd. "But it is good for business. Or at least could be. Maybe we can have a big Elf Walk, or something, during the week between Christmas and New Year. We could advertise it and get more tourists up here. Have little pamphlets with a self-guided tour of all the places that Santa broke into. At least all the *shops* Santa broke into."

At her words, I flinched.

Katie and Anna both looked toward me. "What?" they questioned in unison.

I didn't answer for a moment, eyeing the new display of Watson the Elf mugs. It seemed a crazy notion. So crazy that I nearly discarded it without saying anything. But on second thought, I decided it was less crazy and just more... silly. "What if..." I glanced over to where Carl had finally sat down at one of the tables and the occupants were examining the little elf. "What if that's exactly what this is? Just a... I don't know what you call it, publicity stunt, an advertising ploy?"

Anna and Katie both followed my gaze toward the elf.

I felt that bubbling of excitement and didn't give them a chance to respond. "Katie, do you have a paper and a pen back there?"

She pulled one out from underneath the cash register. "Of course." She also reached over and plated one of the cherry candy cane danishes and placed it beside the paper, tearing off a chunk for herself. "We need this too."

I took the pen and began to scribble. "Okay, who do we have so far? The Cozy Corgi, Cabin and Hearth, Delilah's..."

"The Koffee Kiln," Anna offered, then scrunched up her nose. "*They* got a fruitcake. Now I ask you, why would Santa give Delilah and Carla a fruitcake and not me?"

Katie didn't bother to answer, just nudged the Christmassy danish toward Anna and continued throwing out other places that had been elfified, as she'd said. "Aspen Gold, Pinecone Manor, Prime Slice, and Knit Witt."

"Also Shuttle Bug, Dr. Sallee's home," Anna piped in again, chewing happily on the pastry, as Winston licked at the icing on her fingertips. "Oh, and old Duncan Diamond's home as well. All three of *them* got fruitcake."

"Good point," I jotted down the names on the growing list. "We should also include if they got fruitcake or coal. That might be a clue if it's not actually random."

Katie grinned.

"What?"

Her grin widened as she answered, "Looks like Anna's right. You *are* going to investigate."

"I'm not... I'm just..." I glanced down at the list, realizing that was kind of what I was doing. "We're just speculating, having some fun." I rushed on before she could comment. "The Christmas Cottage was the first place that was broken into. We don't have that on the list yet. What did Santa leave there?"

When neither of them spoke, I looked up in time to see Anna and Katie exchange glances. It was Katie who spoke. "I... don't remember."

From beneath my skirt, Watson growled, and poked his head out the back. Winston joined, his snarl sounding like he was attempting to harmonize.

I turned to find Detective Susan Green, glaring at us, hand on her hips. "You really can't help yourself, can you, Winifred Page? I thought it was only murders you had to stick your nose in."

I flushed, as if I'd been caught doing something embarrassing. "It's not like I'm infringing on your case uninvited."

"Just because the police heard about the latest break-in through the grapevine instead of a call to dispatch—" She cast another quick glare at Anna. "—doesn't mean it's not my case. Luckily, though we've got plenty, I can't sit back and kick my feet up just because we don't have a murder."

"Oh?" I couldn't help myself. "If it's your case, why didn't you come when I called dispatch the night before last?"

"Because it's *not* a murder." Susan snarled toward Winston, "Oh, shut up. I'll put up with it from fleabag down there, but not from you."

Anna sucked in an offended breath.

Susan ignored her before glaring at the reaming curve of the danish. "Seriously? Candy cane pastries? Why must *everything* be so irritatingly cutesy this time of year?" She snagged the remaining piece, popped it in her mouth, and let out an involuntary groan of pleasure as she glanced over my shoulder at the list. "In answer to your question, neither."

"What?" I looked at her in confusion.

"Neither." Susan tapped a finger beside where I'd written *The Christmas Cottage*. "There was only an elf, no fruitcake or coal."

Katie chuckled again and nudged me across the counter. "I know that look, Fred. Murder or not, you're going to look into it."

"Oh, what a shocking Christmas miracle that is." Despite the annoyance in Susan's words, I thought I caught just a hint of a grin forming at the corner of her lips before she motioned from Anna to Carl. "Come on. Get your husband and let's go to your store and file an official complaint. And if that rangy mutt keeps growling at me, I'm going to have it tested for rabies."

As the three of them—four, counting Winston—passed by toward the stairs, Carl looked utterly heartbroken to be pulled away from his captive audience. When I turned back around, I found Katie still grinning at me. I didn't see any reason to protest. "Well, you've got to admit, it is curious. And why, do you suppose, didn't Santa leave fruitcake or coal at Gentry and Susanna's shop."

"No idea. But I'm sure you'll figure it out, as well as who *Santa* truly is." Katie's grin transitioned to more of a smirk as she slid behind the espresso machine. "I'll make you another dirty chai. I imagine it takes a lot of energy to chase around a bunch of elves."

Fresh snow fell that evening as I sat in my over-stuffed armchair at home in front of the fire. With Leo being gone the past week, it had felt like a revival of sorts into my old life, when I'd first moved to Estes Park. Days spent at the bookshop and then long hours reading by the fire while Watson snored each night—at least when I wasn't trying to solve a murder.

In truth, for the past several days, I'd merely been going through the motions. Turning pages in my book, sometimes making it through an entire chapter before realizing I couldn't remember a single word I'd read, and then having to start again. My mind kept going to that manila envelope I'd hidden in my closet right after Halloween, and the effort of batting my thoughts away from it made concentrating on a novel, no matter how potentially engrossing, a near impossibility.

As the snow drifted down in front of my window, thick enough to obscure the forest surrounding my little log cabin, that distraction wasn't an issue, and my psyche practically sang out in gratitude. There was no book in my lap, instead a pile of *The Chipmunk Chronicles* I'd gotten from Percival and Gary—who saved old newspapers to wrap fragile dishes at their antique store. I'd already gone through the pile once, but started over again, making a timeline on the notepad I'd balanced on the arm of the chair.

As I opened the oldest paper, one dated a little before Halloween, Watson's snores broke off halfway through, and he lifted his head to glare. From his spot on the hearth, only half his face was lit by the fire, but it was enough to see the reproach in one of his gleaming eyes.

"I'm sorry, buddy." I leaned forward, trying to balance the newspapers while reaching to scratch his head. "I know these things are louder than a book. I'm not trying to disrupt your dreams."

Just as my fingers nearly made contact, the pile of papers began to slip from my lap and I flung myself backward to keep them from falling onto the floor, accidentally whacking the tip of one of Watson's ears in the process.

Watson sat up, affronted, let out a huff, and then stalked off to the bedroom.

"I'm sorry!" I called out again, feeling just a touch pathetic at the pleading I heard in my voice. "You know me, with my luck they'd have fallen into the fire and burned the whole house down."

A loud chuff issued from the bedroom.

I considered attempting amends but didn't have it in me to get up, hunt for whatever food I thought would appease, and then plead with His Majesty only to have to come back again and get resettled with the papers once more. Instead I refocused and began scribbling.

Within five or ten minutes, I had a pretty good grasp of the situation, and it all seemed to spread out crystal clear. Granted, hindsight is twenty-twenty and all, but if someone had been paying attention, they almost would've been able to predict the events.

The first article, written by George Fletcher—besides being about as dry as year-old beef jerky—briefly reported about an entire collection of elves being stolen from Santa's Cause, the new Christmas shop in town. Two days later, the next article emerged, this time written by Rhonda Biggler, who often reported on town news but frequently with a slightly gossipy and more entertaining style. She described the ins and outs of an altercation between Gentry Farmer, who owned the Christmas Cottage, and Marty Clark, who owned Santa's Cause. I vaguely remembered hearing about the squabble at the time, but I had not paid any attention as I'd been looking into a murder at the Italian restaurant. From the way Rhonda laid it out, Marty publicly accused Gentry of being behind the theft of his elf collection, and Gentry responded by storming into the new Christmas shop, going on a profanity-laced tirade, and punching Marty right on the nose. As it was written by Rhonda and not George, she went into great detail about Marty flailing backward and landing in the middle of a life-sized Nativity set, knocking over a camel and landing safely on top of the manger.

I couldn't help but laugh at the mental image of it.

Another huff issued from the bedroom. Apparently I wasn't supposed to be enjoying myself during my enforced seclusion.

I refocused on the timeline but softened my chuckling. There was only one related article around the middle of November when Santa's Cause put out an advertisement announcing they'd gotten a new collection of Santa's elves in stock.

There was nothing else until the first night in December arrived and the initial elf break-in occurred at the Christmas Cottage. Just like before, George Fletcher reported on the crime. Rhonda Biggler did as well, but she included the fallout in the human turmoil. Gentry accused Marty of doing it to "rub it in his face."

I'd not caught that during my first scan through the article—*rub it in his face*. I read it a couple more times, searching for some context, but neither George nor Rhonda elaborated. Maybe the *it* was simply opening another Christmas shop in our small town. Maybe... Either way, just as Susan had said, the articles also didn't mention anything about fruit-cake or coal.

From then on, George Fletcher had a small article every day in the paper. Just a sentence or two documenting where the elf was left next, and if it was accompanied by a fruitcake or a piece of coal. I compared the articles to the list Katie, Anna, and I had made earlier in the day. Between the three of us, we'd gotten all the details right as far as who had received what, but now I could put them in chrono-logical order, ending with the break-in the night before at Cabin and Hearth. Without even thinking, I dated the next line and left it blank. Undoubtedly, someone, maybe at that very moment, was getting broken into.

Though fewer, Rhonda Biggler's corresponding articles took the more humanitarian approach, as normal. She was silent after the initial break-in until the footage from Delilah's security camera was released that showed Santa tiptoeing around Madame Delilah's Old Tyme Photography shop and perching an elf on top of a tripod then arranging a fruitcake underneath. From that point on, just like Anna had been saying, people took the gifts as a declaration of judgment of the person, or break-in victim, if you were. It made sense. Good little boys and girls got presents, bad little boys and girls got coal.

After letting the final newspaper fall on the pile beside the chair, I refocused on my timeline. The answer was there. Clearly. Anna was right about that as well—it all came down to whoever this Santa was and who they judged to be good or bad.

Although maybe I had been correct. If this continued all the way through Christmas, that meant this person had a list of at least twenty-five people who they felt strongly enough to label as good or bad.

That seemed excessive. In a way, it made more sense for it to be random. Maybe...

If it had been a year or so ago, I might've gone with that. But I was a better judge of character than I had ever been before, and I'd seen firsthand that people could hold grudges for a long, long time.

The clacking of nails on hardwood brought my attention back to the moment, and I looked over to see Watson poke his head out of the bedroom door, his stuffed lion clenched in his jaws. He looked away instantly.

I managed not to laugh, knowing, just like whoever Santa was, my little corgi could hold a grudge. "Come on back, buddy. And bring your lion." I bent down and offered an outstretched hand in a peace offering. "All the newspapers are on the floor. Nothing's going to fall this time. Nothing's going to be crinkling and disturbing your nap."

His gaze slid toward me, then to the kitchen and back once more.

That time, I did laugh. "Not only can you hold a grudge, but you're not overly subtle either. Well..." I groaned as I stood up. "I could use a snack, too, now that you bring it up."

With a little hop, Watson began cantering toward the kitchen, then stopped, clearly having a thought. Just as I reached the doorway, he spun around, hurried to the fire, laid the lion on the hearth, and scurried back to the kitchen, slowing as he reached me, as if trying to keep up appearances.

And my heart utterly melted. "You really are something, you know that, Watson Charles Page?"

He tilted his nose in the air, strolled past me, and plopped down in front of the refrigerator.

"Fine, leftover chicken for you, and for me..." I opened the mint-green refrigerator and peered inside.

Forgetting pretenses, Watson scooted near, close enough to stick his nose in and sniff around. Sure enough, he settled on the Styrofoam containing the fajita chicken.

I wasn't as easily satisfied, as I scanned the cottage cheese, yogurt, and fruit. Instead I opened the freezer and found something much more to my liking—mint chip ice cream. However, when I pulled it out, I noticed the carton of pumpkin ice cream that was wedged behind it. Leo's favorite.

Suddenly, all the theories of elves, fruitcake, and coal evaporated as surely as if they'd traveled up the chimney with Santa. All replaced by that stupid manila envelope I'd hidden in the box containing my crystal-and-gemstone-encrusted boots and stuffed back into the closet.

I put the mint chip back in front of the pumpkin ice cream, closed the freezer, and then sank to the floor with the Styrofoam container of chicken in my hands. After opening it, I offered a strip to Watson. "I should burn it, right? Just like I thought the moment Branson handed it to me."

Watson merely swallowed the chicken whole and then looked up at me expectantly.

I took out another strip but held it in midair, caught in thought. I'd been going back and forth, debating about whatever was in that stupid envelope for over a month. One second deciding to burn it, the next to rip it open and read what it said, and then the next to leave it exactly where it was. "I think that makes me crazier than anything." I met Watson's gaze, and he cocked his head. "I know Branson gave me that to get under my skin, to cause doubt with Leo, or to cause friction between us. And here I am, playing right into Branson's hands. What kind of person keeps a supposed file of dark deeds of the man they love, given to them by their psychopathic ex?"

Watson whimpered.

"Me! That's who!"

Watson whined.

"Oh." I handed him the chicken strip. "Sorry."

He gulped it down, then returned his gaze to the Styrofoam.

"I know I should either burn it or pull it out one night and sit down on the couch with Leo to face it together." With my free hand, I reached out and stroked Watson's head.

Though a trail of drool ran from his lower jaw to the floor, he didn't pull away.

"But what if...?" I shut my eyes, not wanting to finish the thought. "But, Watson, what if...?"

Watson scooted closer so his flank was pressed against my leg.

At the contact, I placed the Styrofoam box on the floor and wrapped my arms around Watson, breathing deep and then letting out a long sigh. "Thanks, sweetheart."

Sheltered in my grip, Watson strained and was able to duck his head down, snag the remaining chicken, and scarf it with a big gulp, but then he settled back into the hug.

"I don't know if I can handle another betrayal. Any more lies," I whispered in his ear, and it twitched against my nose.

I didn't think I could say those words to anyone

else, not even Katie, not even my mother. I was strong, worldly, and I'd handled heartbreak, devastation, and danger. I wasn't supposed to let worry over a man get to me, even if he was the love of my life. At least I wanted to be that person who didn't worry over a man. But the truth was, I did worry.

Sure, I'd lived through my ex-husband's affair and our divorce, my ex-best friend and business partner's backstabbing, and discovering the dangerous double life of the man I dated. Lived through and gotten stronger because of it all. I knew that much was true regardless of what was in the manila envelope. If it revealed that Leo was dark and not the man I truly believed he was, I'd still live through it, and I'd probably still be stronger yet. But some part of me would break, irrevocably, and I knew that with all that I was.

After a while, having reached his extent of physical affection, Watson squirmed.

With a final, quick squeeze, I let him go. Then as an act of defiance, I stood and got myself four scoops of ice cream—two mint chips and two pumpkin—then returned to the overstuffed armchair by the fire.

When Watson disappeared into the bedroom, I thought he'd abandoned me again, but he emerged a second later with his duck stuffed animal, set it beside the lion, and then settled down, resting his chin on both, and instantly fell sleep.

As I ate the ice cream, the manila envelope and all its implications faded away as I refocused on the elf list. Seeing it through new eyes, I recalled my earlier theory from the day. That it had nothing to do with who the Santa person thought was good or bad, but it was all just a publicity stunt, something to drum up business. With that, I turned the page in the notebook and started scribbling again, and all the random thoughts came back to two obvious people—Gentry Farmer or Marty Clark.

When I started to drift off to sleep while the fire burned down to embers, another possibility drifted across my fading consciousness. Perhaps it wasn't Gentry Farmer *or* Marty Clark. Maybe it was Gentry *and* Marty. What better way to drum up business for both of them than to start a war and a scandal? If so, I had to hand it to them—based on Katie's new Watson the Elf mug display, it was working.

I was never the little girl who fancied herself a Disney princess, but the following morning dawned as if I might have actually become one. Okay, there weren't little bluebirds flitting around my head, twittering a morning melody, or mice scampering over the blankets preparing a ball gown, nor did Watson suddenly switch personalities and bring me breakfast in bed. Still, as I looked out the bedroom window and saw the thick, undisturbed, glistening blanket of snow covering the surrounding forest and the silver peaks of the mountains towering over my little corner of the universe, if I'd had Cinderella's charming voice, I might've just broken into song. It was picture-perfect, and thanks to a cozy night's sleep, my brain felt just as crisp and clean as the snow.

The theory I'd fallen asleep to the night before of the whole thing with the elves being nothing more than a dramatic marketing scheme still seemed like a genuine possibility. Gentry and Marty still felt like the most likely suspects. And even the whole puzzling situation was rather comforting. For once I wasn't waking up wondering about who killed so-and-so and who might be next to die. The morning was crisp, Christmassy, and the biggest terror in Estes Park was Santa breaking into a different house or shop every night and leaving elves. For crying out loud, it was like the whole town had stumbled into a Hallmark movie... or a Disney movie, if I was going to stick with the theme.

And that manila envelope—given to me by my murderous ex—hidden inside the box with the crystal-and-gemstone-encrusted boots? Well, that's where it was, *hidden in a box*, out of sight and mostly out of mind. And the wintry perfection outside the window, combined with Watson's soft snores helped whatever contents it held seem a lot less important. Of course, it didn't hurt that Leo was returning from his family's that afternoon. He and I would sit down and look through whatever was in it at some point together. But today wasn't that day, and I was glad of it.

After Watson awoke, giving a disgruntled yawn that revealed he wasn't feeling any of the Disney, or

Hallmark, magic, I opted to skip our frequent morning stroll through the woods. I was more inclined to hurry to the Cozy Corgi to talk over my theory with Katie. And for once, there seemed something rather romantic about leaving the freshly fallen snow pristine, letting the forest animals that lived in my little woods have it to themselves for the day.

The drive into town proved I wasn't the only person who'd awoken in such a festive mood. It wasn't like people were typically cursing or tossing up rude hand gestures most of the time, but there seemed to just be that little something extra as people waved, nodded, and exchanged greetings while passing on the street. I often felt that Estes Park looked like a Christmas snow globe during the winter. Maybe with Santa and his elves making the rounds this season, I wasn't the only one with that particular inclination.

My mood only increased in its winter wonderland merriment as Watson and I walked up the sidewalk, sheltered underneath the red-and-green Christmas garland looping over the street. We were early enough, none of the stores were open and many of the shop owners hadn't arrived, but here and there, one or two looked out the front windows and waved.

We were nearly half a block away from the front door of the Cozy Corgi when the first disturbance of the morning met my ears—an onslaught of barking. Though Watson snarled his annoyance, the easily recognizable baying of Paulie's crazy corgis didn't break the spell I was under. If anything, Flotsam and Jetsam just added to it—more proof that this was actually my home.

The closer we got, the more it became apparent Watson was not coming around to my way of thinking. He growled—a low, quiet thing.

"Relax, not everyone can be as well-mannered as you are." I paused, scratching his head. "And really, they might be more obnoxious, but they have you beat on the friendliness level, so don't be too judgmental."

Watson glared across the street and then up at me in pure annoyance.

"You're right. I'm sorry." I patted his head and stood. "That was judgmental on my part. As far as the friendliness level, you've helped save lives so I'm sure that supersedes the amount of frantic licking those two do." Proving I really was in a mood, I realized I'd just giggled at my own humor.

Still not finding me or the other corgis amusing, Watson's growl deepened the closer we got, and by the time we were standing in front of the bookshop's front door, he was at the end of his leash, straining toward Paws and full-out barking his disapproval to Flotsam and Jetsam.

Pausing with my keys outstretched toward the lock, I looked over to wave an apology to Paulie, then paused again when I only saw Flotsam and Jetsam standing in the doorway of the pet shop, continuing to bark and taking turns pounding their front paws on the glass.

Watson barked again, and that time, with the timbre, it finally broke through my reverie, causing me to really look at him and listen.

It wasn't his annoyed bark, though it was very similar. It was his warning bark, or his worried bark—I couldn't tell. But in that moment, I realized it matched Flotsam's and Jetsam's. That while they were typically frantic, there was a different sound to their chaos as well.

Barely remembering to look both ways across the freshly plowed street, I let Watson lead, and we hopped over the mound of soiled snow at the edge of the sidewalk, hurried across, hopped over the twin mound of snow on the other side, and made it to the front door of the pet shop.

Flotsam's and Jetsam's barking increased by

several decibels. And suddenly this became familiar. Another time I'd entered Paws to a crazed and frantic greeting of the corgis and found one murdered body and Paulie nearly dead himself.

To my surprise, the door wasn't locked. The barking was nearly painful as we stepped in, made even more piercing by the screeching of birds and the whirling of hamster wheels. It truly was a sense of déjà vu. Dropping Watson's leash, I started to rush toward the back room, fully expecting to find Paulie lying there, dying, just like I had before.

I was so caught up in reliving the memory that I nearly rushed past him. I would've, if Flotsam and Jetsam hadn't launched themselves at the figure in the chair.

Paulie sat, secured to the rolling chair by lighted garland that was wrapped around, binding him in place. A Santa hat had been shoved onto his head, low enough that the fuzzy white brim covered his eyebrows, barely giving enough room for his desperate brown gaze to meet mine. A stocking hung from his mouth, a little elf perched in the opening, the pointy blue hat nearly poking Paulie's eye. What skin I could see of his cheeks was streaked with black, and behind him on the wall, written in that same black in giant capital letters was the word *LOSER*. Only then did I realize the black was coal.

My first instinct was to rip the stocking from his mouth, but then I realized it was actually secured with the same Christmas lights that wound around his body, tying him to the chair. It only took a second to find the end trailing to the plug on the wall. I yanked it free, then began unwinding Paulie as all three of the dogs barked and circled us frantically.

"Who was it, Paulie?" I couldn't keep from asking as soon as I pulled the stocking free of his mouth.

Paulie attempted to spit a white piece of fluff stuck to his lips free but couldn't manage. I pulled it off as well, and then he spoke, the words barely discernible in his dry, cracked voice. "Santa. It was Santa."

I froze. "Yes, but you couldn't tell who it was underneath the Santa outfit?"

He shook his head, and his eyes went wide. "Fred, get me free. I can't tell you how badly I need to run to the restroom!"

Susan was so quick, she arrived—followed by Officer Campbell Clifton Cabot—barely moments after

Paulie had returned from taking Flotsam and Jetsam to the restroom as well. She shook her head at me. "I swear, Fred, from day one, I don't know how you're always the first on the scene. Paulie's not even murdered and you're here." She didn't sound overly annoyed, just baffled.

"Well, it was Flotsam and Jetsam that called us over. I'm betting the few other people who walked by this morning are so used to them that they didn't pay any mind." I patted Watson, who sat beside me. "Really, it was Watson who noticed, otherwise I would've shrugged it off as them just being their typical overactive selves."

"They did that for hours." Paulie sat on the floor, his back against the front of the counter, a hand on each of the corgis' heads, which rested on either side of his lap. "Poor boys, they're completely worn out." For maybe the first time ever, they were silent, and both looked like they were moments away from falling asleep.

"Who did this?" Susan turned her attention to me, and though she addressed Paulie, she moved closer to the coal insult on the wall.

"Santa." Paulie's voice was no longer dry and cracked, but he still sounded utterly worn out.

"No." Officer Cabot shook his head emphatically, though his tone was tender as he knelt on one knee, taking a better look at Paulie. "Santa wouldn't do this. You must be hallucinating. Santa's good. Now maybe that evil one, there's that legend of something called—" He snapped his fingers. "—Crumpet, I believe."

The moment he'd started speaking, Susan lifted one hand and rubbed her temple, and she spoke with closed eyes. "A *crumpet* is something you eat, something Katie would make, although I think it's British. You're talking about *Krampus*, who eats naughty—" Her pale blue eyes opened, and she looked at me. I was surprised at the familiar way she spoke to me, as if we were the only two adults in the room. "What's wrong with me? Do you see this? I'm getting weak. I should be screaming at him to get out of my crime scene, not explaining about evil fairy tales." Before I could respond, her gaze hardened, and she looked at her new subordinate. "Cabot."

"Yes, sir, Detective Green, sir?" He stood and saluted.

Susan groaned, then gritted her teeth. "Shut up."

Cabot opened his mouth, paused, snapped it shut once more, then gave a nod and another salute.

When Susan refocused on Paulie, her tone was a little softer, but not much. "Obviously, the person who broke in last night was dressed as Santa, at least I'm assuming Paws was the nightly break in as we've not heard from any other locations. I'm also assuming that this change in modus operandi was because you were here unexpectedly?"

Paulie nodded. "Yeah. The swordtails are sick. I have to medicate them every twelve hours. The boys and I came by to put in the drops."

She cocked her head, then looked at me. "Help me out. Swordtails?"

Paulie's gaze had darted to the wall of fish tanks as he'd spoken, so I made a guess, as I wasn't—despite my utter devotion to Watson—that big of an animal person. "I'm betting swordtails are a type of fish."

"Yeah." Paulie grimaced. "They have Ich."

"*Ick?*" Susan's voice went up.

"I.C.H. Though it sounds like ick." Officer Cabot drew all of our attention back his way. As he spoke, he attempted to pat Watson, who ducked out of the way and trotted around to my other side, out of reach. Cabot merely shrugged and continued. "It's these little white dots that can cover a fish's body. It won't kill them outright, but it makes them extremely susceptible to—"

"I thought I told you to shut up." Susan growled

the words. "If I need a lesson in fish diseases, I'll ask for it."

Paulie narrowed his eyes, thoughtfully, a little smile growing at the corner of his lips as he looked at Officer Cabot. "I didn't realize you knew about fish. I just thought you knew about hamsters and guinea pigs."

"Well, I'm more familiar with saltwater fish than swordtails. My mom had a tank when I was a kid." Cabot beamed and spoke so quickly his words tumbled over themselves. "Really, I love all animals. Being an officer was more my dad's idea. I wanted to be a veterinarian. But my science grades were—"

"Get out!" Susan snarled and pointed at the door.

Flotsam and Jetsam, startled, shot upward and began to bark. They whimpered under Susan's glare and sank back to Paulie's lap.

She gestured toward the door again. "Wait for me in the car, Cabot. If you can't follow directions, I'll write you up, and I don't care if your uncle is the chief of police or how bad your science scores were."

Looking dejected, Officer Cabot saluted again, turned on his heel, and walked out with his shoulders slumped.

For the first time since meeting him, I actually

felt bad for the guy. Apparently so did Paulie as he looked up at Susan. "You should be nicer to him. He comes in here quite a bit to buy stuff for Cujo. I'm sure he doesn't want me to tell you this, but he's under the impression that you think he's stupid. It hurts his feelings."

Susan balked, and demonstrating a Christmas miracle, I thought I saw an expression of guilt cross her face, though it disappeared quickly. "Paulie, if I need your opinion, just like I told Officer Idiot out there, I'll ask for it. And apparently Officer Cabot is more intelligent than I thought, if he's under the impression that I think he's stupid. Because I do. Because he is."

"Susan." I put a hand on her shoulder. Feeling like she was being a little too harsh, even for Susan. On the other hand, for my few interactions with Officer Cabot, the thought of being around him all day made me somewhat sympathetic to her plight.

She shrugged off my touch but softened her tone. "So, Paulie, you came to give the fish medication, correct?"

Paulie nodded.

"Okay. Then walk us through it." Susan pulled a small pad out of her back pocket—until that point Officer Cabot had been taking notes. "Was Santa..."

She sighed with a tight shake of her head. "Was the person dressed as Santa already present, or did he break in while you were here?"

"He was already here, but I didn't realize it. The boys and I entered through the back, so we came through the storeroom, and Santa was over there by the cash register, I think getting ready to hang the stocking." Paulie stroked Flotsam and Jetsam as he spoke. "Of course, the boys were ecstatic, and nearly tumbled all over themselves trying to greet him."

I sucked in a breath, unable to stop myself.

They both looked at me.

"Sorry." I reached down to touch Watson, suddenly so very glad no one had been present when the elf and fruitcake had been left at the Cozy Corgi. "Did... Santa hurt them. Kick them?"

"No." Paulie issued a huge sigh as if relieved all over again. "He shoved them out of the way with his boots, but who hasn't with my boys?"

"What then?" Susan pressed on, clearly wanting to get back on track.

Paulie blinked for several seconds before answering. "You know, I'm not really sure. All night I tried to replay it. There wasn't anything else to do trapped for hours besides try to figure out if there was something else I could have done. But"—he shrugged

—"one minute I saw him, and the next Santa grabbed me and shoved me into the chair and started wrapping me up. Before I could even say anything, he had that stocking shoved in my mouth. I don't even think the boys realized he was trying to hurt me..." A crease formed between his brows. "Well, I guess he wasn't trying to *hurt* me. Otherwise I'd... be..."

When he didn't finish, I wasn't sure what he was thinking. It could be a myriad of things. Maybe the memory of the same night I'd recalled when I came in, the night he almost died. But Paulie had spent years being a perpetual victim, and it looked like that trend wasn't over.

"Were you able to get a punch in, a scratch?" Susan prompted. "Any sort of mark on him that we might look for to let us know that—" She didn't finish as Paulie shook his head, clearly embarrassed. Paulie struggled to lift the large bags of dog food by himself; I couldn't imagine him putting up much of a fight. To my surprise, Susan's tone softened. "That's okay. We'll still figure it out. This definitely ups things. It's no longer breaking in to leave elves with fruitcakes or coal." She gestured to Paulie, then the wall. "We've now got assault and vandalism."

Assault. That was definitely what it was, tying someone to a chair. I met Paulie's gaze again. "Did the person hurt you, Paulie?" I didn't want to insult him any more, but I didn't want anything to be overlooked.

He shook his head. "Not like what you mean. I have some aches, and I'll probably have some bruises where Santa held me down as he tied me up, but he didn't hit or kick or punch or anything. He was rough, but didn't even speak." Sure enough, he flushed. "He was just one man, a big man, but still."

Susan brightened. "Well, that's something we haven't had before. You said he's big. What else did he look like?"

Paulie seemed to brighten as well, and he closed his eyes, clearly visualizing. "Well, he's big, like I said. And he wore boots, like I said."

"What kind of boots, Paulie?" I spoke softly and reached out to touch his knee while still keeping one hand on Watson.

"Um, the big black kind." He glanced down at one of the toes of my boots protruding from the hem of my rust-orange broomstick skirt. "They weren't cowboy boots, not like those."

"So, like... Santa boots," I offered. "The black rounded-toe type, with a buckle?"

He nodded again and kept going, closing his eyes once more. "He had a big belly, and his clothes were red, with white fur trim on the collar and sleeves. Had a thick black leather belt with a silver buckle. He had a big white beard and glasses." Paulie opened his eyes. "He looked like Carl, like when Carl gets dressed to go visit kids at Christmas at the hospital. Except taller. Carl's never very tall."

"So... Santa." Susan sighed and let her hand holding the pen drop to her side. "You're basically describing Santa. Or... Carl, who looks like Santa even without the Santa suit?"

Another nod.

Susan tried again. "Did you happen to notice eye color?"

He shook his head at that. "This will probably sound strange... I could see anger in them, but I can't tell you the color. It was clear he didn't like me. Obviously."

"Could you make out his skin tone?" I continued to speak soothingly, partly worried I sounded too motherly with Paulie, but I couldn't help myself.

"Um..." He appeared to think back once more. "I believe... lighter? It was pretty dark and shadowy..."

"All right, then, so we have a guy who looks like Santa, probably a white Santa, who's strong enough to hold down another man and tie him up while two crazy corgis probably licked his ankles to death." Susan's tone had started to go dark, and I could tell it took her some effort to lighten it. "Sounds like he wasn't overly aggressive, but not exactly gentle with you. He didn't hurt you, and he could've. However"—her hand lifted, almost as if of its own accord, and pointed toward the wall—"this is new, too. And not in keeping with Santa. It doesn't say ho ho ho, or Paulie has been a bad boy, or anything like that."

Paulie angled so he could see over the edge of the counter from a seated position and winced as he looked at the scrolled labeling of *loser* over his wall.

"Paulie..." An idea hit, and my theory from the night before and that morning shifted, but I played it out one step before I completely changed directions. "Have you had any negative interactions, at all, with Gentry Farmer or Marty Clark?"

Susan cocked an eyebrow at me. "Marketing scheme?" When I nodded, she offered a grin. "I've started wondering that myself."

"No." Paulie either didn't catch on or wasn't too concerned about the why of it all. "I don't think I've hardly had any interactions with them."

That's what I'd figured, and I allowed myself to truly change directions then, and gave him a knowing stare. "Who *have* you been having some issues with lately?" I probably shouldn't lead a witness, but I wasn't the actual cop in the room.

His eyes widened in understanding. "Jake?"

I nodded.

Susan looked between us in confusion. "Jake?" Before Paulie could answer, she let out a knowing sound. "Oh. Delilah's Jake."

"Yes." I eyed the five cruel letters on the wall. Yeah, from what little I knew of Jake, I could see him doing that.

We marched en masse—minus Flotsam and Jetsam—from Paws to Madame Delilah's Old Tyme Photography. By that point, the stores had opened, but it was still a little too early for the holiday tourists to be up and about.

I'd planned on going to speak to Jake about how he was treating Paulie, even before this incident, but as we neared Delilah's, my nerves began to tingle. Going as a group had been Susan's idea, one that neither Paulie nor I were overly enthused about. Paulie was exhausted, and about the least confrontational person I'd ever met. And while I didn't *enjoy* confrontation, I didn't hide from it either, but with the strain between Delilah and myself, showing up in this manner was the last way I would've chosen to do things. However, Susan was the official voice of the law, and she thought we'd get a better reaction as a group from Jake if he'd tormented Paulie the night before. For his part, Watson was chipper as we left the pet shop. He started across the street, clearly thinking it was time for a snack from Katie, and quickly grew sullen when redirected down the block.

Susan was right, we did get a reaction.

Jake was behind the counter, scribbling something on a notepad as we walked in. He looked up, a forced, plastic-like smile plastered on his face. "Welcome to—" The minimal pretense fell away instantly as his gaze landed on Susan. Straightening to his full height, Jake swelled to an impressive size, and his eyes went deadly cold. They held there for a second, then flicked to me, revealing no recognition, then to Paulie. A smirk twitched on his lips, but he remained silent.

Susan crossed directly to the counter and laid her badge in front of him. "Are you Jake Jazz?"

It was the first time I'd heard his last name, and I had to struggle to keep a straight face. He might be able to pull off the old-time gangster name if he'd had a few more ounces of class or subtlety.

The smirk stayed in place, but his voice held absolutely no effect. "Do you have a warrant?"

Susan flinched but then laughed. "You require a *warrant* to identify yourself?"

Not a blink. "I require a warrant to answer *any* question from a pig."

As Jake had only moments before, Susan straightened to her full height and swelled to *her* full impressive size, and though I had absolutely nothing to do with Susan's strength, I felt a surge of pride when Jake actually took a step backward. He caught himself instantly and returned to where he'd been, but it was too late—he'd given a little.

"Let's try this again, are you Jake Jazz? And if you feel the need to call me anything, it's *Detective* Green." Susan's whisper was maybe the most dangerous I'd ever heard.

Apparently feeling the same, a low rumble resonated from Watson. I wasn't sure if he was warning Susan or backing her up.

At the sound, Jake glanced toward Watson, noticing him for the first time. "Some canine unit you've got there, Pi—*Detective*."

Another surge of pride as he caught himself.

That time, Susan propped a hand beside the badge on the counter and leaned nearer. "Trust me, unlike you, *his* bite is worse than his bark."

Still Watson rumbled, and from the confusion that crossed behind Jake's eyes, it took him a second to interpret the insult. As he did, his upper lip curled. "Now listen here—"

"Jake, can you help me with—" Delilah emerged from the back, her arms laden down with a heavy assortment of saloon-girl dresses. She halted, her beautiful deep blue gaze taking in the scene and hardening just as dramatically as Jake's had done. She laid the dresses over the back of an artfully worn-down Victorian chair. "What's going on here?"

Watson stopped growling instantly, refocused on Delilah, and trotted toward her, looking back at me questioningly when he reached the end of his leash.

Delilah noticed, and exchanged a cool glance with me.

Maybe I was reading into things, but I thought I read a question there, asking me just how far I was going to push things with her. In answer, I dropped the leash. She had every reason to be upset with me, I'd been meaning to come make a formal apology for taking advantage of her invitation to join her Pink Panthers club in order to get clues about another murder a couple of months before, but I hadn't worked up the nerve. I'd kept shoving a couple of things on the back burner lately.

Watson trotted the rest of the way, and Delilah

knelt, giving him a warm, genuine smile. "Hi there, handsome."

As always, Watson didn't go crazy in her presence like he did with the very select few other people, but instead allowed her to pet him with genuine contentment at her touch.

Delilah spoke from her kneeling position, and somehow managed to convey just as much strength, though not in the same physical way as Jake and Susan only moments before. "And again, I'll ask what's going on here?"

I opened my mouth to respond, but Susan shot a look my way that clearly communicated to let her handle things. "Santa paid a visit to Paws last night."

Delilah's attention flicked to Paulie but didn't remain there more than a heartbeat before addressing Susan again. "Okay. By this point that's hardly news. It's happening every night." She gave Watson a final scratch behind his ears and stood. "If you recall, I've already been paid a visit by Santa and his elves. And I don't remember you going from store to store searching for details when that happened, Detective Green."

"*You* weren't gagged and bound to a chair all night." Though she answered Delilah, I noticed

Susan refocused on Jake as she spoke. "And your store wasn't vandalized."

Jake smirked, and though I noticed, it didn't seem like Delilah had. Flinching, she whipped back around to Paulie and seemed to truly look at him that time, her eyes widening as her gaze settled on the coal spread over his cheeks. "Oh, Paulie, I'm sorry." Delilah and Paulie weren't close. In fact, he got on her nerves and was more than aware of it, but her tone was genuine. "Are you okay? Are your dogs okay?" Her voice went up on that last question. Even though Flotsam and Jetsam also got on her nerves, Delilah was a huge dog lover.

"We're all fine. Thank you." Unlike Susan's whisper before, there was no strength in Paulie's voice. It sounded like he was ready to crawl under a rock and sleep for the next century.

I reached out and touched his arm, and he flashed me a quick smile of thanks.

Watson trotted back and sat at my feet.

"I am sorry about what happened at the pet shop." Delilah joined us at the counter, though stayed behind it on the side of Jake. "But what does that have to do with me?"

"Nothing." Susan turned pointedly toward Jake. "It has to do with your employee. Who, so far, won't even confirm his name unless I have a warrant."

"Jake..." Delilah turned toward him, her expression softening.

"I don't have to answer her." Jake popped up once more, but it didn't seem aggressive toward Delilah, almost defensive of her. "And neither do you. We don't owe this pig anything. She just—"

"Jake!" Delilah barked it out, beating Susan to the punch. "Don't make things worse." She looked at Susan. "I'm sorry, I don't condone that type of language, and I don't see you or the rest of police force that way." No sooner had the sentiment left her lips than she hardened once more. "However, Jake doesn't owe you any explanation or answers to anything unless you do have a warrant. And I don't appreciate you making the assumption."

I looked between them. *What assumption?*

Jake glared at Delilah. "You told *her?*"

Susan snorted before Delilah could respond. "It's not like your record is closed. You weren't a juvenile, *Mr. Jazz.* I don't need your employer to tell me about your criminal past. And as far as your full name, yes, I know who you are. I was just giving you the chance to cooperate."

"Why would I cooperate?" He wheeled back

toward her and then gestured toward Paulie. "There's nothing to cooperate about. I didn't do anything to the sniveling little weasel."

Paulie trembled beside me.

I wish he'd shout, lunge at Jake, try to defend himself. I knew he couldn't, or wouldn't, so I did it for him... couldn't stop myself. "Right there. You act like *that* toward him and wonder why we're here? Just like when I saw you the other night at Habaneros, taunting him about his teeth across the restaurant like you're a middle school bully."

He leered at me, and even before he spoke, Watson growled. Jake didn't even look at him. "Why, lady? Were you jealous of the attention? The next time I see you out stuffing your face, I'll happily make fun of how many portions you clearly—"

"Jake!" Delilah whirled on him, fury in her eyes. "One more word like that and I'll fire you on the spot. No more derogatory comments about police, and *never* talk about a woman's size in front of me. Ever!"

Jake's cheeks went scarlet, and to my surprise, the blush wasn't in rage but in apparent embarrassment, as he nodded and mumbled a barely audible apology to her.

The only other reaction Delilah showed was a

trembling of her hand over the counter, and she quickly pulled it up behind her as she refocused on Susan. "Like I said, you and I have already spoken about who I choose to employ. And we have very different views on the matter."

"This is hardly convincing me I was wrong, Delilah." Undeterred, Susan refocused on Jake again. "Where were you last night?"

Delilah shook her head and tilted her chin, her long auburn hair glistening at the movement. "No. If you're going to do this, do it correctly. With a warrant and legal representation present."

"I have an alibi, anyway, so you're wasting your time." Jake spat the words at Susan. "Trevor and I hung out last night, or are you not going to believe him either because of his record?" He sneered toward Paulie. "Trust me, if I was going to waste my time with rodent boy over there, he wouldn't be in a place to come pointing fingers the next day."

"Stop it!" Delilah smacked the hand that had been trembling back on the counter. "Jake, shut your mouth." She whirled toward the rest of us, but only looked at Susan. "Please leave my store, unless you have a warrant. Otherwise take this up with Jake on his own time, and if he can't get a *decent* legal representative appointed to him, then... then I'll arrange for one."

I gaped at her, utterly baffled.

Susan just scoffed. "You and your strays, Delilah. He's not a basset hound. You've always had horrible taste in men, but this takes the cake. Mark my words. You're going to get burned."

While Delilah's face darkened in anger, she only tilted her chin once more as her lips tightened.

Susan pointed a finger at Jake. "If you so much as look at rodent boy over here wrong again, a warrant will be the least of your worries, trust me."

"*Susan,*" I hissed at her as Paulie flinched again—simultaneously, I noticed Delilah's hand shoot out to grip Jake's forearm, stopping him from responding.

"Sorry." Susan grimaced over at Paulie, then shockingly, threw a heavy arm over his shoulders. "Come on, let's get you to the hospital. I doubt the amount of coal on your face will do anything, but better safe than sorry."

He merely sighed and looked near to collapsing as we left the shop.

SEVEN

Something told me to take a break before giving in to my inclination, to take a few moments to make sure I was levelheaded and intentional. I'd like to say it was my better judgment and self-awareness, but really, who was I kidding? I really just needed caffeine. Either way, the breakfast rush was in full force at the Cozy Corgi, and I was willing to bet, with the way Susan, Paulie, Watson, and I had stomped between Paws and the photography shop, that a crowd had watched from the upper-story bakery windows and a gossip session was in full effect. I settled on that reasoning to ignore my better judgment and need for caffeine, and much to Watson's annoyance, he and I headed in the opposite direction from Paulie and Susan as we left Delilah's and went up Elkhorn Avenue.

What had been a fun, nearly game-like puzzle of figuring out Santa's identity and the reasoning behind his elves had become something so much darker, after seeing Paulie victimized yet again. Granted, Jake was right about one thing, whoever Santa was, they could have done a lot worse to Paulie than cover his face with coal and leave him tied to a chair, but still...

Jake seemed like the perfect suspect, given his overall attitude and clear disdain for Paulie, but he'd offered up another option on a silver platter, and I hadn't gotten the sense he'd done so intentionally. Trevor, the elf artist, had a police record as well. And while a few things over the past few months might have made me more open to the idea of coincidence, no way was I filing this under that category. Trevor didn't fit the skin tone Paulie described, but he didn't seem overly certain about anything, and given he'd been getting tied to a chair at the time, who could blame him?

We were nearly there when Watson paused at the front door of Rocky Mountain Imprints. He caught me so off guard that he stoked my curiosity and I didn't try to urge him on. As far as I knew, he had no feelings one way or the other about Joe Singer, so what had caught his attention?

I'd barely started to lean forward to press my hand against the glass door to peer inside when a figure stepped in front of me, pushed the door from the other side, and bumped against my face.

"Oh, excuse me, I'm sorry. I wasn't watching where I was—" Katie stepped around and halted as she saw us. "Fred! What are you doing?"

"Katie." I rubbed my tender nose. "What are you doing? I... You're not at the bakery?"

Watson jumped up, pounding his front paws on her thigh and snuffling his nose at her jacket pocket.

She had to throw a hand out to support herself on the window to keep from falling. "Good grief, Watson! What's gotten into you?"

He chuffed, then switched sides, sniffing her other pocket, and then let out a thoroughly annoyed breath and plopped down.

I looked from Katie to inside the T-shirt shop, then back down at Watson. "You knew she was in there, didn't you?"

Katie smoothed her jacket and laughed. "And apparently assumed I'd decided to carry around one of his favorite all-natural dog bone tr—" She shook her head. "Goodness, barely caught myself." She turned her narrowed brown eyes up to me. "You still haven't answered what you're doing here."

I glanced down Elkhorn, trying to do the math. "I guess you've been here awhile? You weren't at the bakery?"

"No. I left Nick in charge." She gestured toward the store interior. "I'd scheduled to meet with Joe before the tourists made it downtown. He's making a few personalized Christmas presents for me, and I wanted to go over a couple of design changes."

"Oh, so you haven't heard about Paulie yet? Paws was—"

Joe opened the door, his giant form making me glance up as he took a partial step outside. "Hey, Fred, Watson. Everything okay?"

Katie ignored him. "What about Paulie? Is he okay?"

Before I could answer, Watson repeated his strategy, this time his forepaws barely reaching Joe's knees.

I pulled him down. "Sorry, he's looking for snacks."

"No problem." Joe's low voice rumbled as he bent to pet Watson, who ducked his head and attempted to reach one of Joe's pockets.

"Good grief, Watson. I know we haven't had breakfast, but still." I pulled his leash tighter, earning a glare.

"I've got some crackers in the back." Joe straightened, giving up on petting Watson. "But what about
Paulie?"

A few minutes later, after I'd filled them in, Katie
headed back to the bakery, Watson settled after
receiving a couple of crackers from Joe, and then the
two of us continued on our way to Santa's Cause.

Whereas walking into the Christmas Cottage felt
like stepping back into the Victorian holidays, albeit
updated with electricity and more glitter than imaginable, Santa's Cause had gone with a more present-
day feel. It was almost like a toyshop for grown-up
Christmas enthusiasts—loud, bright, and just a touch
chaotic. Maybe a more apt comparison would be the
Christmas Cottage was the real-life version of "I'll
Be Home for Christmas," and Santa's Cause was
more along the lines of "Rocking Around the
Christmas Tree." Or, perhaps, I felt that way simply
because that particular frantically cheerful song was
playing as Watson and I entered.

I had to admit, though not my style, Santa's
Cause had its charm.

Christmas trees were spread everywhere; it was a
perpetual forest. The most common was the tradi-

tional evergreen variation, but scattered throughout were solid white ones and shiny metallics of red, silver, pink, and rainbow hued. I caught sight of Marty Clark on the far side of the shop, boxing up a Nativity set that appeared to be made out of gold-encrusted pinecones for a young couple, and I slowly headed in that direction. Halfway there, my attention was captured by a shiny baby-blue Christmas tree, completely covered in hippopotamus ornaments.

"Watson." I barely breathed his name, afraid the vision would dissipate. "You see that too, right?"

He didn't answer, and I didn't look down to check.

I had many skills—a high retention rate of anything book related, could eat pastries nearly quicker than Katie could bake them, and was surprisingly good at solving murders. However, I was woefully unskilled at present shopping. I could start scouting for Christmas gifts in February, and by the time Christmas Eve rolled around would still have no clue what I should get anyone, but there in front of me was the answer to every single Christmas present for Katie Pizzolato from now until the end of the world.

Stretching out a hand, I cupped the hippo ornament with a red-and-green-striped innertube around its fat belly. Not imaginary. It was heavy, and the details were exquisite, even considering it was a hippopotamus. A glance at the price tag brought reality into sharp focus, but then another hippo, two branches higher, pulled my attention. It stood with its four feet pressed together primly, and on its tossed-back head rose a unicorn horn with a donut skewered on the tip. A unicorn hippo! If I'd been at Rocky Mountain Imprints, this Christmas tree would've made sense. I'd lost count of how many hippo shirts Katie made Joe Singer design for her.

Maybe there was a whole underground cult of hippo lovers I never knew existed. And it didn't stop there. There were hippos covered in birthday cake, hippos with angel wings, hippos dressed as Santa, hippos in bathrobes and curlers, and... I sucked in a gasp and knelt down to where Watson was sniffing a hippo on the lower branch.

"No way." I twisted the ornament too quickly and accidentally scraped across Watson's nose.

He sneezed, took a step back, glaring at me, and then sneezed again.

"Sorry, buddy." I barely spared him a glance.

This hippopotamus was lying on its back, and perched on its rounded mound of a belly, a corgi in a Santa hat, the hook looped through a small ring on the cotton-ball top.

"Pretty cute, right?"

The voice from above startled me so that I dropped the ornament. Luckily, it was still latched onto the tree and swung harmlessly in midair. I looked up to see Marty Clark's handsome fiftysomething face looking down at me. All thoughts of elves and investigations fled my mind. "Where did you get these? Did someone in Estes Park make them?"

"No." Marty shook his head and sounded apologetic. "They're mass-marketed, I'm afraid to say, but they are premium quality and from a high-end distributor."

"But..." I refocused on the ornament. "It's a hippopotamus... with a corgi."

Watson sneezed again, then trotted from where he'd been standing between the two of us and stood on the other side, lest Marty decided he might want to attempt petting a dog, heaven forbid.

"Fat animals are always popular Christmas decorations. Hippos are a go-to." Marty smiled at Watson but didn't attempt to reach across to touch him.

"Corgis have been increasing in popularity the past couple of years. And they aren't exactly known for being svelte. It's a natural combo." His grin shifted to me. "You sound like it's a giant coincidence? Do you have a pet hippopotamus at home as well?"

"Not hardly, although Watson eats enough to probably qualify." Laughing, I stood. "It's just that my best friend and business partner is completely hippo obsessed. It's like these ornaments were made for her, and then to top it off, to find one with the corgi of all things."

"Ah, yes." Nodding, Marty picked up a hippo with a mermaid tail. "The baker, correct?"

"Yes, Katie. Do you know if she's seen these?"

"I couldn't say. I don't think I've noticed her in here. If the shop is open, typically I'm here as well, but she might've slipped by me." He placed the mermaid hippo back. "Did you just find a Christmas present?"

"I think a whole bunch of them." I might regret it, and while I wasn't exactly scrimping by, I didn't have unlimited resources either. Whatever. I decided to throw caution to the wind; it was Katie, after all. "If I take the entire collection, will you get another shipment in or will this be it for the year?"

"All?" His smile grew, and though I was certain there were dollar signs in his eyes, he still sounded casual enough. "I imagine you'd like these to be the only ones I carry this year? So that your friend won't see them?" Marty kept going without giving me a chance to nod. "I can do that for you, especially considering you're another shop owner downtown. We need to stick together, and there's a mountain wildlife line I've been considering bringing in that's perfect for Estes—elk, bears, chipmunks, mountain lions, that sort of thing. I'll just switch the two."

I groaned. "Okay, here's the other part of this bargain—don't let me see those. My boyfriend is a ranger at the national park. It's like you're trying to make me go broke. Next you'll tell me you have a Judy Garland and Barbra Streisand collection for my uncles."

"Well, I do have a *Wizard of Oz* tree." Marty laughed good-naturedly. "If it makes you feel any better, do you know about why we're called Santa's Cause?"

I started to shake my head, then realized I had heard. "Oh, yes. A percentage of every sale goes to charity, correct?"

"Yes, a large percentage." Marty beamed in

pride, though there wasn't a touch of arrogance or martyrdom in his tone. "Since this is my first year up here, this season we're spreading it out, giving to several different local charities, but for each season after this, we'll pick one recipient. It makes a bigger impact that way, but I wanted to start off all equally. So, see? You can feel good about splurging for your baker, boyfriend, *and* uncles."

"That's pretty amazing. And really great business practice, and a clever name." I glanced at the tree, starting to experience buyer's remorse, but then, at the sight of the hippos, I could practically see Katie's smiling face and excited jiggle as she opened the adorable ornaments. I could just spread out the collection for a couple of years or something. And it wasn't a bad idea to get others presents all at once. Plus... if some of the profits went to charities...

"If you're having second thoughts, it's okay." Marty reached out and touched my arm kindly.

"I am, but..." I took a final look at the unicorn hippo with the donut and then toward the one with the corgi. "No, let's do it. They're too perfect not to."

"Okay then." Marty clapped his hands, the decision final. "While I ring you up at the counter, unless there's more you'd like to see, I'll send my nephew over to untrim the tree, as we say. Each of the ornaments comes with its own collector's box."

"No, I'll wait for Leo and my uncles, for now." Thoughts of presents flew out the window. *His nephew.* Feeling ridiculous, I suddenly remembered we'd not come for Christmas shopping in the first place. Well... two birds, one stone, as they say. I followed Marty to the counter, and as Watson and I waited, he hurried back across the store and found his nephew. I recognized Finnegan from the other night at Habaneros. Seeing the two men together, I would never have guessed they were family. Where Marty was handsome, kind-looking, and appeared young for his age, Finnegan was slightly unkempt, hard, and already seemed used up. However, though I was searching for it, I saw no spark of irritation or negative attitude at being told what to do by his uncle.

As Marty returned, I noticed a large glass case beside the cash register, and I pointed to it. "These elves have been getting around town a lot lately."

"Yes. And apparently made an appearance at your shop the other night." A furious blush rose over his cheeks. "I'm so sorry."

"Nothing was taken. It's all right." I decided there was no time like the moment to switch directions, I wasn't sure if gossip had reached this far up Elkhorn about Paulie or not, but I decided to see if I could surprise him and get a reaction. "Unfortunately, the same can't be said for the pet shop. It was broken into last night, and in addition to the elf, Paulie was tied up to a chair and had coal rubbed all over his face, not to mention it was used to graffiti the walls."

"What?" Marty's dark eyes went wide, and the flush over his cheeks vanished instantly, leaving him pale. "Is he okay?"

I studied him for a heartbeat, I thought I believed his reaction. He seemed both shocked and genuinely upset. "Shaken, but fine other than that, as far as we know." I studied the elf nearest to me, little more than a white puffy beard and a crimson red Santa hat. "Do you have any theories on who took them? Who's been leaving them around town?"

Marty changed in an instant once more, bristling, and a barely discernible snarl behind his words. "I'll have you know, Finnegan's turned a page. He made a new start here, and I'm proud of him. If you're here to accuse my nephew, you can take your money and leave the ornaments."

Watson snarled protectively below me, but Marty either didn't notice or wasn't concerned.

For myself, I tried to catch up, confused. "Finnegan has... had trouble with the law?"

Marty's gaze darted behind me to where I imagined his nephew was taking the ornaments off the tree. "A person shouldn't have their past used against them. It's *in the past*. He's turned a corner."

That was a yes if I ever heard one. And a huge confirmation of suspects. So... Jake has a past with the law, and he'd disclosed, however unintentionally, that Trevor had the same past. And now Finnegan. So, all three friends had that in common.

"I'm not accusing your nephew of anything, Mr. Clark." Did I keep pushing? I'd barely asked myself the question before I leapt in. Doing so was my nature, and I'd also discovered that when people were agitated, sometimes they were more prone to show their true colors. "According to Mr. Jazz, he and Trevor, the artist of these"—I gestured toward the elves—"were together last night. I wonder—"

Marty snarled again, and elicited a similar action from Watson once more, not that he noticed. "Jake Jazz." He sneered. "Ridiculous name. I can't say I approve of Finnegan, or Trevor, for that matter, hanging out with the likes of him, but they're grown men. Trevor is the gold standard of what any parent would hope for their child, and Finnegan is becoming more like him every day. He's turned his life around, though he's had everything stacked against him since the day he was born. I couldn't be prouder of the man he's becoming. If Mr. Jazz has half a brain cell, he'll take a page out of Trevor's book, just like Finnegan has."

I'd heard the phrase "mama bear" in regard to how protective a mother could be of her children, and though I heard aggression in his tone, I felt like that was the case with Marty Clark in regard to his nephew.

Before I could say anything, he leaned forward and punched the countertop with his finger. "You asked if I had any theories? My guess? Gentry Farmer." Another jab at the counter. "*He's* the one that stole them in the first place, angry that I opened up the store, jealous that I got the exclusive contract this year with Trevor Donovan."

I went along, it was one of my theories after all, though it involved Marty as well. "It seems that would backfire. With all the publicity the elves are getting, he would almost be doing you a favor."

Though I feared Marty would make the natural leap to think that I was suggesting *he* might be behind it as well, that didn't seem to click. "Gentry isn't smart enough to put that together. He's nothing but a bully. Him and his gang of friends. I should've pressed charges the day he came in and punched me. But I wanted to keep the peace. Not be seen as a troublemaker being one of the new shop owners in town. Clearly that was a mistake. With people like Farmer, sometimes they only learn and respond to force."

"Uncle Marty?" Finnegan stepped up to us, flipping his head to get a red lock of hair out of his eyes while both hands were busy holding a large box filled with smaller boxes, each with a different image of a hippopotamus on it. "You okay?"

Marty flinched, looking like he'd been caught, then took a shaky breath. "Yes." He took another breath, calmer this time, and clapped Finnegan on the shoulder. "Yes. Like I told you, we all lose our tempers from time to time. It's what we do with it and how we respond that defines the kind of man we are."

Finnegan nodded awkwardly and seemed uncomfortable. I couldn't blame him. He was a grown man getting a lesson more suited to a twelve-year-old, and right in front of a stranger.

Marty stared at the box of hippo ornaments, and I wondered once more if he was going to refuse to sell them to me. He didn't, and within ten minutes, I was loading them in the back of my Mini Cooper, and the few that wouldn't fit, into the footwell of the passenger seat. The whole time, Watson pranced around my feet, knowing that we were finally getting ready to be at the bookshop and treats would soon be overflowing.

EIGHT

In a sure sign more schools were out for the winter holidays, there was barely a moment to sit down for the rest of the morning and the entire afternoon at the Cozy Corgi, and it wasn't simply people wanting to gossip about their speculations around Paulie. Though we didn't reach the level that occurred during summer, the steady stream of tourist families, couples browsing hand in hand, and grandparents picking out presents, kept Ben and me on our toes.

As if making up for his rather spoiled demeanor at Rocky Mountain Imprints, Watson was nearly filled with Christmas cheer, at least after he finally had breakfast and a snack or two. My typically grumpy fluffball actually wandered around the shop —and not always at Ben's side—allowing the customers to pet, take selfies, and patronize him with baby talk.

We had the perfect level of busy that allowed me to be present and cheerful with the customers while letting the details unfolding over the past several days tumble around the back of my mind with a pleasant buzz.

As I gift-wrapped the Alice Borchardt *Legend of the Wolves* trilogy for a rather prim woman—who made it very clear that she would never stoop so low on the literary ladder as to read about werewolves and she had some guilt around indulging her sister's obsession—I pondered the relationship between Trevor, Finnegan, and Jake. What were the chances that the three friends, each with their own criminal past, had nothing to do with the string of break-ins, especially when two of them were immediately connected to Santa's Cause and the elves? Maybe they were low-hanging fruit, but I ultimately decided I'd be foolish not to consider them. I'd do a quick Google search to see what I could pull up about their pasts and then run it by Susan.

While I helped an older gentleman decide on the newest of Carla Hall's cookbooks, I fell back to considering that it all might have been a ploy between Marty Clark and Gentry Farmer. There was no doubt it was good publicity, and judging by the conversations I'd heard in the shop, even if the tourists were taking sides, they still wanted to visit both shops. However, despite that, it seemed that Santa's Cause was getting the better end of the bargain, if that was the case, as many of the tourists talked about wanting to own one of the elves for themselves. Not to mention that I didn't pick up on any sort of insincerity when Marty spewed hatred of Gentry. It was possible for them to have entered an agreement and still despise each other, I supposed, but I doubted it.

It wasn't until a young couple expecting their first child in the next week or two bought half my selection of children's picture books and the top one—*Narwhal's Otter Friend*—caught my eye as I slid the stack into a bag, that one detail of Marty's diatribe came back to me. As he'd been ranting about Gentry being a bully, he'd included his "gang of friends" in that accusation. I supposed that was open to interpretation, but it was pretty common to see Gentry in the presence of Pete Miller, Jared Pitts, and Joe Singer. Clearly Gentry had a temper, and from what I'd seen, Pete did as well. As I thought of it, I recalled well over a year ago Jared having an outburst of temper on the softball field and punching Pete Miller in the face. Though I tried to picture Jared doing anything like that to Paulie, I just couldn't. And Joe? He was a nearly silent friendly giant, if I'd ever seen one. Still... the good old boys club was a true and real thing.

By the time late afternoon rolled around, Watson had resorted to his typical self and napped on top of his ottoman by the fire. It was late enough no sunlight streamed through in his favorite napping spot by the front windows. Ben and I reshelved misplaced books, straightened Christmas decorations, and got ready to close for the day.

Just as I was considering following Watson's direction and curling up in front of the fire with a mystery novel, Katie came down the steps, holding up a platter. "Fred, Ben, come try this. You'll never scoff at fruitcake again."

It showed my true faith in Katie that I didn't doubt that statement to be pure fact.

As Ben and I took simultaneous bites, we rewarded her with twin groans of ecstasy.

Katie scoffed. "Oh come on. Now you're just being overly dramatic on purpose."

In response, I took another bite and unintentionally groaned again as the juices from a rum-soaked raisin combined with cinnamon and clove.

"No way." Ben didn't take a second bite, but still

spoke with his mouth full. "This is seriously great. Not dry or bricklike at all!"

Katie burst out with a laugh. "Now *that's* high praise."

"Well, more than just that, but I mean..." Ben shrugged as he took another bite and kept right on talking. "I know you're you, but I thought it was a rule fruitcake *had* to be dry."

"Not a rule." Katie inspected her own slice of fruitcake. "Sometimes I do break the cherry rule and use Bing and Rainier, but I wanted the bright Christmas colors today, so I went with the traditional candied red and green."

I finally joined the conversation. "It's seriously wonderful. I think I might want to try it for breakfast, toasted with butter or something."

"Now *that's* a brilliant—"

When I heard the door open and shut behind me, cutting Katie off, I silently wished I'd locked up a few minutes early. It always seemed, without fail, customers who arrived moments before closing tended to stay a long time and never buy anything. I took a second or two to make sure I had on my best "Welcome to the Cozy Corgi" smile.

Before I could turn around, Watson let out a bark and leapt off the ottoman with so much force it slid across the hardwood floor and hit the nearby bookshelves. As if he were a different dog, he moved so quickly there was nothing more than a blur as he streaked toward the front door and collided with someone, losing himself in a frantic mess of cries and whimpers.

"I missed you too, buddy."

A thrill shot through me at the sound of Leo's voice. I turned to see him kneeling to greet Watson, whose frantic whimpers were accompanied with bounces as he lathered Leo's face with kisses. I wasn't sure I'd ever seen anything so perfect in my life as the two of them together. Then another wave washed over me, this time a strange mix of pain and pleasure. I'd missed Leo, but I hadn't realized quite how much until right then. The hidden envelope pierced my thoughts, trying to steal my joy at seeing him. I shoved it away, mentally lighting a match and tossing it into the boot box.

Then Leo's honey-brown gaze lifted, as he continued to pet Watson, and found me. I tried not to flinch and wasn't sure if I'd succeeded. He'd only been gone a few days, but I could swear he'd aged. Tight lines crinkled around his eyes—as he was several years younger than me, those were typically smooth. Then he smiled, a warm, beautiful thing that softened his handsome face. Even from a distance, I could see him sigh and relax.

That was all I needed to know. Right there. I wasn't going to give the envelope another thought. There was no deceit in that reaction. It was clear Leo's world was better because I was in it. And the same was true of mine.

Leo stood as I crossed the store, though Watson never stopped bounding and pawing at his legs. I barely started to say hello before he wrapped his arms around me, pulled me close, lowered his head to my neck, and took a deep breath. Then another, before I felt him relax. "My Lord, it's good to see you. And smell you. Shampoo, books, coffee, clove."

I laughed, and though some part of me was self-conscious knowing Katie and Ben, maybe even Nick by that point, were watching, I pulled back and kissed him, and felt myself relax along with him. Watson's bounding now included pawing at my legs as well, accompanied by desperate whimpers. "You're just smelling the bookshop and Katie's baking."

"No." He didn't argue more than that as he ran a thumb over my cheek and gave another sigh. "I'm not. I'm really not."

Watson's whimpering was so intense that it

pulled our attention back down, and I almost expected to see tears in *his* eyes. As one, Leo and I sank down and lathered attention on him, both of us getting kisses across our faces as we caused a flurry of dog hair and wagging nubbed corgi tail.

"Good gracious, if I wasn't already in the Christmas spirit, you three would put me there." Katie stepped up, the Pacheco twins standing a little behind her. "Luckily, I am, though you're about to give me a sugar high."

Leo stood and gave her a warm hug. "Good to see you, my dear. Looks like you've been busy baking, as always."

Katie held up the tray after the hug was broken. "Nothing says welcome home like fruitcake!"

Leo balked, then laughed. "Are you sure that's what fruitcake says? I was pretty certain it whispered something more along the lines of, *I'm forced to buy you a Christmas present and I hate your guts, so here you go. Don't choke on the sour candied cherries.*"

"Insult my baking again, Smokey Bear, and you will be choking on something, I guarantee you." She smacked his shoulder. "Shut up and try this. And then spend the next ten minutes telling me how brilliant a baker I am, and that I can even make candied cherries taste good."

"Do you see that?" Leo looked down at Watson. "Do you hear the threats? Are you going to allow such treatment?"

Watson merely whimpered joy and glanced at Katie, then back at Leo, who chuckled.

"Hmmm." Katie's eyes twinkled. "I wonder..." She passed the tray of fruitcake to Nick and then turned back to Watson, hands on her hips and her voice switching to a singsong playful tone that always got Watson revved. "Treat?"

Watson didn't seem to notice, he just kept bouncing, pleading for Leo to squat back down.

"Treat?" Katie tried again, clapping her hands that time. "Does Watson want a treat? I'll get you one of your favorite treats!"

Watson paused midbounce, turned a wide-eyed, frantic stare at Katie, clearly considering, and then went back to Leo, bouncing once more.

With a loud, satisfied laugh, Leo sank to the floor, legs spread, and wrapped Watson in a bear hug, sending him into pure Corgi heaven. "Now *that's* love, isn't it?" Still hugging Watson, though having to twist his face to keep from getting a tongue in his mouth as he spoke, he angled toward Katie. "I say let this boy have his favorite treats, please, madam, and I'll even pretend to like your fruitcake."

Katie had started to whirl but whipped back around after a couple of paces. "Pretend? *Pretend?* You haven't even tried it yet."

A little less than an hour later, with snow falling outside the cabin window, the lights twinkling on the Christmas tree, the fireplace crackling, emptied Penelope's bags on the coffee table, and bellies satisfied, Leo, Watson, and I sat curled up on the couch. Leo's back was against the arm of the sofa, I sat between his legs, my head reclined on his shoulder, while Watson sat between my legs, curled up in the material of my fuzzy Christmas nightgown and snoring softly.

"You sound so tired. And looked even more so when you got to the Cozy Corgi today." Realizing how that sounded, I rushed to correct myself. "Not that you didn't look handsome, it's just—"

He chuckled softly, the low vibration of it rumbling through me. "No, I didn't. Not a chance. I didn't even feel human at that point, but I'm back to myself more every minute."

I rubbed his arm and sank deeper against him, wanting to comfort. "I'm sorry that going home has that effect on you. It's supposed to be the opposite, where you feel loved and supported."

"Hardly." Another laugh, though this one dark. However, when he spoke again, he sounded more like himself. "Technically, I've just come from home, but it's not home, never was." Leo sighed and took a long, soft breath, as if breathing in the scent of my hair. "Although, if we're speaking *technically*, I guess Estes Park is home, but it's not, not really. It's you, Fred. *You're* home. I couldn't breathe easier when I crested the mountains and Estes Valley came into view, no matter how beautiful it was. My spirit didn't still, surrounded by the forests I love so much. Only you, seeing you, feeling you, smelling... well... everything *you*. You're home."

My eyes stung, but I held the tears at bay. However, my voice cracked, betraying me. "I feel the same." I did. Completely. No matter the fears and worries that had been whispering. If anything, the truth of the sentiment only strengthened my internal debate of what to do. "I don't think I could be happier or more content than right now." I pulled his arms tighter around me.

Leo lowered his head so that it rested on mine and breathed deep once more. "Can we just sit like this forever? Let all the stress and worry and struggle of life lay buried under the snow outside and then melt away with the rest of it in spring?"

"Yes, please."

And we did. For a little while. No thoughts or worries or what-ifs entered. There was only the warmth and crackle of the fire and Watson's harmonizing snores. The Christmas lights twinkled in time with the falling snow on the other side of the window, and the warmth of each other's bodies lulled us into a meditative, dreamlike state.

For a little while.

Then Leo's stomach growled.

"You know," Leo murmured beside my ear, "don't tell Katie this, but I could really go for another slice of that fruitcake right now."

I laughed, started to angle up to look at him, but then didn't want to disrupt Watson or fully break the mood. "I was actually just thinking the same thing. Which is practically disgusting considering we *just* had cheeseburgers, fries, and malts. I swear that girl has a superpower. Who's heard of fruitcake being good? I actually read a mystery once where fruitcake was the murder weapon."

He chuckled, the low rumble from his chest radiating through me pleasantly. "No you didn't."

"I have! I promise!" I settled for pulling his arm

tighter around me. "You know me better than to think I'd lie about a mystery novel."

"That's true." I felt Leo shrug. "Sounds like you got yourself involved in another mystery since I've been gone. Not that I'm surprised."

What remained of our illusion of being suspended from the rest of the world faded, but returning to normal life with Leo was pretty sublime on its own. "It was just kind of a fun one, after the elf was left at the Cozy Corgi a few days ago, along with a fruitcake—which was not on par with Katie's, by the way. It was nice to have something to puzzle over that didn't have life-and-death attached to it, you know?" The memory of finding Paulie that morning, wide-eyed and helpless flitted through my mind. "Doesn't feel quite so fun anymore."

Leo pulled me in tighter yet, not needing any further explanation. "Paulie is safe. It's not life-and-death. And from what you and Katie said earlier, it sounds like you have some... good leads."

There was a strange tone to his last words, and I looked up then, causing my legs to shift and Watson to let out an annoyed grunt in his sleep. "What does that mean? You think I'm on the wrong track?"

He hesitated, then shook his head, but instead of looking at me, stared into the glowing fire, casting shadows under his sharp jaw. "No... but"—another shrug, and another grunt from Watson—"I don't know, it just seems kind of convenient that the elf artist and the Christmas shop owner's nephew both have criminal pasts of some sort. I mean, everyone would look at them with their pasts. They'd have to be pretty dense to try to pull that off without knowing they'd be suspects."

"I was thinking that earlier today, low-hanging fruit, if you will." Though it seemed off, it was the only option that made real sense. "Don't forget that they're also friends with that Jake Jazz character who works at Delilah's. He's horrible. He's got a criminal past as well. Maybe it's obvious, but it also seems like too much of a coincidence to not be connected."

Leo was silent for a little bit, and I could see his thoughts turning, so I waited. When he finally spoke it was hesitant. "I've had a few interactions with Jake. I won't say that I don't have concerns about him, and I even warned Delilah about them, but we all need second chances."

Despite my earlier promise, the manila envelope called out from the other room.

Before I could give in to the impulse of getting it and opening it with Leo then and there, he kept going. "That's one of the great things about Delilah. I know she has her faults, but it doesn't matter if it's one of her basset hounds or a person, she doesn't write them off just because of choices they made in the past or because the rest of the world rejected them." He finished the sentiment with a long, tired sigh.

Repositioning once more, I turned to face him.

Watson, chuffing his annoyance, stood as I turned, and looked down at the hearth. After a second, he surprised me by not punishing us with his absence and crawled over my lap to sprawl in the tight wedge between Leo's and my legs. Automatically, both of our hands lowered and we stroked him as we spoke.

"You sound... almost as if you're taking this personally." I wasn't sure how far to push. "That by wondering about Jake, Trevor, and Finnegan, I'm... I don't know exactly, insulting you?"

With a flinch, he looked back at me, this time the fire shadowing half his face. "No, not at all. What I'm feeling has nothing to do with you, and I don't think you're insulting me or anyone else." The lines around his eyes that I'd noticed when he arrived at the shop returned. "If anything, I think I'm insulting myself by considering them, or insulting myself by not wanting to consider them." He let out a heavy laugh and shook his head. "Sorry. I'm just tired. And... glad to be home with you. To really and truly be home."

Stealing one of his hands from Watson's back, I linked our fingers together. "Family was that rough this time?"

He nodded, eyes squeezed shut. "I spent the whole time lecturing Mom to stop giving my brother chance after chance after chance." He chewed on his lower lip for a moment. "Ronnie doesn't deserve it. I know that's horrible, but he doesn't. And Mom just continues to play the victim, over and over. It's like as soon as she was free from our father, Ronnie stepped up to fill the role, and she welcomed it. If anything, Ronnie's worse."

"I'm sorry." I didn't know what else to say. "I wish I could fix it or..."

Leo laughed gently and gave me a soft smile. "That's what I wish. I keep looking for ways to fix it. Part of why I moved away, I mean, outside of wanting my career. But at some point, everyone's an adult, they're all making their own choices. If I could make it for them, I would, but I can't." He lifted his other hand, but Watson didn't seem to notice, and Leo cupped my cheek as he frequently did. "I start to lose myself when I'm there. Or at least who I want to be. That never happens with you."

Still not knowing what to say, I simply covered his hand with mine and let my head sink into his touch.

After a while he gave another shrug. "I guess I'm overcompensating with even suggesting those three guys are too obvious. It is hard to believe that it would be a coincidence that all of them would have that past, have a friendship, and not be at the center of the drama of the elves that one of them makes, for crying out loud." Another laugh. "I guess in this sense, I'm taking Mom's role, refusing to see the obvious."

I twisted slightly, pressing my lips to the palm of his hand. "Well, like we've said. It's not life-and-death, so..."

"Maybe, maybe not." He grinned, looking like Leo once more. "Like you said, the fruitcakes they are leaving weren't made by Katie. Maybe each one is a clear attempted murder. It's just that no one has been dumb enough to actually try and eat one."

I laughed with him. "You're not the first one to suggest that."

Though his stomach continued to rumble, Leo didn't bring up food again. "You know, you're right. I was beyond worn out when I got home. I feel a billion times better now and have transitioned to pleasantly tired." Another chuckle. "Okay, maybe a *bit* more than."

"Bed?" I shifted, finally leaving his embrace to turn to look at him, disturbing Watson and earning a huff. "We can go to sleep early, and by the morning you'll be the charmingly handsome, fresh-faced park ranger again."

He snorted a laugh. "As long as you think so, I'll be good with that."

NINE

The next morning dawned just as beautifully as the one before—with the thick new layer of snow, maybe even more so. After reading the sweet note left from Leo, who'd already reported to work, I leaned closer to the bedroom window to get a better angle of the mountaintops over the trees and pulled back before my nose touched the pane. Even without the contact, the cold was palpable. Only then did I notice the crackling frost growing from the corners. Even that was beautiful—the jagged snowflake pattern making its way over the glass.

A loud, exaggerated yawn sounded from behind. Turning, I found Watson stretching, his tiny front legs pushed out in front of him like he was trying to reach something over the hardwood floor while his hind legs remained in his dog bed, his rump in the air, and his nub of a tail appearing to reach just as insistently. With his jaw wide open, and even his tongue seeming to stretch, I couldn't hold back a giggle.

Watson froze, his brown gaze darting in my direction. Despite his position, he managed a scowl.

The irritation at being caught in such an undignified manner, and Watson's internal debate about what to do about it, was so evident that I couldn't help but laugh again.

He straightened abruptly, chuffed, started to grab one of his stuffed animals from the bed, then apparently decided there wasn't time, and sauntered out of the bedroom, casting the final glare over his shoulder as he disappeared out of view.

"You know," I couldn't help but call after him, "I've seen you sniff other dog's butts and eat out of the garbage. You can't put on airs with me, mister." I hesitated, waiting to see if I'd get any response. There was none. I chuckled again, but it ended with a shiver, causing me to refocus on the window. Gorgeous, yes, but clearly bitterly cold, which was unusual for Estes. I thought Watson and I would take one of our morning strolls through the woods, but I discarded that idea instantly. Grabbing my robe, I decided to have a leisurely breakfast instead.

After brushing my teeth and washing my face, I

found Watson waiting in the kitchen. He sat in front of the mint-green oven, his back to me, staring up at the cooktop in full expectation.

"It's a good thing I don't have children." I bent down to scratch his ear as I joined him, a little surprised when he didn't weave away out of pure principle. "If they were even half as spoiled as you, they'd be utter menaces to society."

Watson did weave then but angled his head so he nudged my hand roughly upward with his nose.

"I got it, Your Highness, I got it. You want break-fast. It's like you think I'm here to serve you." I scratched his ear again just for good measure. "And... you're probably right. Besides, who knows what today has in store. We both had to wait hours before we had breakfast yesterday. Let's be preemptive, shall we?"

By the time coffee was brewed and my scram-bled eggs and toast were plated, my moody corgi had forgiven my laughter at his expense and gazed up at me in pure adoration as I added a boiled, unseasoned egg to his reheated baked chicken.

"Yep, that look right there." I had to settle for scratching Watson's haunches as his head was already lowered so he could inhale his breakfast. "One of the many reasons I'm wrapped around your little finger, or your barely there tail, I should say."

He either ignored me or didn't hear over the sound of his slurping, not that it mattered.

I settled down, doing a little slurping of my own as I took a long draft of heavenly coffee, enjoying the heat while the tie-dyed flamingo-curtained kitchen window framed the snow falling outside.

Just as I'd taken my first bite of egg, the-Leo-specific chime sounded from my bedroom. The phone was on silent, but I'd set it up so Leo would ring through. I hurried to get it, surprised as he didn't often text when he was on duty at the park.

Check this out! I'm betting Athena had a hand in it. What do you think? And good morning, so glad to be home and with you again!

I sighed a quick moan of contentment as warmth that had nothing to do with the furnace or fireplace wrapped me in an embrace. I allowed myself to revel in that for a few moments before focusing on the photo of a newspaper article below Leo's text. As I returned to breakfast, Watson trotting along at my feet as if he'd known it was from Leo, I zoomed up on the image, making the text easier to read Rhonda Biggler's column as I ate.

Let's be honest, I'm the first one to admit that I've rather enjoyed the nightly break-ins around town since the first of December. I'll even go so far as to say part of me hoped my own home would be the recipient. Who would have ever dreamed of actually wanting someone sneaking into your house during the dead of night? But the idea of Santa coming in, letting you know whether or not you've been a good boy or girl with a fruitcake or piece of coal, and leaving one of his charming little helpers, was magical. Really, it's something from when we were younger, probably a lot of us would have hoped for that, and the sound of reindeer hooves on our roofs to boot.

But it turns out Santa is nothing more than an overgrown schoolyard bully. Things took an ugly turn when he broke into Paws. As I'm sure most of you have heard by now, our own Paulie Bezor was tied up, tormented, and terrorized by this delinquent.

Up until this point, the Estes Park police, I feel, haven't shown an investment in bringing the nightly crime spree to an end. I'm not casting blame, as I previously stated, there was something charming about it all. Now, however, I'm certain we can all agree that physical assault and vandalism cross the line.

So, hear this, Santa. *The Chipmunk Chronicles* has narrowed your identity down to two possibilities. Both of you are new to Estes, both gainfully employed at two of our shops downtown. And both of you have criminal pasts, which are public record. So, locals, do your research, it isn't hard. Do the math and put the pieces together and then go to the shop owners and inquire why they support those who make our town unsafe, hostile, and as far away from Christmas cheer as possible.

Santa, take your elves and get out of our town, or like the villagers of old, we will gather up our pitchforks and drive you away!

Somewhere during the reading, I had paused with a forkful of scrambled eggs halfway to my lips. The morsel fell off, but I barely paid it any mind as I placed the fork down and scanned the article again.

I was certain Leo was right. Athena was behind this, and I would be surprised if she didn't pay for it with her job. It wasn't written in her style, and it still had Rhonda Biggler's voice—though on steroids—but

I could hear Athena's motherly defense of Paulie behind every word. Not to mention that she practically called out Jake Jazz and Finnegan Clark by name.

This wasn't good, not good at all. There was no doubt Athena would pay a price, especially since the paper's majority stockholder, Ethel Beaker, held a grudge against Athena to begin with. Not to mention the conflict it might cause between her and Paulie, as he'd been clear he didn't want any of us to stir the pot by defending him.

Then there was the whole issue of Delilah and Marty. The photography and Christmas shops had practically been named as well. I wasn't familiar enough with the laws around libel to know if the article had crossed that line or not, but it had to be close.

And what about Santa? If either Jake or Finnegan was behind it, from what I'd seen from them—or Jake at least—I had the feeling the article would be seen as a challenge. And if neither of them was actually the culprit, then whoever was dressing up as Santa would surely feel emboldened, knowing someone else would take the rap.

"See?" I looked down at Watson, who was staring up as if he could see my plate through the bottom of the table, waiting for me to drop some more scrambled eggs. "It's a good thing we had breakfast at home. It looks like it's going to be a long morning."

He whimpered, refocused on me, and then back to the underside of the table, whimpering again.

I tossed him a chunk of egg—it really was a good thing I didn't have children. Figuring it was high time to get downtown, I stood. With a swipe of the screen, the article went away and I noticed it hadn't just been Leo contacting me. There was a missed call from Katie an hour before and two text messages. I clicked on them.

Come straight down when you wake up, Fred. We've been broken into again. It's not just fruitcake this time.

The second message had come through a few minutes later.

I'm pretty sure this is my fault.

When Watson and I arrived downtown, there was still over an hour before opening time, not that the Cozy Corgi would be opening that morning.

Watson growled and went on high alert the second we entered the bookshop. Maybe he could smell whoever had been there dressed as Santa, or perhaps he just felt the anxiety in the air. Maybe both.

I didn't have the heightened sense of smell or the innate intuition of a dog, but even without Watson or the text messages, I would've known something was off the second we walked in. Everything in the bookshop was in perfect condition, just as I left it the night before—the books were still on the shelves, the holiday decorations were in place and their lights twinkling merrily, even the cash register was untouched. However, no piped-in Christmas music greeted us, and there were no fresh aromas of yeast, cinnamon, and butter.

After Watson and I hurried up the stairs, I stopped, tears instantly burning in my eyes as I took in Katie standing in the middle of her ruined bakery. I barely even noticed the Pacheco twins, Susan, or Officer Cabot.

Katie's pale face turned at the sound of my gasp, and she stiffened. I knew my best friend well enough that I could see the state she was in. Her short frame stood rigid and tense, and though there was strain over her features, her eyes were clear and dry. She was hard as stone and in her warrior mode.

That changed the second her gaze met mine.

Her shoulders slumped, and tears began to course down her cheek. "Oh... Fred..."

She didn't get anything else out before I hurried over and wrapped her in my arms. She began to shake. At our feet, Watson whined and pressed his weight against our legs.

Holding her close, I scanned the bakery as I murmured reassuring nothings. The walls were covered in coal and soot. The antique tables were overturned. Several of the legs of the rustic log chairs were broken, shattered as if stomped on or hit with a baseball bat or iron bar. The overstuffed couches intermingled through the space were slashed, stuffing pouring out like internal organs from a wound.

Maybe the worst was the kitchen and bakery itself. The glass of the cases was shattered, and whatever had been used to break the wooden chairs had been unleashed on the equipment. My gaze fell on the beautiful espresso machine, now looking like a smart car run over by a semi.

"We have insurance, Katie. We have insurance." I stroked her hair, my fingers accidentally yanking her curls. "It's just stuff. We can redo it."

"I know." Pulling back, she released me, wiped her eyes, and took a steadying breath before she continued. "I'm being silly. You're right, the important thing is that it's just stuff, no one's hurt." She moved away, and for once, Watson trailed along beside Katie, keeping sentinel for her. "But..." She stopped by the counter, where an elf sat with a large chunk of coal in its lap between seafoam-green shoes and partially covered by its fluffy beard. "This is..."

Nick had moved closer as well, and as he stared at the countertop, he put a hand on her shoulder. I wasn't surprised to see a tear roll down the sensitive young man's cheek.

I let out another gasp of horror as I joined them and saw that it wasn't just random smears and streaks of coal that covered the marble, but words. A fury ignited inside me as I read them. Horrible words, not just because of some of their vulgarity, but because they were directed specifically at Katie. Words about her weight, her looks, her... I stopped myself from reading the rest and turned to her again. "They're just words. They're not true. And I swear to you, I will find who did this."

Susan stepped forward, saying out loud what I'd already been thinking. "We'll definitely find who did this. It's not like we don't already know."

Katie shook her head, curls flying. "It's not the

words." She wiped her eyes and reached a hand out as if to touch the scrawling coal script.

Susan grabbed her hand swiftly but gently. "Remember, don't touch anything."

Katie nodded and pulled her hand back. "It truly isn't the words. They're awful, but they're nothing I haven't heard before. The majority of them aren't anything *most* women haven't heard before, but..." Her voice broke. "The marble, Fred. That will never come out. It's ruined."

I started to remind her that it was just a thing, replaceable, then recalled the countless hours she'd searched for that specific marble, the trips she'd taken to Denver, touring stone galleries. The respect and awe she had for a material that came from so deep in the earth and had taken so long to form. It was what she was most proud of in her bakery and what the rest had been built around. I didn't have words, so I just wrapped an arm around her again.

Officer Campbell Clifton Cabot joined us at the counter. "I'll bleach it for you, Miss Pizzolato. Bleach takes care of everything, my mama always said. That or duct tape. But I don't think duct tape will help here."

Before Katie could respond, Susan wheeled on

him. "Cabot, if there was ever a time to keep your mouth shut, this is it."

He gave a nod, flushed bright red, and stepped back. To my surprise, though, he didn't follow her directions. "They're not true. Those words, Miss Pizzolato, they're not true. You're as pretty as the day is long and just as sweet."

Susan had opened her mouth, clearly intending to bark at him again, but stopped, a look of surprise in her pale blue eyes.

"Thank you, Campbell." Katie sniffed, but smiled at him. "I don't think bleach will actually help, but I do appreciate you trying."

Sometime later, after we'd sent the twins home, Katie, Watson, and I took shelter in the mystery room. Watson, true to form, curled up on his ottoman and napped. Katie and I simply sat on the antique sofa and stared into the crackling flames, both lost to our thoughts while Susan and Campbell finished their work upstairs.

It was only the awareness of how much Katie was hurting that kept me in the Cozy Corgi. Everything in me screamed for action. In truth, it was probably good that Katie needed me, because it wasn't research, snooping, or gathering gossip that I was inclined to do. I wanted to storm across the street, burst into Delilah's shop, and use one of her heavy old-time cameras to beat Jake Jazz across the head. I was used to my temper, but it was rare that I had any inclination toward physical violence. But I was willing to bet I wouldn't feel an ounce of hesitation if I saw that man's face. As always, my father came to mind along with the ache of the loss of him. How many horrific cases had he endured and solved? Cases much worse than cruel words on stone, and I knew the kind of man he'd been, the pure fighter-for-justice soul he had. Not once had he given into the desire to take matters into his own hands, to act as judge and jury. Instead, he ensured that he'd find every shred of evidence to guarantee the evil would pay for their crimes.

Even with the thoughts of my father, it took all my strength to remain in control. How a person could say such horrible things to anyone was beyond me, but especially Katie, of all people. It was inconceivable.

And again, it was such a clear, exaggerated form of bullying. Just like with Paulie. And although his victimhood-past was very different from what Katie had experienced, both of them had been on the receiving end of torment, gossip, and ridicule. But people like Jake Jazz? It was like they could smell it, like a lure that called to them, tempting them to come wallow around in it.

And the words scrawled across that marble? My hands clenched into fists as they flittered through my mind. I knew that they'd do the same in Katie's as she tried to fall asleep each night, seeing the names and disgusting terms for her so bold in that deep black coal against the beautiful muted white of her marble. All the insults and...

I paused for a second, realizing what the insults were missing. Everything had been about her looks, her size, or a host of other stereotypical insults thrown at women. None of them were about her past or the secrets of who her parents were that she used to keep hidden.

Without thinking, I turned toward her. Trying to add it up.

Clearly feeling my gaze, Katie shifted, looking at me and lifting a brow. "What?"

I shook my head, not wanting to dredge it all up, but then couldn't stop myself. It wasn't like she wasn't sitting there thinking about it all anyway. "You said in the text that you thought it was your fault. I just assumed because of your past, but—"

Catching myself, I started again. "Your *parents'* past, I mean. But... there was nothing written about—"

"No." Her cheeks flared, and she looked away, staring into the fire. "I didn't mean that. I just..." She sighed and then was quiet for so long that I didn't think she was going to finish, and I couldn't bring myself to push. When she finally spoke again, her voice was so unusually quiet that I had to strain to hear it over the crackling of the fire and Watson's soft snores. "Last night, well, early evening, really, I was finishing up with last bits of Christmas present designs with Joe. As I was leaving the shop, Jake and Finnegan were coming from..." She shrugged. "Well, I don't know where they were coming from, not that it matters. Anyway, I bumped into Finnegan, accidentally elbowed him in the stomach. I don't know how it all happened." She closed her eyes, reliving it. "I was moving too fast, there was a bit of ice on the sidewalk, they were right there. It was just a quick, silly collision. It irritated Jake, and he instantly launched into calling me all sorts of names like... well, you saw them on the marble."

Horrified, I reached out a hand, placing it on her knee, my fury increasing. "Katie, how in the world is this your fault? You're not responsible for the names he called you. You didn't do anything to deserve him saying anything about—"

Katie laughed, and though there was still a dark shadow in her eyes when she looked at me, there was also a touch of reproach. "Winifred Page, you know me better than that. Number one, it's nothing I haven't heard before, and two, like I give a flying croissant crumb over what some idiot thinks about my waist size." She blushed again but didn't whisper. "It's just that... well... Joe must've heard because he stepped out the front door right in the middle of it, and I..." Her blush grew. "Well, I got embarrassed. It's one thing to be called that stuff. Like I said, no big deal, and I can stand up for myself. But for him to hear..." Her gaze darted away. "For *anyone* to hear... it's humiliating."

In that moment, though I wouldn't have predicted it possible, a realization cut through my anger, leaving me feeling a little amazed. How had I missed it? Or maybe it was new, I wasn't sure. But either way, it was as obvious as the blush over Katie's cheeks that she had a crush... or feelings... or something... for Joe Singer.

"Well." Katie chuffed out a laugh of a breath. "I guess I took a page out of your book and completely lost my temper. I... slapped him. Jake, I mean. Not

Joe." Another laugh at the thought, and it sounded a bit more like herself. "I told Jake *exactly* where he could go, where he could get off, and how quick he could get there."

"Good!" I laughed as well, and relief flooded through me, seeing the proof that Katie's fighting spirit was still in her. "He deserved it."

"Yeah. He did." She gestured upstairs. "Now I'm paying for it. I wish I'd just kept my mouth shut."

"Oh, don't you worry about that."

Susan's voice startled both of us, and Watson as well, as he woke up with a bark and a growl.

"Calm down, fleabag." Susan rolled her eyes but didn't move from where she leaned against the doorway, arms crossed, and she clearly had been listening to us. "We'll make him pay. For you and Paulie. And really, just for being creepy. It's one thing to be insulting and rude, it's another to leave weird little elves all over the place. Who does that?"

Perhaps it was because I was finally starting to get ahold of my temper, or at least figure out steps to avoid igniting that particular fuse to begin with, but I suggested Susan—with or without Officer Cabot—speak to Jake Jazz on her own. It was also just as likely I couldn't handle sticking my foot in my mouth in front of Delilah again. I really should have made time to go over to the photography shop to attempt to repair the damage I'd done during her Pink Panther meeting, but as with a few things lately, I'd slipped into avoidance. Such avoidance wasn't typical for me, but... who knew? I decided to blame it on the holiday season. Either way, with everything going on with the elves and Jake Jazz's involvement, now wasn't the time to try to repair things with Delilah.

Plus, I had a different target.

While Katie started the process of contacting the

insurance company, I fixed Watson's leash to his collar, and we headed through downtown. If anything, the day had only gotten colder, probably due to the breeze that was treating Elkhorn Avenue like a wind tunnel. Even as I passed the toyshop with its hand-carved wooden toys filling the window ledge, none of my Christmas spirit returned. Although I did pause a couple of seconds to take in the spectacularly garish, yet charming, window display of Victorian Antlers. My uncles—Percival mainly, I was willing to bet—had gone with a Dolly Parton "Hard Candy Christmas" theme.

From inside, Gary waved from atop a ladder as he hung decorations for their party later that night, motioning for us to come in. But Watson pressed on, his head lowered nearly to the sidewalk, determined to get out of the cold. I offered an apologetic wave as I was dragged along. Even the wind didn't manage to fully sweep away the sound of Dolly Parton and Kenny Rogers wailing "I Believe in Santa Claus" from inside the antique store. Yep, definitely Percival's doing.

When we stepped out of the cold and into Santa's Cause, Mariah Carey made it a little more subtle with "All I Want for Christmas Is You," but not much. My temper flared as the door shut behind me and I saw tourists milling about the practical forest of multicolored trees as if nothing had happened. Like it didn't matter that the Cozy Corgi was closed, that Katie's beautiful bakery had been destroyed, and that there was no chance she'd be making Christmas pastries like she had planned.

Watson gave a giant shake of his entire body, flinging little ice particles of sleet that had covered his fur as we walked over to a couple of the glass shelves and displays.

I patted his head. "Good boy."

It might've been petty, but it was better than giving in to my temper. Although that faltered yet again when I realized most of the sleet had landed on a display of glittery porcelain penguins. The melting water droplets merely made it look more authentic.

Scanning the shop, I searched for Finnegan, or his uncle. I couldn't spot them, but I was distracted by a couple of the employees helping the tourists. They were dressed as elves, complete with red-and-green felt hats with bells on the end, white wide-brimmed collars, thick black belts, and finished with yet more bells on the toes of their pointed elfin boots. How had I overlooked that detail when I was in before? Surely that wasn't a new addition. No one had that low standard of decorum.

Watson growled and backed up, his rump bumping into my leg when one of the employees scurried by, the bells on their shoes chiming frantically.

Of all the nerve.

Another one of the elves peeked around a plastic life-sized Nativity set done entirely out of flamingos —that any other time I would've simply *had* to have purchased for my stepfather—and started our way.

It was at that moment I noticed Trevor Donovan exit from the back room, carrying a box toward the counter. With a wave toward the human elf, I made a beeline across the shop, Watson scurrying along at my heels, trying to keep up.

Trevor looked up in surprise, one of the now hated elves in his hand, the long pointy red hat woven through a couple of his fingers. "Oh! Um..." His eyes squeezed shut for a second. "Winifred, right?" Without waiting for a response, he glanced down and smiled. "And Watson."

"That's right." I nodded briskly, unable to start out with niceties. "Are Marty or Finnegan Clark here?"

He hesitated, then shook his head. "No. They'll be back soon. They're meeting Pastor Davis."

"Pastor Davis?" I hadn't seen the preacher of

Estes Valley Church in several months, and I found the man charmingly endearing. Even so, the mention of him didn't manage to water down my mood. "Is Finnegan going to make a confession or something?"

Trevor flinched and set the fuzzy little elf on the counter. "Um... No? I'm not sure what he'd... confess about?" Instead of meeting my gaze, Trevor bent one knee to focus on Watson. "They're picking up more Christmas lists of families in need from Pastor Davis. We hang them on the giving tree by the front." He reached out to pet Watson, who, though I caught an audible grumble, allowed his chest to be scratched.

I started to make another smart-alecky comment, then caught myself. That wasn't going to help. And even though Finnegan wasn't here, since he'd gone out to eat with them at Habaneros, it seemed Trevor was friends with Finnegan and Jake. Maybe he knew something. "I'll wait for a little bit. I have a couple of questions for them."

Still not looking at me, Trevor nodded, and when Watson finally backed away, he stood once more. "That will work. Make yourself at home. Let me know if I can help you with anything." With that, he returned to unboxing the elves and filling in some of the empty spaces on the display.

Settling back into myself, I opted to take the

"catch more flies with honey" route with Trevor Donovan. Easing into it, I decided to play twenty questions, even though I knew the answers from the research I had already done into the elves. "What brought you to Estes Park this year?"

He glanced over at me, as if surprised to find me still standing there. "Um... what?"

"Well..." I shrugged. "From what I understand, you're not part owner in Santa's Cause or anything, right? You simply make these elves." I mentally patted myself on the back for managing to say the word without a sneer, though the image of one of his creations sitting on Katie's ruined marble flashed in my mind. "Typically, the artists of the things we sell in town don't accompany their creations."

As intended, he eased instantly, clearly falling into a rote answer to a frequently asked question. "Part of my marketing strategy. Each year, I pick one tourist town known for their Christmas draw, and they get exclusive rights to sell that season's elf collection. This is my fifth year doing so."

"Why Estes?" I made a quick sweeping gesture around the shop. "We get plenty of tourists, but really, we're not that big of a shopping mecca, and while we do have some high-end stores, most of them are run-of-the-mill tourist-type caliber and hardly exclusive."

Trevor seemed uncomfortable again. "I thought I'd change tactics. Just to see. Historically, you're right. I've only done the more Hollywood-elite type resorts like Aspen and Vail. I even went to Verbier, Switzerland, last Christmas."

That was a huge switch, and though I would pick Estes Park any day over any other mountain town, from a business perspective, it was quite the drop in prestige. Not that I was going to say that. "Well, Estes is lucky to have you. I know both Gentry and Marty were desperate to carry your elves in their shop." I made another gesture around the store. "What made you choose to give the contract to Santa's Cause instead of the Christmas Cottage, which is a lot more established and well-known? Marty's commitment to giving some of the profits to charity?"

"Oh no." Trevor flinched again, clearly having not meant to speak quite so freely or emphatically, and gave me a self-conscious laugh as he looked my way once more. "I mean, yes, that's a huge value to me, and if I'm being blunt, good for my brand. But it was clear that Marty simply... um... wanted me... er... the elves, that is, more." As his nerves increased,

Trevor's speech sped up. "Marty's actually providing housing. Finnegan and I have a little cabin close to—"

"You live with Finnegan?" I hadn't meant to interrupt but couldn't help myself.

He nodded, but shut his mouth, not offering any more details.

Just hearing Finnegan's name again reignited my temper, and I leaned closer, allowing some of my aggression to be heard. "I did notice you hanging out with Finnegan and Jake when you and I met the other night. Are you aware of how your friends treat women?"

He flinched again, looked at me, his dark eyes wide, and then once more focused on his elves. "I... no... I..."

"What do you mean?"

Flinching myself, I turned to see Marty, the handles of a large paper bag gripped in one of his hands.

His gaze flicked from me, to Trevor, to Watson, then back to me. "You're not very subtle, Ms. Page. Are you trying to imply my nephew had something to do with the break-in at your bakery last night?"

I felt Watson's weight against my leg as he sat at attention, and I regained my footing somewhat.

"Interesting that *that's* where you went. Why? Do *you* think your nephew had something to do with Katie's bakery being destroyed?"

"I most certainly do not." Despite his anger, there wasn't hostility in Marty's tone, just a simple hardness. And though he addressed Trevor, he never took his gaze off me. "But we don't need to take my word for it. Trevor, can you attest to Finnegan's whereabouts last evening?"

"Of course." Trevor still sounded nervous. "We were home all night."

As if hearing his name, Finnegan also arrived, each of his hands also clutching the handles of paper bags as he did a quick scanning assessment of the situation. When his gaze landed on me, it was hard, like his uncle's, and while I also saw nerves like with Trevor, there was also a defiance. "I'd heard you fancy yourself a detective. You and your dog. If you're going to accuse me of something, you might as well do it to my face. But I have to question your ability, if you think that I look like someone who enjoys dressing like a big fat elf from the North Pole."

Looked like Marty was about to say something, but I couldn't tell if it was to me or Finnegan. I didn't give him a chance. "Actually, I'm not that concerned about the bakery. Or any proclivities you might have of dressing up as Santa Claus." Despite my best intentions, I stepped forward, pulling myself up to my full height, and was a little satisfied when Finnegan took half a step back, a lock of unkempt red hair falling in front of his left eye. "I think it says more about you that you would stand by and watch your friend degrade, bully, and attempt to humiliate a woman. Or anyone, for that matter."

"Now, Ms. Page—" Marty sounded on the edge of temper as well, but he didn't get to finish.

"I... she..." Finnegan sputtered for a moment, shaking his head. "I didn't even get a chance to try to defend your friend. Jake barely said anything at all, and she completely lost her mind on him."

Trevor kept his attention focused solely on his elves, and Marty slowly turned toward his nephew. "Excuse me? Are you saying—"

Once more, I didn't give Marty a chance, nor could I keep myself from jamming my finger sharply into Finnegan's chest. "*She* lost her mind? Are you kidding me? What did you want Katie to do, stand there and take it as Jake insulted her? Did you think it was funny? Is that how you get your *jollies, Santa*?" Everything clicked in that moment. I supposed it had before, but more pieces fell into place. Finnegan was directly involved; I could feel it. "Are you going to pretend that it's merely coincidence that the very things Jake said to Katie were scrawled over her marble countertop this morning?"

Maybe the jamming of my finger was too far, as Finnegan took a step forward as well, closing the distance between us, and didn't seem concerned at all about Watson growling dangerously below. "That's just a coincidence. I guarantee it's not the first time she's been called those things. Anybody with eyes can see she's—"

I slapped him, hard. Partly out of my fury at him in the moment, and partly just to stop him from saying whatever he was getting ready to about Katie.

Finnegan stumbled back, a hand going to his cheek, then, his own fury leaping in his eyes, lunged toward me.

"Don't!" Marty stepped between us, shoving his nephew in the chest, pushing him back.

For a second, it looked like Finnegan was going to try to dodge around his uncle, but then stood where he was, trembling.

Finally, Marty looked back at me. "You need to leave, or we're pressing charges for assault."

I barked out a laugh that sounded worthy of Susan. "Oh, please. Do that." Knowing there was no more to accomplish, and that things would only deteriorate, I cast one more glare at Finnegan. "You heard correctly. I'm good at getting to the bottom of things. Enjoy this Christmas. It will be your last one outside before returning to a cell."

He started to lunge again, as did Watson.

Marty shot out a hand once more, restraining his nephew, and I held firm to Watson's leash, more to keep him out of Finnegan's kicking range than to stop him from biting.

And with "Holly Jolly Christmas" playing over the speakers, and my head held high, I strolled purposely out of Santa's Cause, Watson growling and snarling over his shoulder the whole way.

ELEVEN

"Leo, I had such high hopes for you." Percival, clothed in a silver rhinestone-encrusted tuxedo with tails so long they could've doubled for the back of a ball gown, clapped Leo on the shoulder and shook his head exaggeratedly. "Okay, if I'm being honest, maybe my hopes weren't high, but there was a whisper of a prayer you might help my darling niece up her fashion game a little bit by the mere act of being in love." He sniffed and gave a once-over down Leo's body. "But it seems the opposite has occurred. She's dragging *you* down with her. And it doesn't matter how handsome you are, if you're invited to a party where the invitation clearly states holiday costume or formal attire required, you *don't* wear plain slacks and a sweater."

"I told you." I shoved Percival's narrow shoulder playfully, raising my voice to be heard over the music. "I didn't notice it said anything about how to dress on the invitation. And considering the day we had at the bookshop and bakery, I think it's impressive we're here at all."

Percival hummed, considering. "All right, that's the best excuse you've ever had for showing up in yet *another* broomstick skirt and peasant blouse. But you could have at least worn the fancy boots your sisters and mother made for you. You need a little bling at Victorian Antlers' first annual holiday party."

My stress level spiked at the mere mention of those boots and what I knew was concealed in the box with them. Luckily, Gary offered a distraction as he joined our small group. "This is *not* going to be an *annual* thing." The sparkling tuxedo that covered his wide ex-football-player build was red-and-white stripes, like a candy cane. He used an actual three-foot-tall cane, also done in swirled red-and-white stripes, to gesture toward the built-in speakers in the ceiling. "You sealed its fate when you insisted on playing the entire Dolly Parton and Kenny Rogers Christmas album on repeat, and it's so loud this party isn't going to last long enough to even count as a first. Everyone is wincing. I feel horrible for Watson—he's behind the counter with his head literally buried in a crate of tissue paper."

"Oh, poo." Percival snatched his husband's cane. "Watson's never social, and I spiked the eggnog with *plenty* of rum, so soon everyone will be dancing along." Despite the protest, he glanced around the antique shop, and a look of concern crossed his face before he grimaced. "Fine, I'll be right back." Percival whapped Gary on his backside as he hurried away. "But it's not because you said so."

Chuckling in his ever-good-natured way, Gary smiled at Leo and me. "Watson doesn't actually look too annoyed. He's still making his way through the pile of buffalo jerky Leo hid around the workspace. Happy as a fat, furry clam can be. But still, it's good of you to attend after the day you had, Fred. I tried to talk Percival into canceling, with everything going on, but after the grand opening of Santa's Cause and then the Christmas Cottage's party the other night, I'm afraid Percival was feeling Victorian Antlers was a bit overshadowed."

Leo chuckled as well, demonstrating one of the ways he and Gary were similar—both even-keeled and soothing. "Between the music and the trimmings, I'm not sure anything could overshadow Victorian Antlers at the moment."

Percival and Gary had gone all out. I couldn't imagine how much they'd spent on decorations.

Everything was oversized and sparkly. Giant glitter-encrusted pieces of candy hung in staggered clusters from the ceiling—peppermints, gumdrops, and replicas of the old-fashioned hard Christmas candies that went along perfectly with the Dolly Parton theme. Draped over the gorgeous Victorian antique furniture, stiff, wide streamers had been fabricated to look like red-and-green striped ribbon candy, complete with smaller clusters of fake sugared cranberries.

"It's a lot, I have to admit, but—" The volume of the music dipped suddenly, making it sound like I was yelling. The entire crowd let out a collective sigh of relief. Adjusting my volume, I continued, "The decorations are a lot, Gary, but I have to say, it is rather magical. It's like stepping into a Christmas version of Willy Wonka's chocolate factory."

He grinned. "It should be. Percival practically spent our entire retirement decking this place out." Gary refocused on Leo. "Are you off from park ranger duty on Christmas Day? Do you get to spend it with family?"

Leo flinched, just slightly, but his smile was back in place so quickly I doubted Gary noticed. "I am off on Christmas Day. But I just got back from seeing my family. I'm hoping to crash your celebration again, if that's all right with you."

Another warm laugh left Gary, and his large dark hand came up to pat Leo's cheek. "My dear boy, that's what I meant. *We* are your family."

"Oh. Of course. I'll—" Emotions stole Leo's words, but he nodded.

Though I wasn't surprised in the slightest, gratitude towards Gary flooded through me. To my whole family, really. They might be eccentric and strange in a lot of ways, but I couldn't imagine there being more love anywhere. I slipped my hand into Leo's, interlocking our fingers, and leaned against his arm.

He gave three silent squeezes, his nonverbal way to say *I love you.*

"*There!*" Percival rushed back with a flourish. "You can't say I never listen to you. And Watson was fine, enough like himself to growl at me for no reason. Makes me want to hunt my mistletoe headband you hid from me." He shoved the cane back into Gary's hands and started to turn. "No time for that, though. I need to make the rounds again and greet... oh!" His eyes widened, and then he beamed. "Now *that's* how you do it. If Katie can pull that off after the day she's had, neither of you have any excuse."

We turned as one and saw Katie walking in. She spotted us instantly and waddled our way. She was dressed in a full penguin outfit, just a few brown curls escaping under the orange bill of the beak over her eyes. She wore a red bow tie with green polka dots, but other than that—and her face peering through—she was a full-fledged penguin. The orange flipper-like contraptions covering her shoes appeared to make it both challenging to walk and to maneuver her way through the crowd without tottering over.

"I can't believe you're here!" I gave her a quick hug.

She returned the gesture, the large pointed wing covering her arm flapping against my back. "I almost didn't. But I ordered this outfit a week ago, and what good would sitting at home moping do? Plus, since the Cozy Corgi obviously won't be having our holiday party, I figured this is second best." She tilted her chin, causing the beak to nearly collide with Percival's hooked nose. She winced an apology. "Not that anything Victorian Antlers does is ever second best to anything." She continued before my uncle could launch into whatever diatribe he'd opened his mouth to begin. "Besides, it's all going to work out. The insurance is covering everything, and I've managed to get a construction crew to come in tomorrow and start gutting the bakery. They think they can have us up and running again in a week."

"A week?" Leo gaped at her. We'd stopped by the Cozy Corgi on the way to the party, and he'd been astounded by the damage. "I told Fred I was betting Valentine's Day would be the soonest."

"Where there's a will, there's a way." She grinned, though it seemed just a touch off.

"I thought the insurance said it would take a few weeks for the payout to occur, maybe even longer because of the holidays." Although, I'd been so furious about the interaction with Finnegan, maybe I misunderstood when Katie explained earlier that afternoon.

Her cheeks flushed. "Well... Joe... is lending me the money." She sped on. "It's just a loan. And I'm going to pay him interest as soon as the insurance settlement comes in. He offered, and, well"—Katie shrugged—"I'm not going to let some stupid elf keep me from my dream bakery any longer than I have to." A smile beamed over her face. "I'm going to make it even better than it was before. I might've had a little breakdown this afternoon, but I wiped the tears and have already started planning. It's going to be gorgeous."

I couldn't help myself, I hugged her again. "I adore you."

"That Joe Singer, he's proof what they say..." Percival propped both his fists on his hips, casting a glittering, refracted rainbow around us at the movement. "The homelier the face, the purer the heart."

We all gaped at him, but it was Gary who chided first. "Babe!"

"What?" Percival shrugged. "The man ain't pretty, but he's sweet as the day is long." He batted his eyelashes. "Granted, we can't all be as lovely as I am. It's no wonder I'm such a scrooge."

As ever, when he wanted to, my over-the-top uncle was able to turn an insult on its head. With his tall, gangly scarecrow frame, balding head, and bony, exaggerated features, Percival had never been accused of being handsome, and he had no problem laughing at himself just as much as anyone else.

Before we could reply, however, Percival's eyes went wide, then narrowed as he stared across the shop toward the front door again. "I told that woman to leave that rabid animal at home. I never dreamed she'd actually bring it, especially if they're coming from playing Santa at the hospital. Goodness knows how many sick children that vile creature devoured this evening." He hurried away, still mumbling.

We watched him storm over to Mr. and Mrs. Claus, who'd just entered Victorian Antlers. Anna and Carl Hanson looked like Santa and Mrs. Claus on any given day of the year, with their short round bodies and white and poufy hair—Anna's on top of her head, Carl's in the form of a beard. But in their authentic red velvet costumes, trimmed in white fur, even a nonbeliever would swear they could hear reindeer in the distance as they looked at the couple. The one addition, this year, was Winston—wearing a reindeer-patterned diaper, clutched, as ever, over Anna's heart. The small, scraggly dog snarled and hissed at Percival as he drew nearer.

"Excuse me." Gary offered an apologetic smile and headed off himself. "I better intervene before my husband ruins the relationship with two of our closest friends in the world."

Maybe sensing Gary would need reinforcements, Mom and Barry emerged from the other side of the shop where they'd been talking with Zelda and Verona's families. They, too, were dressed as Mr. and Mrs. Claus, though the tie-dyed version. Even as they attempted a greeting, Winston lunged, nearly biting Barry's nose, but Barry just sidestepped and laughed it off.

"I always thought *Watson* was the hardest dog to

please that I've ever met." Katie weaved and dodged as she spoke, trying to keep the scene in view as taller people passed by. "Actually, I know Watson's gotten along with Winston at this point, but if he saw one of his heroes treated that way, he might just put an end to Winston then and there."

"Speaking of, I should go check on my little grump." I looked toward the workspace, which was still free of people behind the counter. "I debated leaving him at home, but trying to get out the door without him is hard enough on my own. When Leo is with us, it's a near impossibility."

Instead of chiming in with a joke or an agreement, Leo was staring at Katie, his head cocked.

Katie gave up trying to see the fallout from Winston's presence and turned back to us. She flinched when she noticed Leo's expression. "What?"

He shook his head, a slight blush rising to his cheeks, but his expression cleared. "Oh, nothing." Another headshake. "I mean, I'm just relieved that you're taking things so well. I know how much you love every inch of that bakery."

Though that clearly hadn't been the only thing he'd been thinking, either Katie didn't realize, or she intentionally skipped over it. "The bakery is the bakery, and not dependent upon how it's decorated. It will be just as good, if not better, than before." She whipped toward me, trying to grab my hands with hers, forgetting about her costume and only managing to whap me in the face with her flippers. "Sorry!" She giggled but didn't slow down. "I was online and think I found a new marble. Totally different than the gorgeous Carrara I had, which I have some feelings about, but if we're going to start fresh, I think the bakery counter should be fresh too. It's a leathered Velluto, three inches thick. I'm going down to Denver tomorrow to see it in person." Katie shook her head as if in disbelief at her own words, her excitement growing as the three of us weaved our way through the crowd toward the counter. "It was strange, as I searched for my first countertop like Fred looks for clues, but as soon as I saw this one, I just felt it, you know?"

I supposed I shouldn't have been surprised how quickly Katie rebounded and chose to find the positive. She'd faced a lot harder than a little name-calling and destruction of property.

Leo grinned conspiratorially at me, clearly coming to the same conclusion about Joe Singer that I had reached.

The three of us stepped behind the counter, and

Watson, a partially chewed piece of buffalo jerky clenched in his teeth, raced from beneath and collided with Leo's legs as if he hadn't seen him only fifteen minutes before. Not missing a beat, Leo fell to his knees and wrapped Watson in his arms and a flurry of baby talk.

"You know, Fred. I don't know if you'll ever be truly certain if Leo loves you for *you* or your corgi." Katie giggled again, then launched into more of her plans for the bakery.

As we chatted, the merriment in Victorian Antlers increased, the volume of the chatter nearly reaching the levels of the music before. Maybe it was genuine Christmas spirit, or perhaps Percival had been as liberal with the rum in the eggnog as he'd claimed... or both.

After a while, we were joined by Paulie and Athena.

Leo, Katie, and I all gaped at Paulie, but it was Katie who stood, wrapped Paulie in her flipper-clad arms, and surprised me again when I could hear tears in her voice. "One of the many reasons I love you, Simon Paulie Bezor."

"Well, I couldn't let him win, could I?" Paulie, dressed in identical fashion to the elf that had been hanging in the stocking stuffed in his mouth, hugged Katie back. "I've faced a lot meaner than Jake Jazz."

Watson growled and took a sheltering position, peering out behind Leo's legs.

Though my own emotions were riding high, I knelt and scratched his head. "I can't blame you entirely, buddy. It's not every day you see a giant penguin hugging a giant elf."

"Here, this will help." Athena started to kneel down beside me, then caught herself, placing a steadying hand on my shoulder. "On second thought, at my age I'm not getting on the floor unless I have to." Instead, she lowered her gorgeous deep cranberry-colored purse to the floor, and a little white head poked out.

Forgetting the overgrown penguin and elf entirely, and even the buffalo jerky that had been clenched in his jaws, Watson let out a bark and gave Pearl an exuberant lick across her face.

Letting out a happy yip of her own, the toy poodle leapt gracefully from the purse, and she and Watson began their ritual of sniffing each other as they turned in circles. As the five humans watched, enamored, they finally calmed and trotted off to curl up together under the counter.

No sooner had they settled, than Watson scurried back to us. He snagged the forgotten buffalo jerky and hurried back to Pearl, where they gnawed on it together.

"I'll never get used to seeing him share food." I realized that I'd clutched my hand over my heart. The night really was getting to me, between the show of strength from Katie and Paulie, and now the sweetness of the dogs. "It's a beautiful ending to a rather hard day." I turned to Athena. "Speaking of beautiful, you're even more stunning than usual."

"I'll second that!" Leo chimed in.

Never the shy one, nor falsely modest, Athena batted her fake eyelashes, gave a slow twirl, making the plum-colored gown, trimmed in deep cranberry-hued lace, flare slightly. "Thank you both. I took the Victorian Antler party as an excuse to go shopping."

"And that's why I dressed like a penguin." Katie made a motion, covering the entirety of Athena. "If I tried to wear that exact same dress, I'd look like a blueberry tart exploded."

"We all would." I let out a very unladylike snort of agreement.

"I don't know..." Leo scratched his chin. "I think I might be able to pull it off."

Laughing, Athena leaned in and gave Leo's arm a squeeze. "I have no doubt that you could, darling."

Suddenly, it hit me that the full Scooby gang, as some people called us, was together again for the first time in a while, and I couldn't let the moment pass, even if the night should only have been focused on Christmas cheer. "So..." I leveled my gaze at Athena, growing serious. "You're behind the Biggler article this morning, right?"

She batted those eyelashes again. "What article?"

Paulie the Elf laughed, just a touch wickedly. The motion caused the ridiculously poufy beard covering him to shake like an avalanche. Since it was attached to his huge green hat, it slid over his eyes, unintentionally completing the look. He lifted the brim, one twinkling brown eye gazing out. "That's not what Rhonda told Ethel Beaker today, in any case."

Katie grew serious right along with me. "Oh, come on. There's no way Ethel will believe that."

"She doesn't have to." Athena offered an uncon-cerned shrug. "As long as Rhonda sticks to her story, Ethel doesn't have cause to fire me unless she wants a lawsuit."

Leo joined in, and just like that the Scooby gang was once more official. "Maybe so, but she could fire Rhonda."

Athena shook her head, the intricately arranged curls of her hair glistening in the reflected Christmas lights. "Apparently not. Rhonda says she has some dirt on Jonathan, though she won't share what it is. And while I don't think Ethel's overly proud of her son, there's no way she'll allow him to be associated with any scandal if she can help it."

Katie and I exchanged glances, both wondering what Rhonda might have on Jonathan. It wasn't the first time we'd heard of secrets in Jonathan's closet.

"It's not only Ethel, but you could get into some legal trouble with Delilah and Marty. You practically named their shops as being responsible." It seemed Leo had other concerns, and he looked back and forth between Athena and Paulie. "It sounds like you're both convinced Jake Jazz is behind it all. I think we need to be a little more careful jumping to conclusions because a group of friends all have criminal records."

"I'd *love* to see Delilah Johnson try to take on Athena. She'd get mopped across the floor." Katie didn't give anyone else a chance to answer. "And, come on, Smokey Bear. I know you're all about second chances and stuff, but between the way he treated me and Paulie, is there any doubt? The very things he called me were scribbled on my marble."

"I think it's him *and* Finnegan Clark," I chimed in as well, also not giving Leo a chance to answer. "When I was at Santa's Cause today, I could just feel it. And that was *before* he tried to get aggressive with me."

"He what?" Paulie sounded shocked.

I barely looked his way before I realized Leo was staring at me openmouthed. "What?"

"He got *aggressive?*" Fury lit Leo's typically calm eyes, and it seemed all notions of second chances flew out the window. "You didn't mention that."

"I said he *tried* to get aggressive." I placed a hand over Leo's. "His uncle got between us. Besides, I can handle myself. Not to mention, Watson was there."

At the sound of his name, Watson grunted and looked up from where he'd been napping with Pearl. Seeing that there was neither danger nor morsel to be found, he snorted and went back to sleep.

Getting going again, Katie patted Leo's leg. "You men are all the same. Instantly entering caveman and superhero mode when your lady's been insulted." She blushed instantly, as if she hadn't meant to say the sentiment out loud. "Not that you shouldn't, of course." She flicked a hand toward the dogs. "I guess it's natural. I bet Watson might even growl at *you* if you insulted Pearl."

Athena snorted, somehow even managing to make that sound ladylike. "Watson needn't bother. If someone insults my Pearl, *I'll* be the one growling."

We all laughed, and I joined in a few seconds late as I'd been studying Katie. The way she'd said it made me think Joe Singer had had a thing or two to say about Jake Jazz and Finnegan Clark. I reevaluated my assumptions of why Joe had wanted to walk down to the Cozy Corgi with me after the Christmas Cottage's party. He'd not been feeling things out between Leo and me, but maybe trying to ask about Katie... It looked like the feelings were mutual.

When Katie caught me staring, I switched directions. "I think I might swing by Santa's Cause in the morning. I also had the feeling Trevor, the elf artist, might know something as well, and if I can get him alone, without Marty or Finnegan interrupting, I might be able to weasel something out of him."

"Really?" Katie's blush faded. "Every interaction I've had with *him* has been fine, not that we run into each other that much, but he's always seemed friendly."

"I agree. He struck me that way as well, but he also seemed nervous." I exchanged meaningful glances with the four of them. "And it turns out, part of the reason he chose to give the elves to Santa's

Cause, was because Marty is giving him a free place to live... *with* his nephew."

And that set off a whole other torrent of speculation. While the majority of Estes Park locals milling around Victorian Antlers laughed and partied, growing steadily louder, and even singing along with the unending loop of Dolly Parton and Kenny Rogers, the five of us exchanged theories about the goings-on around Santa's Cause and even circling back to the conflict between Marty and Gentry. By the time we helped ourselves to a couple of rounds of eggnog, the stressors of the past couple of days vanished, and the theories grew more and more ridiculous, culminating with a conspiracy of giant penguins teaming up with Santa's elves to ruin Christmas in Estes Valley.

The following morning was as bitterly cold as the day before, but as Watson and I walked toward the Cozy Corgi, he trotted along, as spry and cheerful as a newborn pup. He'd been that way since the night before, and we hadn't even had breakfast yet!

As I retrieved the keys with one hand, I used the other to bend down and scratch Watson's head. "I never dreamed a social event would leave you in such a great mood. Although, let's be honest, we both know it was more because of Pearl and an endless supply of buffalo jerky."

Watson glanced up with a hopeful whimper, whether at the mention of Pearl or the promise of buffalo jerky, I wasn't certain.

"Sorry, buddy. All we've got this morning is a cutting breeze and a quick moment for one of Katie's dirty chais and a pastry before we see if we can catch..." I froze, keys halfway lifted to the door as my brain caught up with why the bookshop was dark inside.

What in the world was wrong with me? I'd simply been going through the motions and moving quickly in the hopes of reaching Trevor Donovan before Marty or Finnegan arrived at Santa's Cause. A momentary shot of sadness coursed through me, picturing Katie's bakery, but I shook it off, remembering what her plans were.

Katie was probably already on her way down to Denver, ready to check out her Velluto marble the second the stone-gallery doors opened. And *she'd* doubtlessly been smart enough to begin her early morning with caffeine. I was also willing to bet the Pacheco twins were more than likely still warm and snuggled up in their beds—Ben probably snuggling with his Persian cat, Cinnamon.

Grumbling to myself, I stuffed the keys back into my purse and then turned to trudge the couple of blocks to the Christmas store. Certainly it was my imagination, but without the promise of the dirty chai, the windchill dipped a good thirty degrees, and though I wore winter tights beneath my mustard-yellow broomstick skirt, I might as well have been clad in only a bikini. *That* thought only made me more irritable.

For his part, Watson continued frolicking along at my side, clearly not disturbed by the winter wind or the stress of his mother in a two-piece bathing suit. Dogs really did have it good.

I'd left the house early enough—giving time for that elusive dirty chai and pastry—that all the other shops were dark as Watson and I passed. Clearly I was wasting the journey. The elf artist wasn't going to be at the Christmas shop yet, but... without a second plan, I continued on, passing Rocky Mountain Imprints, Bushy Evergreen's Workshop, and Victorian Antlers. I glanced through the still dark windows of my uncles' antique shop, picturing the raucous Christmas celebration from the night before, which only made me think of Athena. Never mind that she was nearly twice my age, I bet Athena Rose could pull off a bikini.

Mollifying myself that given the choice between rocking a two-piece or having unlimited access to Katie's pastries, there was absolutely no doubt which I'd choose, which only proved I was already living my best life.

Watson and I arrived in front of Santa's Cause. Sure enough, the windows were dark. "Well, we might as well head home. I'll whip us up a quick breakfast to go and a coffee, and we'll come back." I checked the time. "Although that will take too long if I hope to catch Trevor by himself."

Watson whimpered.

"I know. I shouldn't have said breakfast." I started to bend down once more to pat him, expecting to find Watson looking up at me plaintively.

He wasn't. Though he whimpered again, he was staring straight ahead at the door of the Christmas shop.

Only then did I realize that while it was dark inside, the front door was slightly ajar. I glanced at Watson again, then really listened to his whimper, which clearly had nothing to do with his desire for breakfast. Despite the lack of caffeine, Watson's reaction managed to do what the frigid breeze hadn't, and I came to full attention.

Somewhere in the back of my brain a little whisper suggested I call Susan, but I shoved that aside just as I pushed open the door and poked my head in. "Hello?"

No answer, but Watson followed suit, stepping all the way inside the door. He instantly went rigid, lowered his ears, and began to growl.

Knowing what I'd find, I pushed the door open the rest of the way, started to reach for the light switches, and caught myself just in time. So that I wouldn't leave fingerprints, I pulled out my cell phone and turned on the flashlight.

Though it was hard to tell from the strange shadows the Christmas trees cast under my direct beam, nothing looked out of place or destroyed. If it hadn't been for Watson's continued growling, I probably would've assumed the door had simply been left unlocked by mistake and the wind had blown it open or something. But unless the wind had gotten a whole lot colder during the night, it wasn't responsible for the dead body I knew was there somewhere.

We found it, lying on top of the counter, the cash register and a case of elves at his head, and his feet slightly hanging off the other end. For some reason, I expected it to be Trevor, probably because he'd been the whole purpose of my early morning visit. But as I shone the light over the body's face, it wasn't the artist I saw.

Finnegan lay there, as peacefully as if he were sleeping. He could have been, except for the caved-in portion of his skull at the temple. That, and the fact he'd been laid out as if in a coffin. Despite the wound, with the way his red hair fell back in a smooth sweep from his forehead, Finnegan looked more presentable than I'd yet to see him.

His body was arranged plank straight, with his arms folded and his hands crossed over his chest. Instead of a Bible or a cross clutched in his hands, however, there was an elf, its tufts of white beard poking through Finnegan's fingers, and the long trail of its red hat hanging toward Finnegan's neck. Perched atop those interlocking knuckles sat a solitary lump of coal.

No fruitcake for Finnegan Clark. Clearly Santa had judged him to be a very, very bad boy.

"See, Detective Green? You can be wrong about things too. Which is nice to know." Officer Campbell Clifton Cabot looked up from the other side of Finnegan's body and offered an oddly friendly smile, considering the situation, to Susan, who stood beside me. "You thought Finnegan was responsible for the break-ins. Except, had he bashed in his own head, I doubt he'd have been able to lie down all nice and pretty like that afterward."

"Really, Sherlock?" Susan leaned forward with a sneer. "You *don't* think it might've been some sort of

Christmas miracle he achieved? He is holding an elf, after all."

"Oh..." Officer Cabot tilted his head, inspecting Finnegan's face. "I hadn't thought of that."

"You—" Susan clamped her mouth shut, her jaw twitching, and she closed her eyes. If she had been the type, I would've assumed she was praying for strength. Finally, with a shake of her head, she turned to me, not opening her eyes until she bypassed Cabot and had me firmly in view. "You said the front door was unlocked, just like with the other break-ins?"

"Yes." I nodded. "Although the door was ajar, so maybe slightly different." I motioned toward Finnegan's head, which was clearly visible now that the Santa's Cause lights had been turned on. "There's blood on his wound, but none around him, hardly even any on the countertop, so he wasn't killed here." Though that wasn't all that unusual.

"Really, Sherlock? You think?" Susan got the words out, then squeezed her eyes shut and shook her head again before taking a deep breath and letting it out in a sigh. "Sorry. You didn't deserve that. I'm apparently a little on edge. And repeating myself." She darted another glare toward Cabot. "Yes, I agree. We can't find blood or any other sign of

foul play anywhere else in the shop. Mr. Clark
wasn't killed here."

I gaped at her, dumbfounded.

She flinched. "What? Do you disagree with that
now?"

"No. Not at all. It's just that..." I didn't finish the
thought, figuring pointing out that Susan Green had
just apologized to me without prompting wouldn't go
well. "Um... it's just that... um..."

"If the victim was murdered somewhere else,
then it would make sense that our killer probably
used a vehicle of some sort to transport Finnegan's
body, unless he was killed at one of the nearby shops
and carried over," Officer Cabot jumped in,
sounding excited to be building on our theory. "That
means, if we can locate a vehicle with some of his
blood in it, we've found our killer." His smile
widened. "Or... if we can find the home, shop, or
warehouse, or somewhere with a lot of blood in it,
along with the murder weapon—I'm guessing a lead
pipe, by the way—then we've also found our killer."

"A lead pipe?" Susan stared at him over
Finnegan's body.

Officer Cabot just nodded. "Yeah. That's a very
popular murder weapon."

"Did you actually attend the police academy or just play a whole bunch of rounds of the Clue board game?" Susan kept muttering as she scribbled once more on her notepad. "You're probably getting ready to suggest Miss Scarlet killed him in the conservatory."

"I did go to the police academy," Officer Cabot answered, full of sincerity. "But my roommate and I played a lot of Clue at the time. Very insightful that you would know that."

In a newly acquired habit, Susan massaged her temples. "How I miss the days when my greatest annoyance was a busybody bookseller and an over-abundance of corgi fur."

As if knowing he'd just been referenced, Watson growled, rising from where he'd been curled up at my feet.

I started to bend down to comfort him, then at the commotion coming from the front door, realized the source of Watson's agitation.

"Let me in right now or I'll knock you into the middle of next week!" When I leaned around, angling to see past the Christmas tree, I found Marty Clark arguing with another officer, who stood guard at the door. "I don't care if you are the police. This is *my* shop."

"Let him pass, Officer Lin." Susan raised her voice, then lowered it once more. "Here we go."

"Thank you!" Marty bit the words out and stormed past Officer Lin, then made a beeline in our direction. "Don't you think this is a little overkill? Every night someplace is broken into. There's no reason to put up a barricade and stop morning tourists from coming in because of some stupid elf. If you recall, this was the very first place Gentry Farmer broke into when he stole my elf collection and—" Marty's tirade came to an abrupt end a few yards away from where we stood.

Other than the murmuring of the crowd outside, Watson's continued growl was the only sound as he repositioned himself in front of me, clearly thinking the angry human stomping toward us might be coming for his mama.

Marty halted, and when his gaze flicked from Susan to the partially hidden body, the blood drained from his face. Confusion lit in his eyes, and he started to shake his head. "Who..." Before he finished, his attention pulled downward and held on Finnegan's tennis shoes. Marty shook his head, a hand coming to cover his mouth. "No..." It was almost more of a question, and then a defiant demand as he hurried forward again once more. "No. No!"

His movements startled Watson, who lunged, and I stepped back, barely snagging Watson's leash in time to drag him along with me.

Marty shoved Susan—who'd been standing in front of Finnegan's upper body, blocking his face— out of the way. Though she stumbled, she caught her balance easily enough, and to my surprise, didn't retaliate.

Marty froze again, inches from the counter, wordlessly shaking his head as he stared at his nephew. Then tears silently streamed down his cheeks.

At the sight of Marty's grief, my own eyes burned, and still gripping Watson's leash just in case, my other hand rose of its own accord and covered my mouth.

He reached toward Finnegan's cheek, but his fingertips stopped just short of touching Finnegan's waxen skin, and then Marty crumpled to the floor, collapsing on his knees, covering his face. The tears that had been silent broke free, and he began to wail.

THIRTEEN

"You guys should see it." Katie sighed wistfully as she took a slice of pizza from the box. "Well, I guess you will see it soon enough. It'll take your breath away." She took a bite and spoke in between chews. "The Bianco Velluto was even prettier in person than online. Whiter than what the bakery had before, but the leathered texture softens it. Such depth, with little veins of crystal subtly running through it. Kind of like peering down through the frozen surface of the ocean."

Leo grinned from his spot beside me on the mystery room's antique sofa. "Granted, I'm just a park ranger for the Forest Service, and I've not ever been stationed anywhere by the ocean, like at Point Reyes National Seashore or anything, but I don't think there are too many oceans that freeze all that regularly."

"The *Arctic* Ocean, smarty." Katie pointed what remained of her pizza slice at him.

"And..." Feeling the need to help my best friend out, I searched my geographical knowledge base and came up wanting. "The... ocean around Antarctica too, I bet. But there isn't an Antarctica Ocean, I don't think."

Leo held up his hands. "I stand correc—"

"No, it's the *Southern* Ocean!" Katie beamed, once again pointing with her pizza slice, though this time at me in gratitude. "Though technically it's the combination of the Indian, Pacific, and Atlantic Oceans. It's where all three of them meet."

"And the Google Queen strikes again." Leo laughed good-naturedly, tore off the edge of his crust, and tossed it to Watson, who sat at his feet, displaced from his ottoman by the gargantuan pizza box.

I sighed contentedly, feeling relaxed for the first time all day. Katie had called on her way back up from Denver and wanted to meet us at the Cozy Corgi to go over bakery remodel plans. Leo had suggested the pizza. Even with stumbling upon another murder that morning, and knowing the bakery lay in shambles above us, my mystery room never failed to soothe—with the mystery-novel-filled bookshelves lining the small room, the crackling of the river rock fireplace with the lighted garland over the mantle, and the other Christmas decorations glittering throughout the rest of the darkened bookshop. "I'm just glad you're excited about the new marble. You spent so much time picking out the Carrara, I was afraid you'd feel like a friend had died."

Katie clapped her hands excitedly, accidentally sending a glop of pizza sauce across the room. She grinned as Watson scrambled, slipping in place over the hardwood floor for a few seconds before going off in search for wherever the morsel landed, then refocused on Leo and me. "That's the best part." She made a face. "Well... tied for the best part. I was lamenting about the Carrara to the stone guys, and they asked to see pictures of the damage. They think we can salvage a large percentage of it. I'm going to have them make some small open-air shelving for the bakery, maybe a couple of smaller tabletops, and on the really little pieces, they said they could turn them into bookends and little tiles for coasters, so it's not really gone!"

"I'm so glad, Katie." My heart warmed even further at her happiness. "And I'm not surprised, not really, at how quickly you've rebounded and are turning everything into a silver lining, but... it's impressive."

She waved me off, cheeks pinking. Before Leo could chime in with his agreement, Katie swiveled directions. "So, how was your day? Did you get to talk to Trevor this morning? Did he spill the beans on Finnegan and Jake?"

Watson waddled back into the mystery room, licking his chops, having clearly found the runaway pizza sauce. He settled beside Leo once more and looked at the three of us expectantly for more flinging food games.

Leo and I exchanged looks. "You didn't text her?"

"No." I shook my head. "I was with Susan for hours and then with Athena at the paper." I looked to Katie. "*Paulie* didn't text you?"

"Actually, now that you mention it, he did call while I was at the stone gallery, but I was too busy with—" Katie fluttered her hands. "Who cares? What happened?"

"When I went to see Trevor this morning, Watson and I found Finnegan." As I spoke his name, Watson moved a little closer to me, probably hoping for some of my pizza. "He was dead, on the counter, and holding an elf and a piece of coal."

Katie blinked. "Finnegan?" She didn't wait for a response before she continued. "Okay, that throws me off a little bit. I'd already chalked him up to being responsible for the elves based off your gut feeling last night. Your gut is never wrong."

"Well, *that's* not true." I pushed on before she or Leo could contradict. "But... I'm not convinced he wasn't responsible, at least partly. Jake is still very much alive. And remember I said I spent a lot of time with Athena this afternoon?"

Katie nodded.

At Watson's pleading eyes, I caved and offered a bit of crust as I continued. "It turns out, *The Chipmunk Chronicles* was broken into last night as well."

"We all saw that coming." Katie didn't look impressed but repositioned herself on the corner of the ottoman as she took another slice. "If they attacked the bakery just because I defended myself against their bullying tactics the night before, of course the newspaper was bound to get ransacked after that article."

"That's just it." Leo had snagged another slice as well but spoke before he took a bite. "*The Chipmunk Chronicles* wasn't ransacked, not like with Paws or your bakery. There was just an elf left on Rhonda Biggler's desk, holding a piece of coal."

"And unlike Santa's Cause, the paper's office had surveillance." I lifted my brows toward Katie. "They can see Santa, plain as day, enter, do a couple of quick fiddles with the security system, and then make a special delivery."

Katie lifted a finger, opened her mouth to speak, then paused. She looked like she was going to try again, paused once more, and then took a bite of pizza before finally speaking with her mouth full. "Okay, I'm confused. Are we thinking Santa—aka, Finnegan—broke into the newspaper and then was murdered at the Christmas shop?"

"Oh, that's the other factor. He was killed some-where else and taken to Santa's Cause." I joined Katie in talking with my mouth full. "So on one hand, it's back to status quo with the break-in at the paper—no vandalism, no destruction of property, just an elf and either coal or fruitcake. In this case, coal. But the pattern cracks by there being two break-ins in one night. Not to mention things escalated once more, from vandalism, destruction of property, and assault on Paulie, to *murder*."

Katie was nodding along as I rattled everything off, making little nods with every point. "Okay, then if we go with your theory that Finnegan and Jake were working together, and let me tell you, I can get behind that in a heartbeat, maybe there was some sort of conflict after one of them dressed up as Santa and hit the newspaper. Then Jake killed Finnegan and dropped him off at the Christmas shop, making it look like just another run-of-the-mill elfing. Except for the whole murder thing, of course."

Though I shook my head, Leo spoke up before I could, as I'd just taken another large bite of pizza. "That's what Fred and Susan thought as well. Susan brought Jake in for questioning. But Jake has an alibi. He and Trevor were together until late."

Katie shrugged. "Okay then, he broke into the newspaper early, hung out with Trevor, then killed Finnegan later."

I jumped in. "No, he has an alibi for after Trevor as well. He was with Tiffany the rest of the night?"

"Tiffany?" Katie pulled a confused expression, and then her eyes widened. "Tiffany? As in Carla's barista at the Koffee Kiln?"

Leo and I nodded as one.

"Gross!" Katie made another face, this one disgusted. "What is she? Sixteen? She's in high school?"

"Try nineteen, and she graduated a while ago, it seems. Remember she was in school around the same time as Ben and Nick." I couldn't help but laugh. "We're all getting older."

"Oh. Either way, it's still gross. Jake has gotta be

in his late twenties or early thirties. Granted, not as gross as murder, I suppose." Still, Katie wrinkled her nose. "So, where does that leave us?"

Before I responded, I grabbed the final slice of pizza, handed it to Leo, and then slid the pizza box off the ottoman. With a huff of relieved irritation, Watson hopped up, did a circle, and then lay down, though he kept his gaze fixed on Leo's pizza.

"*Trevor* doesn't have an alibi, at least not one after hanging out with Jake, so the time frame could work for him. There's no proof connecting him, so Susan couldn't hold him or press charges." I shrugged. "I think he's a valid suspect, though. You know how we wondered if Marty and Gentry were doing this all for publicity? It could easily be Trevor's motivation as well, making a name for his elves."

Proving to be just as much of a pushover as me, Leo passed a giant piece of sausage to Watson as he spoke. "Maybe so, but I wouldn't think you'd want your elves associated with murder. Breaking and entering and leaving *gifts* like Santa, sure, there's a bit of whimsical charm in that, but not murder."

Katie nodded in agreement. "The same for Marty and Gentry, too. Talk about ruining your Christmas shop's reputation."

"Well..." I looked between the two of them but

addressed Leo first. "I actually spoke to Susan on the phone right before we all met here, and I didn't have a chance to tell you before the pizza arrived." I included Katie at that point, glancing back and forth between them as I spoke. "It's way too early to get Finnegan's complete autopsy report, of course, but some of the preliminary stuff is in. He was definitely dealt a killing blow to the head, the speculation is something heavy and metal." I felt a smile start to grow at the memory of Officer Cabot's lead pipe theory but kept it at bay. "They're guessing an iron poker like you'd use on a fire, or something similar. However, he also had some bruising around his ribs that looked like it was done by fists." I met Katie's gaze and held it. "Unusually large fists."

A crease formed between her brows. "I suppose that rules out Trevor. He's pretty average in stature, but Jake's big enough. I don't know if I'd say *unusually* large, though—" Her expression went slack, and her eyes widened, but only for a heartbeat. "I guess it will be someone who has a vendetta against Marty, otherwise why kill his nephew and leave the body at Santa's Cause. Maybe we shouldn't stop looking at Gentry Farmer." She finished the thought lamely, then stared off into the fire.

Leo met my gaze, almost seeming pained, and

confirming that he and I were on the same page and that Katie, as much as she didn't want to be, was as well.

Joe Singer was unusually large, and probably had unusually large fists to match the rest of him.

Katie cleared her thoughts and angled her gaze upstairs. "You know what? Why don't we order another pizza and invite the twins over to join us? I bet Ben will have some good artistic ideas on the redesign. And Nick can help me catch anything bakery related I might overlook."

And keep anyone from any possible Joe speculation. I kept that thought to myself, however.

FOURTEEN

Watson snorted peacefully in a curled-up ball on the hearth, his head resting on the stuffed lion he'd retrieved from the bedroom. His other favorite stuffed animal, the duck, had, for whatever reason, not been found worthy that evening. As the fire crackled behind him, I let my gaze wander, my mind meandering as I inspected the ever-growing collection of Watson paraphernalia covering the mantle. Bypassing the old-time photo of Watson and me from Delilah's shop, and the hand-knitted version of Watson done by Angus Witt, I settled on the wooden replica of Watson, whittled by Duncan Diamond two Christmases before.

Though Leo, Watson, Katie, the twins, and I had spent a couple more hours at the Cozy Corgi—daydreaming and mapping out different possibilities for Katie's bakery—I'd basically slid into autopilot.

Katie had been genuinely excited as we'd tossed around different ideas, not holding back since she got to start from scratch, but I sensed that even some of her enthusiasm was forced. She'd not confirmed that she had feelings for Joe, and I hadn't asked. But that didn't change the obviousness of it all.

I couldn't help but have a sense of loss. Katie was my business partner and best friend. There was nothing we didn't talk about by this point; we had no secrets. Except... neither one of us were the kind to get all giggly and twitterpated about a man. We might've discussed my relationships with Branson and then Leo, but it was never the type of gushy moments between girlfriends like in a romantic comedy. In truth, I'd barely thought of Katie's romantic life at all, other than when I thought she'd been starting something with Leo. Granted, romantic astuteness was never my forte, but now that it seemed she was developing feelings for someone, a few of those giggly moments might've been nice.

A clattering in the kitchen pulled my attention away, and I peered over my shoulder. "Everything okay in there?"

"Yes! Just being a klutz," Leo called back. "I dropped the knife I was using to cut some of Watson's chicken. You stay there."

At his name, Watson sprang to attention and hurried off to the kitchen.

My focus was captured by the forgotten stuffed lion, partially silhouetted from the fire behind it, but illuminated in twinkling flashes from the Christmas tree across the room. If it had any advice, clues, or comfort to offer, it didn't make it obvious. Instead I returned my attention to the whittled version of Watson and the memories of Christmases past.

I'd considered Joe Singer to be a suspect in the murder of Duncan Diamond's son. The Diamond's toyshop and Joe's T-shirt store were next door to each other, and Joe had more than enough motive. It seemed weird that we were there again—with the beauty and joy of Christmas lights, holiday music, and snow, and I was once more deliberating about a man I considered a gentle giant, for murder.

But was he? A gentle giant? Factually, I didn't know Joe much better than I had two years ago. He designed and produced all the Cozy Corgi merchandise, but our conversations never went any deeper than that. Most of the time there wasn't even conversation required. More than anything, I simply associated him with all of Katie's ridiculous T-shirt designs and custom gifts.

"Here we go!" Leo walked back in, carrying a heavily laden tray and proving there was nothing klutzy about him as he glided across the living room with Watson twirling and weaving in and out of his feet without so much as stumbling. "I might've gotten more than just chicken for Watson."

I gaped at the spread as he placed a veritable charcuterie of cheeses, meats, crackers, and jam, as well as a small dish of chocolates, on the coffee table in front of the sofa. "I know I should ask how many people you think you're serving right now and pretend that I could never possibly eat that all, but neither of us would be fooled."

He shrugged as he sat down. "What would be the point of that? I'm not a great cook, but I've proven more than once that I know how to cut meat and cheese. Why waste that skill?"

Laughing, I squeezed his knee and then gave him a quick kiss. "I must have really zoned out. I didn't realize you were gone long enough to do all of that."

"Like I said, I've got skills." He winked, taking a moment to kiss me back. "And I'll pretend I'm not hurt you didn't miss me desperately. You're not Watson, after all, and you've got murder to think about."

Watson looked back and forth between us expectantly, then chuffed in annoyance, deciding we'd had more than enough time.

"Oh, sorry, buddy." Leo lifted the plate of sliced chicken and laid it on the floor.

"I wasn't actually thinking about murder." Absentmindedly, I watched Watson inhale his food as I spoke, then flinched, hearing my own words, and looked at Leo. "Well, that's interesting. I was actually sitting here thinking about Joe and how I'd wondered if he might've killed Declan Diamond two years ago and finding it strange that he's suddenly a murder suspect at Christmas once again. But if my Freudian slip is to be believed, maybe I don't actually think he is a suspect in this murder."

"It's hard to say." Proving that the two of us talked about murder more times than we could count, Leo spread some jam on a cracker and then began stacking a variety of meats and cheeses on top, as if we were merely discussing the weather. "I'm a little bit embarrassed, but I don't know Joe very well. I'm even more embarrassed that I didn't notice Katie developing feelings for him. I have no idea how long that's been going on."

I grimaced and followed suit, fixing my own

morsel. "Same, although now that it's right in front of my face, I'm not sure how I didn't see it coming. All the time they spent together coming up with T-shirt designs."

"Still, you're not getting a gut feeling about him?" Leo took a bite, sending crumbs of the cracker dustings to the floor. Watson had some of them licked up before they even made it all the way down.

"I don't have a gut feeling about him at all." I considered. "Although maybe that's a feeling in and of itself. He just seems like a nice guy. I don't have a strong reaction one way or another."

"Exactly the same for me." Leo considered, but only for a moment. "But if we weren't talking about a murder possibility, I think I'd be okay with the two of them." He rushed ahead, as if correcting himself. "Not that Katie needs me to be okay with anything, though I can't help but feel protective of her. And I think I'd..." He considered again, then shrugged. "Okay, I'm not sure of a better way to say that, or a more empowered way to say it. I feel okay about it. From everything I know and have seen, which isn't that much, Joe seems like a good man, someone who would treat Katie wonderfully."

I agreed, completely. "I think that's where the

glitch comes in. He's a good man, as far as we know, and we both feel like he would... care for Katie, as you said." I met Leo's eyes. "But maybe this is part of caring for Katie. He was there when Jake and Finnegan said all that stuff to her the other night. Even you—and you're not violent in nature at all—I think would have a hard time staying passive if you heard someone saying those things about me."

Leo's expression hardened instantly. "Yeah..." He didn't elaborate, started to take another bite, then paused, causing Watson to whimper. Leo ignored him, looking at me. "But... we're thinking about this wrong. Unless I'm misunderstanding, Finnegan was there when it happened and didn't stand up for Katie, but it was *Jake* who said those things, just like happened with Paulie. *Jake* is the one who's verbally abusive. Finnegan and Trevor are just his buddies who go along for the ride. Not that that makes it okay, but if Joe was going to go after somebody, wouldn't he start with Jake?"

"Good point." I thought about that for a second, then leaned back, relieved. "I think you're right. And I'm glad of it. Maybe those bruises didn't come from Joe."

He sighed. "I'm glad of it too. Katie deserves

some happiness. Not that I ever really thought she even wanted a relationship."

Laughing, I reached out, grabbed his hand, and gave it a squeeze. "Sometimes, even when we don't want a relationship, one comes along and takes us captive whether we want it to or not."

"I know that's how it was for you. But not for me." He squeezed my hand back, three times, and held my gaze. "I wanted you from the moment I met you and Watson, you on a mission with that owl feather."

Warmth spread through me, the kind that had nothing to do with the nearby fireplace. Though it was silly to do so, I was tempted to hurry into the bedroom to my mostly empty jewelry box and retrieve the silver bracelet shaped like an owl feather Leo had commissioned. I might've done so if not for the memory of what else was put away in the bedroom. I gave that thought a hard pass, refusing to let it steal any more from me, from us. "So, we're not making the determination whether Joe Singer is capable of taking vengeance for Katie's honor or not. We're simply saying that if he were to do so, it would be directed at Jake, not at Finnegan."

Leo blinked, justifiably thrown off from the abrupt transition of sinking into a romantic moment and diving right back into murder. Though he let go of my hand to fix another combo of meats and cheeses, passing a slice of each to Watson, his tone didn't betray if I had hurt his feelings. "I'd say that's a fair assessment. So, then we're back to who killed Finnegan, where, and why they laid him out in the Christmas shop?"

Thankfully he'd gone smoothly along, and I latched on. "Exactly. The two most likely scenarios are the Christmas shop feud, and that the three friends who all have criminal pasts..." I raised my hand as if trying to say I meant no harm. "I know we shouldn't judge people from their past mistakes, but it's too big of a coincidence for all three of them to have criminal records and for them to be a weird version of the Three Amigos."

Though he looked like he wanted to argue the point, Leo just nodded, but still picked up on the other option. "I can't say I know Gentry Farmer all that much better than Joe, but he has a bit more of a reputation. He's got a temper, and since we're talking about clichés of friends, he's in the same group as Joe, and Joe's the only one we think *doesn't* have a temper. Pete Miller and Jared Pitts definitely do."

"Yes, I thought about them before. That maybe they were all ganging up on Marty for opening a competitive Christmas shop and also stealing the elf collection from Santa's Cause. However, you brought up my gut feelings a while ago—it's not Jared. I know he went off on Pete in the middle of that softball game forever ago, but... I don't know, it's not him."

"I agree. And I don't think it's Joe either. But it could be Pete and Gentry. I'm not accusing either of them of murder, but..." He shrugged, like he was only half convinced of his theory. "It would explain why the killer moved Finnegan to Santa's Cause—talk about ruining any possible reputation as a cheerful Christmas shop."

I started to nod and remembered other details. "I know murder is bad enough, but that scenario is beyond cruel if we're just considering it being a business feud gone bad. That's not just a random body they laid out on the counter. It's Marty's *nephew*."

Leo grimaced, and as if it were moving of its own accord, seeking comfort, his hand dropped to Watson's head and began to stroke.

For just a second, Watson looked disappointed that there was no accompanying snack, but then remembered it was Leo, *his Leo*, and nuzzled against the touch.

"In that case, and I hate to say it"—once more it

looked like the words cost Leo—"we're back to the three friends with criminal records. Maybe it has nothing to do with elves, really. And more to do with some altercation between two of them. I don't guess we can say, but we've seen Jake's temper, and there's more than enough evidence of his cruelty."

"I agree." I had no problem picturing Jake murdering someone. "And the bruises could fit. I've not paid much attention to Jake's hands, but he's a pretty big guy. So not only might he be responsible for the bruising, but he'd be able to move the heavy weight of a dead body from the murder scene to the Christmas shop."

Leo hummed in agreement. "I hadn't thought of that. It wouldn't be easy for one person to move Finnegan's body. He wasn't exactly a small guy either. He and Jake were both pretty stacked. But again, we're forgetting, Jake has an alibi, remember? Tiffany."

I replayed Leo's words from several moments before. *Maybe it has nothing to do with elves...* "That's true, but... alibis can be faked, and smitten girlfriends, especially ones so much younger than the *bad boy* in question, can be easily manipulated or intimidated into providing one. And maybe, if that's the case, Jake didn't have to move the body by himself."

Leo grimaced. "You think Tiffany moved the body with him?"

"I hadn't thought of that, but it's a possibility." I drummed my fingers on the table, causing Watson to glare. "I was referencing Trevor." I checked the old clock on the mantle, a little past ten in the evening, then refocused on Leo. "I know it would be nice to have a sweet, romantic night at home, but would you mind if I—"

"Take a visit to see the elf artist?" He just grinned and shook his head. "Darling, we both know if we attempted a romantic evening right now, your mind would never stop working overtime. Honestly, at this point, neither would mine."

I stared at him, suddenly feeling a touch overwhelmed.

Leo flinched. "What?"

I had to take a moment and cleared my throat before I continued. "You're... just perfect. And you... *get* me, accept me."

Those beautifully strange-colored eyes of his stared deeply into me. "Getting you, understanding you, *that's* how I know how lucky I really am." He kissed me again, this time slow and long before finally pulling back and waggling his eyebrows. "Okay, where do we start?"

After having to clear my throat again, I gave Leo a grin of my own. "Well, I know it will annoy Susan, but I think I'll give her a call, see if she'll give us his address."

FIFTEEN

Susan answered on the first ring, I hadn't even made it back to the couch from retrieving my cell phone. "You're there, aren't you?"

Maybe she'd been expecting a call from someone else and hadn't looked at the display. "Susan, this is Fred."

"Well, obviously." She bit the words out, instantly annoyed. "You called *me*, not Cabot. I know how to read."

"Hey, *I* know how to read." Officer Campbell's muffled voice came through all the same.

I pushed on, *without* mentioning that I knew of her snarky label for me on her cell, afraid I'd lose Susan to some diatribe against her new partner. "I'm at home. I'm calling about Trevor Donovan. I was wondering if you could give me his address. He lives... lived with Finnegan Clark."

"I'm aware of that too, Fred, obviously." She didn't give me a chance to reply. "I thought you didn't listen to police scanners?"

"I don't. Why?" I shot Leo a wide-eyed "You should hear this" expression.

"Then how did you hear about Trevor?" Once more, she rushed on. "You know what, never mind. Just meet me at his place. And..." There was a brief pause, followed by an exasperated sigh. "Can't believe I'm actually asking for this again, but bring the fleabag. He's annoying but useful. At least when he can stop eating."

She started to give me the address, the whole reason I had called, but I interrupted her. "You're already going to Trevor's house? Right now?"

"Yeah, Cabot and I were wrapping a domestic altercation when we got the call. At this rate, unless you hold me up, we'll beat the ambulance."

"Beat the ambulance? What—"

She was rattling off the address before I could finish, then hung up.

I scrambled to write it down before I could forget.

"What was that?" Leo leaned nearer, looking as I scribbled.

"I'm not sure. But we're heading to Trevor's.

Watson too. We're meeting Susan, Campbell, and... an ambulance."

The little house where Finnegan and Trevor had been living was near enough that when we arrived, the ambulance was barely pulling to a stop in the driveway. On the few minutes over, Leo and I had settled to the obvious conclusion that Trevor had met the same fate as Finnegan.

Jumping out of the Mini Cooper, the three of us hurried up the sidewalk, bordered on either side by red-and-blue lights flashing over the snow.

Maybe because of the unexpected snacks of meat and cheese, or Leo's mere presence, Watson bounded along with us, acting as if we were going on a late-night adventure. He paused as we neared the front door, and he shoved his head in a deep drift as he often did when playing in the snow, but I urged him through.

Susan was standing over the body on the hearth, which was almost curled up in the same position Watson had taken in front of the fire. She barked orders to Officer Cabot, who darted out of the way as the paramedics hurried over. Noticing us, she gave an approving expression, then looked back down at the body.

Only when I heard Trevor's voice did I realize he wasn't dead. "Just like I told Detective Green, I think I can stand on my own. I'm not as dizzy anymore."

Leo and I exchanged confused looks as Watson still tried to get back through the door, never the one for crowds.

"You've lost a lot of blood, Mr. Donovan. It's true that head wounds bleed a lot, but it's impossible to assess how much damage has been done, if any." The paramedic laid a large hand on Trevor's thin shoulders, which reminded me of the bruises on Finnegan's torso. "Let's move slowly. Do you remember what happened?"

"Of course I do." Though there was a weary quality to his voice, Trevor was insistent and gestured toward Susan. "I was trying to tell *her* that when you all burst in. I really am okay."

The paramedic knelt, unwilling to be rushed. "Did you trip and hit your head on the fireplace, or is it hazy like you blacked out?"

Only then did I notice the spray of blood against the bricks beside the opening of the fireplace and then a large pool of it over the hearth. It was dim enough in the room I hadn't recognized it for what it was.

Despite the paramedic's restraining hand, Trevor gestured up toward the mantle. "I *didn't* fall. I interrupted *Santa*."

I followed the gesture, and in what had become commonplace, found a little elf that was barely more than a mossy green hat, nose, beard, and matching shoes sitting smack-dab in the middle. Beside him was a cellophane-wrapped loaf of fruitcake.

"Like I tried to ask you"—Susan stepped forward once more—"what was this Santa character doing when you walked in on him? And did you see his face?"

"He was—"

The paramedic cut him off again and glared at Susan. "My apologies, Detective Green, but your questions will have to wait. We need to get him to the emergency room, do an MRI of his head to make sure there's no bleeding or swelling."

"Now listen—"

"Once the doctors clear Mr. Donovan, then you can have your time."

Officer Cabot stood, jaw completely unhinged as he gaped at the interrupting paramedic. I couldn't quite blame him. A person didn't interrupt Susan

Green unless they were an idiot or had nerves of steel.

Even so, Trevor kept talking as they loaded him on a stretcher and wheeled him from the house. "I walked in, saw the elf and the fruitcake, knew Santa had been here, but I thought he was gone. When I walked toward the elf, I heard a noise, turned around, and there he was. He shoved me, and I fell."

"Did you see any features?" Susan followed after the gurney. "The color of his eyes, any identifying characteristics about his nose or body size?"

The straitlaced paramedic took the opportunity when they reached the doorway and slid in front of Susan, cutting her off. "You can ask your questions *later*, Detective."

I joined Officer Cabot in staring, expecting to see a murder in real time, and could have been bowled over with a feather when Susan, though shaking in obvious rage, remained where she was and closed her mouth. It wasn't until the ambulance doors shut that she finally turned around and faced the rest of the room. "Now, *he's* what I wished for in a partner."

"I can tell you what to do. Be aggressive." Cabot stepped forward, his voice shaking. "Green, get out your pad and take some notes about the—"

Susan glared, and a growl escaped her chest.

Watson echoed the sound.

Officer Cabot stepped back and lowered his head.

Susan nodded toward Watson. "Thanks for the support, fleabag."

He growled again.

She ignored Watson, gave a sharp, welcoming nod toward Leo, and turned to me. "So, what is this? I don't get it. If you didn't discover Trevor sprawled in front of his fireplace, why did you call me?"

"I wanted his address, like I said. He was the reason I went to Santa's Cause this morning, and I decided I still wanted to talk to him." I looked at the bloodstained fireplace and hearth, its presence making what normally would have been cozily crackling logs look sinister. "I had no idea another elfing had happened or that Trevor was hurt."

"An elfing? Really?" Susan wrinkled her nose.

"That's what Katie calls it."

Officer Cabot grinned at me. "That's a pretty good term for it, I'd say. In fact, I—" His shoulders slumped, and his gaze dipped toward the floor after another glare from Susan.

Leo had walked toward the fireplace and stood in front of it with his head cocked.

"Don't touch anything, Lopez." Though Susan

used her commanding tone as she always did, there was none of the implied "because you're an idiot" undercurrent she often gave to others.

"I won't." Leo turned, looked at her, then angled back to me as he pointed. "Check this out."

For a second I thought he was gesturing toward the blood, then realized it was the tool set beside it. A dark bronze stand with three hooks. On two of them, a brush and shovel hung, each in matching bronze and with wooden handles. The third hook, however, was empty. "The poker."

Leo nodded. "Didn't you say Finnegan was killed with something like a lead pipe to his head?"

"Me!" Officer Cabot spoke up again, pointing at his chest like an overgrown five-year-old. "That was me. I'm the one that said that. Lead pipe, like in Clue."

That earned him another growl from Susan, but she stepped forward, gave a cursory glance around the room, and then met my gaze. "How much you want to bet your boyfriend just found the murder weapon?"

"Well, technically, he *didn't* find the murder weapon," Officer Cabot started off conversationally, then finished hurriedly when Susan whirled on him.

"That's only where the murder weapon is *supposed* to be."

Clenching her jaw, she looked back at Leo, then Watson. "Good job, Lopez. Now, fleabag, see if you can sniff out anything interesting. Preferably something *not* edible."

We took our time, covering ground slowly after Susan and Campbell secured the scene, made notes, and took pictures. Watson didn't show any more interest in anything other than a few different trails of crumbs in the kitchen.

It wasn't until we'd admitted defeat and stepped back outside that Watson perked up again. Instantly, he snorted and shoved his face back in the snow mound by the front door.

Campbell chuckled. "Ah... that's cute."

"Yeah, adorable." Susan didn't spare Watson a glance as she passed by. "Only thing the fat hamster solved this evening was how to ruin the hem of my slacks with corgi hair."

"Come on, buddy." Leo bent, scratching Watson's rump. "Let's go to your mama's. You can cover me in dog hair on the ride home."

At Leo's touch, Watson pulled back and started to follow.

I did as well, but something about the hole where

Watson had shoved his face caught my attention. Not trusting the dim illumination of the porch light, I pulled out my cell, tapped a button, and aimed the beam of light in the hole, instantly discovering what Watson had been trying to show me the minute we'd arrived. "Susan, you're gonna want to see this."

She hurried back, leaning above me. When she nearly slipped, she caught herself with her hand on my back. She grunted in way of apology, then leaned closer. "Well, I'll be. Flecks of blood in the snow, didn't see it buried under the fresh stuff." Angling, she offered Watson a grin. "Good job, fleabag. I bet you just discovered where Finnegan was killed last night." She actually reached out to pet him.

Watson looked on the verge of allowing it, then growled, and moved out of her reach.

Susan simply nodded. "Sometimes I actually kinda like your style, fatso."

SIXTEEN

Watson trotted beside Leo as he headed out to the parking lot, then looked over his haunches at me questioningly.

"Sorry, buddy, we're staying here." I motioned him back to where I stood at the hospital entrance with Susan and Officer Cabot.

Leo knelt, ruffling Watson's fur with both his hands. "It's already midnight, and I've got to be at work early in the morning, buddy. Stay with your mama."

Looking back and forth between us, it truly appeared like Watson was taking in what Leo had said and was debating. Whether that was true or not, to my surprise, he offered Leo a final lick on his hand and then sauntered over and sat by my side.

Maybe I was overly tired after the day's events and being up well past my bedtime, but I felt my eyes burn. He never got as excited to see me as he did with Leo, or with my stepfather and Ben either. But time and time again, Watson showed that above anything else, he was Winifred Wendy Page's corgi, and I was Watson Charles Page's human. And really, could it get any better than that?

The police officers had turned to head back inside when Leo paused and let out a sharp laugh. "What am I thinking? We both drove here in your Mini Cooper."

"Oh! Right!" I started to reach into my purse to snag the keys. "That's okay, you take it. Your minutes of sleep are dwindling fast. It doesn't matter what time I get home. With the Cozy Corgi closed, Watson and I can sleep in."

Leo hurried back. "No, I want you to have a car. I'll use the Lyft app and have them take me to your cabin. I can grab my Jeep and be on my way."

"It's Estes Park and after midnight. There's not going to be any of those ridesharing people driving around at this time." I forced the keys on him.

"Well, that's going to be doubly true whatever time you get done here." He pushed the keys back at me. "No way am I leaving you without—"

"Oh, good Lord. You two are as nauseating as a Hallmark Christmas movie. I don't know if you or

Christmas Connection has more sap." Susan made a gagging sound and shoved Officer Cabot toward the parking lot. "Here, do something useful for once and take our sleepy park ranger wherever he wants to go. And then pick up a dozen donuts on your way back. Fred and I will be hungry."

Cabot nearly stumbled under Susan's force, but caught himself and looked back with panic in his eyes. "But... you just heard them. It's after midnight. Where am I going to get a dozen donuts?"

Susan shrugged. "Don't know, don't care. Just do it. And actually, make it two dozen." She sniffed. "Fred likes her carbs. Her fat dog probably does too."

Before either Leo or I could protest, Officer Cabot's gaze narrowed. "Wait a minute... how do you know *Christmas Connection* was sappy? I agree, but kind of liked it." He sucked in a breath, eyes widening. "Oh... you watch Hallmark Chris—"

"I will kill you." Susan took a step forward, and I could swear the muscles rippled under her uniform.

Officer Cabot saluted, spun around, and grabbed Leo's hand. "Hurry!"

Leo laughed, allowed himself to be pulled along, and gave an overly exuberant wave toward me that I had a feeling was more directed at Susan.

Apparently, she felt the same, as she called after

them, "I have no problem taking out a park ranger either. Lots of places to bury the body in the woods!" Her scowl deepened as laughter floated back to us, laughter that sounded like it was coming from *two* men. Pretty daring on Officer Cabot's part, and was probably laughter he'd pay for dearly later. "Come on." She whirled around and stomped toward the front doors, which slid open automatically.

Within a few minutes, we got the update on Trevor, who'd already been wheeled back for an MRI scan and some other assessments. Susan, Watson, and I settled in the waiting room, the two of us humans with Styrofoam cups of steaming coffee. As much as I loved caffeine, I had a strict rule about not having any of it after five thirty in the afternoon. I knew I'd regret the choice, but also hoped I was tired enough that it would simply help me function while I was at the hospital, and that I could crash when I got home.

"So..." Susan took a long draft from the coffee, her pale blue gaze darting to me, then settling on Watson—who was sprawled on his back in the middle of the floor, legs spread, looking like roadkill as he snored away. "Things must be going pretty well for you and Leo. It's almost a year since you've been together, right?"

I nearly dropped my coffee, and for the life of me, couldn't find a single word to say, couldn't even force out a sound.

After a second or two, she looked over at me again, brow cocked. "Did I bring up a tough subject? Are you guys not doing good?"

My mouth moved that time, which might've been an improvement. Hadn't I just been thinking that evening that Katie and I should probably have more conversations around relationships and romance from time to time? Now... here I was... doing that very thing... with *Susan Green*, of all people.

"Oh, never mind." She rolled her eyes, sat back, and took another long swig of coffee. "Just trying to kill time."

Maybe that was part of it, but Susan didn't small talk, *ever*. If I wasn't mistaken, she was actually either genuinely interested or simply trying to be... a friend. And both were Christmas miracles worthy of a Hallmark movie all of their own.

"Branson left me an envelope with some stuff in it about Leo." I hadn't meant to say it, *couldn't believe* I'd said it. I hadn't even mentioned the envelope to anyone, not my mother or Katie. It'd been a constant battle to not let myself think of it.

"What?" Susan sat up so quickly, a little of the coffee splashed over the side and hit the linoleum floor.

Watson scrambled up, huffed in annoyance, then moved over several feet and regained his undignified sleeping position.

Susan either didn't notice or didn't care. "Branson was here again? These stupid elfings are related to the Irons family?"

I didn't point out that she just used Katie's term without irony. "No. For once, the Irons family option hadn't even entered my mind, which probably means that's exactly what it is." I forced my gaze to meet hers and hold. Despite it feeling overly intimate, I needed to see her real reaction, and though she wasn't the one I would've picked, it was a relief to finally share it. "Branson's not back. He gave me whatever the information is when he cornered me in the woods outside my house right after Halloween."

"Thank Saint Nick and his horde of tacky elves for that." Susan sighed and sat back in her chair, but then she instantly straightened again. "Wait a minute, *what* does it say about Leo? Was it bad?

True, or just stuff Branson made up, doing one of his mind games to mess with your relationship?"

At some point, I might stop being surprised by Susan Green. For as harsh and closed off as she could be, sometimes her matter-of-factness was a gift, and allowed her to cut right to the heart of the issue without pomp and circumstance. "I... don't know. I... haven't opened it."

She gaped at me, and then a smile formed at the corner of her lips, and she began to laugh.

Another reaction I hadn't expected.

Susan laughed so hard that she set the Styrofoam cup aside and actually had to wipe her eyes. "That is the most ridiculous thing I've ever heard. You are, hands down, the nosiest busybody who has ever wandered the face of this green earth."

I flinched.

And once more, Susan either didn't notice or didn't care. "But with this, when your murderous ex-boyfriend gives you information he claims might be dirt on your current boyfriend—" She did some quick figuring. "—over a month and a half ago, and you... what? Stuffed it in some book in the Cozy Corgi and pretended like it didn't exist?"

The room seemed to be getting hotter. "I stuffed

it in a boot box in the closet of my bedroom, actually."

Once more, she threw back her head and practically howled.

After a few more seconds, though I couldn't explain why, I began to chuckle along, and then... before I knew it, and much to my shame, I realized a few tears were making their way down my cheeks.

That Susan noticed, and it killed any ounce of laughter she had. "Oh no, none of that. I don't do tears." She shook her finger at me. "Why don't you bleed, or get shot, or have a car wreck, do something, like, useful. *That* I can deal with."

I chuckled again and wiped my eyes. "Sorry. I've just been a little stressed with it. And feel—"

"Stupid?" Susan offered without hesitation.

And this was why I should've spoken to Katie, not blurted it out to Susan. "Yes. Pretty much."

"Well, good, then you haven't completely lost your marbles." She sniffed and straightened. "Either open the dreadful thing and look at it with Leo or toss it into the fire and don't think of it again."

I looked back up at her in surprise. "You think that's an option? *Not* opening it?"

Her expression conveyed the term *stupid* again, but she didn't verbalize it. "Everything's an option.

But those are the only two that make sense. If it was me, I'd rip it open and read it and..." She hesitated, brows knitting. "At least I think I would. But like I said, we both know Branson Wexler and the games he's played. And trust me, I got to hear and see first-hand his obsession with you." She lifted a finger like I was going to protest, but I wasn't about to. "And yes, I call it obsession. I know he calls it love, but that monster wouldn't know love if Cupid jammed his arrows up both his nostrils and in his ears. Not one thing he said can be trusted. That includes whatever he gave you about Leo."

I blinked. She'd spoken so fast about something that had been broiling around in my mind for so many weeks that I struggled to parse through it. "So... what are you saying? Open it and read it even though it might be nothing but lies and just an effort to hurt Leo and me, or that I should toss it into the fire and never think about it again?"

That time, Susan opened her mouth and no words came out. Finally, her shoulders slumped once more, and she returned to her slouched position in the chair. "I don't know. I think... if it were me... I'd move. Change my name, get some plastic surgery, ditch the dog for a... goldfish or something sensible... and start life fresh somewhere else. And that time keep your nose only in yours and the goldfish's business, and *that's it!*" She clapped her hands definitively.

At the noise, Watson sprang up and gave a startled bark.

Susan leaned toward him and clapped her hands again. "Goldfish!"

Watson snarled, trotted over to, and took shelter behind my chair, settling down out of Susan's view.

For the first time in weeks, a sense of relief settled around the envelope Branson had given me. No answers about what I should do, which was irritating since I was always so decisive, but it helped, knowing that Susan—who was equally as decisive as me, even if our decisions typically went opposite directions—also had no idea what I should do. Somehow... that eased the pressure. I smiled at her. "Thanks, Susan."

She grimaced, then sniffed. "If you really want to thank me, when you run away to start your new life, take Cabot with you."

I laughed, settling back into my chair and letting one of my hands drift over to allow my fingertips to scratch Watson as he returned to his snores. "That partner of yours is something, and I can see why he drives you crazy, but he seems genuinely sweet."

"Yeah. He is." She rolled her eyes. "Unfortunately, sweet people are often stupid. And he's no exception to that rule." She glanced at the clock on the wall. "Speaking of, what's the moron doing? Making donuts himself?" Susan shifted with a grunt, once more leveling her gaze on me meaningfully, and thankfully went back to our normal topics of conversation. "Speaking of stupid, your whole family and Scooby gang are always talking about that gut of yours. What does it tell you about this one? Who's Santa?"

"I wish you'd ask me at least *one* question I could actually have a definitive answer to." I shrugged and glanced up, noticing the solitary string of Christmas lights bordering the waiting room. They looked like someone had attached them with Scotch tape, and three quarters of them were burnt out. *Very* un-Estes Park like. "Here's the abbreviated version of what we're playing around with. It could easily be a matter of promotion around those elves. For a while, we thought it might have actually been Gentry and Marty, dreaming up the feud together to boost both of their shops, kind of like free advertising."

"Yeah, that's where I was leaning as well, but

that theory pretty much died the second Finnegan did?"

"Exactly." I nodded at Susan's assessment, and continued, "There are a few other options, but the main one I'm leaning toward at the moment, are the three friends. Not necessarily because it makes any sense, but because there's too much coincidence, and that never sits comfortably with me."

Susan grunted her agreement. "How so in this case?"

"Well..." I used my fingers as I went through the list. "We've got Trevor Donovan, the artist whose elves are at the center of all of this. He travels from fancy resort town to fancy resort town each Christmas, trying to make a name for his expensive elf collections. Now he's here. Estes is great, but it's hardly exclusive. And just like with Marty and Gentry, from his perspective, this could have all been an advertising ploy as well."

"Sure, if you want your product associated with murder and are willing to go so far as to allow yourself to be attacked."

"Right, there is that." I pressed down on my second finger. "And then there's Finnegan, the owner of Santa Cause's nephew, roommate to Trevor."

"And now dead body," Susan chimed in helpfully.

"Yes, and now dead body." I depressed my third finger. "And finally, Jake Jazz, the slightly older of the three, and if I had to guess, the ringleader of the friendship, or at least the one with the power. From what I can tell, he's not connected to the Christmas shops, or the elves, in any way other than his friendship with Trevor and Finnegan. But he's also the most hostile and verbally aggressive. In addition, it seems—while this doesn't play out, as far as I know, with each of the gifts left with the elves—that there's a correlation between people he's had conflict with or bullied who end up getting coal."

Susan considered, weaving her head slightly from side to side as she did so. "But that theory falls apart with Finnegan and Trevor. If anybody should be getting fruitcake, if Jake is behind this, it's his friends. Though why someone determined leaving fruitcake is a good thing is beyond me."

I nearly told her she needed to try the fruitcakes Katie had made and she'd change her mind but didn't allow myself to get distracted. "All this brings us to the coincidence, and what I can't let go of. All three of the friends have criminal records. Whether they are ones acquired as an adult that are public knowledge, or a juvenile record that we've only heard about through the grapevine. That's got to mean something."

"*That's* what I've been telling Delilah, what I told her the minute she ignored me about hiring Jake Jazz to begin with." Susan growled, more to herself than me. "Women like her drive me nuts. Keep giving worthless men chance after chance after chance. It's not like she's related to him and has no choice."

It would've been easy to point out that Susan's hostility might be more based on her frustrations at supporting her... less than stellar brother, but I figured she was already aware of that, so I stayed on topic. "I think that becomes even more important if you look at the three men individually. Granted, I don't know any of them very well, but on the surface, they don't seem like a natural fit. Trevor Donovan, a young artist who is trying to make his living by doing nothing more than making elves and is solely focused on his career. Finnegan Clark, who's getting a fresh start handed to him by his uncle and has nowhere else to go but up. Maybe those two would be friends in real life; maybe they wouldn't. I'm not sure. But it makes sense, given their situation as roommates, and their connection through Santa's Cause as well. But when you throw Jake Jazz in the mix, you get a different picture. He has absolutely no association with Christmas, Santa, elves, or otherwise. He's big, burly, and mean. In any other situation, Trevor looks like a guy who would be one of Jake's victims, *not* a friend. It makes a little more sense that Jake and Finnegan would get along. While Finnegan wasn't as overtly abusive as Jake and seems more to go along with Jake's bullying than prompting it himself, I have seen firsthand that he can dish it out just as strongly."

"So..." Susan drummed her fingers on the side of the Styrofoam cup. "A coincidence as all three of them are connected through various criminal pasts, but in truth, that's not such a strong connection. Plenty of other people in town have criminal pasts. So why have these morons become the Three Amigos. I hadn't thought of it this way, but as you were speaking, it sounded like the glue that held them together was Finnegan Clark."

"Yeah. I think you're right." I almost thought I felt an answer there, but it wouldn't come. I shrugged. "I don't know what to do with that. Especially since we're currently waiting for Trevor in the hospital right now, and Finnegan is dead."

Susan's eyes widened. "Maybe that's the connection as well. Though one out of their hands."

I tried, but I didn't follow. "What do you mean?"

"It's not just that they have their criminal past in common, but two out of the three of them have been Santa's victims." She looked at me meaningfully. "So far…"

A little jolt coursed through me. "You mean… Jake Jazz might be next on the list?"

"Sure, save the meanest for last." Susan paused, then shook her head, as if disagreeing with herself. "Although if that's the order of things, then it's already been messed up. If you go from most helpless to most aggressive, you'd start with Trevor, not Finnegan. Not to mention that, between the two, Finnegan got the worst deal. Typically, in such cases, things would escalate with each victim, not decrease or be all over the place. Somebody took vengeance out on Finnegan, they didn't on Trevor. But I bet there's a long line wanting to do so on Jake."

All good points, and all led me uncomfortably back to Joe Singer. Sure, my gut didn't suspect him, but at the end of the day, feelings were just feelings, not facts. And while the escalating pattern didn't make sense if you looked at it from Susan's perspective, it did if you looked at it from Joe's. Trevor was present during the bullying of Paulie, and maybe part of some conversations or insults around Katie, but he was the most innocent of the three, and was merely knocked out. Finnegan was also an observer of the bullying, and at times, a participant—especially around Katie—and he was beaten and killed. If Jake was next to receive the rewards of his horrid treatment of people, he would get the same as Finnegan, yet somehow worse.

As much as I didn't want to, if there was even a chance that Jake Jazz was on the list, then I needed to share the possible Joe Singer theory with Susan. No matter what my gut said, and no matter if it would hurt Katie.

Just as I opened my mouth to tell her, the door to the waiting room opened, causing Watson to bark again. The nurse stepped inside, cast a disgusted glance at having a dog in the hospital but didn't say anything as she looked at Susan in her police uniform. "The doctor asked me to let you know Mr. Donovan is out of testing and able to speak to you now."

SEVENTEEN

"He's right in here." The nurse started to push open the door when the sounds of rushed footsteps over the linoleum and heavy breathing made us all turn around.

Officer Cabot was speeding through the hallway, two large flat red-and-green-striped paper boxes in his hands. "Drunkin' Donuts was closed, but I woke up the owner and had him make a fresh batch." He panted, coming to a stop in front of us, holding up the boxes. "Well, two batches, so there'd be some variety. We have regular glazed and coconut covered."

"Coconut covered!" Susan practically choked. "You could only pick two varieties and you chose *coconut* covered?" She peered in the top box, sneered as she slammed it shut, and yanked out the promised glazed of the lower level. "I'll take these."

As Watson sniffed the air below us, I gaped at Officer Cabot in surprise. "You woke up old Mr. Logan and made him bake donuts in the middle of the night?"

Cabot nodded. "Sure did. Just flashed my badge."

"Really?" Susan had been turning back toward the room but halted, giving her new partner an appraising once-over, then a satisfied nod. "Nice work. Didn't think you had it in you. Now get in here and—"

"I'm sorry, the limit is two visitors at a time." The young nurse interrupted and started to close the door in Susan's face. "I was already pushing things by allowing three of you to come in, especially when one of those three is a *dog*. I'm afraid we just can't—"

Susan bristled, then straightened and took her time reaching her hand into the box and pulling out a glazed donut to hold between them. "My partner just woke up old Mr. Logan, who's a hundred and fifty if a day, and he needs to see how a proper questioning of the victim is done. Fred is annoyingly astute with these things, and the fat, furry fleabag... well... I don't have an explanation for that and find it annoying myself." She shook the donut in the nurse's face. "So don't push me."

The nurse looked like she was about to protest, then blinked and shook her head in apparent confusion. I couldn't quite blame her. I'd not been completely able to follow Susan's logic either. Finally, with a sigh, the nurse tossed up her hands and walked wordlessly away.

Susan grinned, took a shark-worthy large bite, and disappeared inside.

Campbell looked over at me, his volume barely a whisper. "I also paid Mr. Logan two hundred bucks for his trouble, and I didn't show my badge until he asked to see it. I think he's going to decorate with police stars in icing on some of tomorrow's... er... today's donuts."

With a chuckle, I gave him a conspiratorial wink as he held the door open for Watson and me. "My lips are sealed." Hopefully, Campbell had gotten the nonalcoholic kinds. Jed Logan liked his booze, and a good half of his recipes, as the name of his donut shop suggested, had alcohol in them, but I decided not to ask.

Susan already had a hip propped against the windowsill beside Trevor's bed, and had apparently asked him how he was doing.

"Good, the doctor thinks..." Trevor glanced over

as Watson and I entered the room, followed by Officer Cabot.

"Keep going." Susan spoke with her mouth full.

"Right, okay." Though he looked uncomfortable, Trevor shifted and continued, "They say the MRI is fine, no bleeding or swelling in the brain, that really it's just a superficial head wound. They wouldn't even be keeping me here overnight if I didn't now live by myself."

"Good news." Susan took another bite and gestured toward Officer Cabot. "Care for a donut, Mr. Donovan? My partner has fresh-baked coconut ones, apparently."

"No. Thank you." Trevor kept his gaze on Watson, who slowly circled Officer Cabot's legs, looking up in clear supplication.

"Do you mind?" I looked toward Officer Cabot, and he lifted the lid, allowing me to pull out one of the donuts. Tearing off a little of the underside, void of any icing or red-and-green-coated coconut, I tossed it down to Watson, then refocused on Trevor. "That's good news. So glad you're all right."

"Yep, it's great," Susan chimed in before Trevor could respond. "No bleeding or swelling in the brain, sounds to me like your memory should be crystal clear." She grinned—just like the bite of donut before, the expression was shark-worthy.

Trevor shifted. "What would you like to know?"

I moved to the side of his bed Watson followed beside me, and I spoke up before Susan could offer some condescending retort. "How about you run through what happened for us again?"

"Okay..." Trevor swallowed, and his dark gaze flitted from Susan, to Officer Cabot, to me, and then finally fixed lower on Watson. "Well, like I said. I got home and realized I'd been broken into. I saw the elf and the fruitcake on the mantle, so I walked over." He nodded as he spoke, as if Watson would agree with him. "I heard a noise, turned around, and saw... Santa. I think we startled each other. He pushed me, I fell. I don't know how long I was out. When I came to, I pulled out my phone and called 911. Then... you all came."

Something about the scene had bothered me, though it wasn't until that second, I realized what it was. "Oh, right, you had a fruitcake with your elf."

Trevor nodded, and Susan looked at me quizzically from the other side of the bed, as if I was daft.

"I'm just putting the pieces together. You had fruitcake but were still hurt by Santa." I hurried on. "The other people he's harassed or hurt, like

Paulie and Finnegan, received coal with their elves."

"I get it. The fruitcake proves that Santa wasn't there to hurt Mr. Donovan." Officer Cabot beamed in his childlike way. "Which further goes to prove that Santa was merely startled by Mr. Donovan, that it was only an accident."

"Which further goes to prove?" Susan cocked an eyebrow. "Really? Who speaks like that?" She refocused on Trevor. "Besides, we got that much at your house. What else do you remember?"

Even as she said it, I realized it was true. We hadn't connected the dots to the fruitcake necessarily, but none of it was new information. Nor did it actually answer what bothered me about the scene. I thought it had, but that whispering voice remained, taunting that I was missing something obvious.

Trevor licked his lips again, swallowed, and then shook his head. "I... don't know. What else is there to remember?"

Then it clicked, truly clicked. It wasn't something I'd been missing; it was a sense of déjà vu that I hadn't quite picked up on. I'd done this before. Susan and I both had. And Watson, as well, for that matter. I eyed Trevor and tried to keep from sounding interrogational. "I guess I'm just a little surprised. If you were startled and fell backward, hitting your head on the corner of the brick of the opening of the fireplace, I would've expected a little more damage than just a cut on the back of your head."

"There was blood everywhere, Miss Page." Campbell spoke up softly, as if he didn't want to insult me.

Susan was staring at me with narrowed eyes, but I could see her wheels turning and her willingness to follow along.

Though I offered a quick smile to Cabot, I didn't let up on Trevor. "There was a lot of blood, but even as the paramedics said, head wounds bleed a lot. Still... falling backward, unable to stop yourself, and hitting the corner of a brick? That's really lucky to only have a cut."

"I guess so. Especially considering I was knocked out." Trevor had been looking at me but refocused on Watson. "I think he wants some more donut."

I felt Watson's paws lightly pounding right above my knee, and I was certain Trevor was right, but I pressed on. "That's a good point. It's weird that the blow was hard enough to render you unconscious and nothing more. No skull fracture, no swelling of the brain, no internal bleeding."

"Maybe it was a Christmas miracle." When Susan spoke that time, the sharp quality had morphed into something more snakelike, and confirmed that she was fully on board with me now.

"Maybe it was." Trevor offered a smile, or at least something that looked like it was desperately attempting to be a smile. "Pretty perfect for a guy who makes Christmas elves to receive a Christmas miracle."

"Are you sure you were standing when you were surprised by Santa?" I moved a little closer to him. "Maybe you were sitting by the fire, relaxing, and when you were startled by Santa you fell backward from that distance? That would explain it merely being a cut. Not as far to fall, the impact against the brick would be lessened."

"Um..." Trevor rubbed at the back of his head, which was covered by a solitary wrap with gauze. "Maybe?"

Watson pounded on my thigh again, not overly hard, just a reminder, but I took advantage of it and lurched forward a little, catching my balance on the bed rail, bringing me closer to Trevor, then ripped off a larger chunk of donut and passed it to Watson before returning directly to Trevor's gaze. "I imagine if I threw myself against the bricks, I'd probably sit down first. I think it probably would even take me a little time to work up the nerve to throw myself backward at all."

His eyes widened, both in shock and fear.

Any doubt that I'd had, not that there'd really been any, vanished. I *had* done this before. Another supposed victim in a hospital bed who'd actually done it all to himself. "This would've been more believable if you'd committed further. Starting with the fruitcake. You probably should've chosen coal, and even though it would've hurt, made yourself fall from a bigger height, or even—" My gaze flicked to Susan, just for a second as I replayed the memory of the other pretend victim from months before, and then back to Trevor. "—stabbed yourself in the leg with a knife or iron bar or something."

Susan grinned. "From my experience, iron bars and shrapnel are very popular when inflicting wounds on yourself, and they're easier to control the damage, unless you hit an artery..." She moved forward as well, blocking Trevor on the other side. "Speaking of metal objects that can hurt, we noticed that the iron poker was missing from your fireplace set?"

Trevor had been about to speak, but flinched, his

brows creasing in what appeared to be genuine confusion. "My what?"

"The iron poker, from your fireplace set." Susan spoke patiently, calmly. "It's one of those tools on your hearth. You probably even bumped into them as you threw yourself backward."

"There's also that little issue of the blood in the snow outside your front door." I mimicked Susan's position.

"Blood?" Trevor's eyes widened even further.

"Officer Cabot..." Though she addressed her partner, Susan didn't take her gaze off Trevor. "Can you remind me, have we had any dead bodies lying around Estes Park who were beaten with an iron poker, or a lead pipe, or something, and definitely left a trail of blood somewhere?"

"We sure have, Detective Green." I hated to admit that I was surprised when Campbell's tone suggested he was tracking right along with Susan and me and not needing any other clarification. "I believe that was Mr. Finnegan Clark."

"Oh, right!" Susan snapped her fingers, still staring lasers into Trevor. "And... Cabot, help me, I'm pulling a blank, where did Mr. Clark live again?" Once more, she snapped her fingers as if trying to think.

"I believe he was roommates with our current victim, Mr. Donovan."

Trevor appeared to be on the verge of hyperventilating and stared in horror at Officer Cabot, who had taken position at the foot of his bed. Finally, he settled on me once more. "I honestly don't know about the blood. Or that iron poker thingy. I didn't notice it was missing. We never even used it."

"Why don't you fill us in on what you *do* know, Trevor?" I smiled, hoping I'd been able to capture some of Susan's shark skills.

Watson leapt up once more, this time his forepaws landing on the side of the bed, and he looked back and forth between us. I simply laid a hand on top of his head.

"Fine. Yes, I did this to myself. Santa wasn't there." Trevor let out a breath. "I knew people would start to think that I had something to do with Finnegan, so I..."

"You might as well tell us why, Trevor." When he looked at me with unconvincing innocence, I pressed on, going with my gut, though by this point it was obvious. "Were you worried that people would assume you'd be willing to kill someone if you're also the type to break into stores around town, leaving elves as you vandalized and assaulted?"

Susan didn't give him a chance to answer. "And why did you kill Finnegan? Did he threaten to turn you in, or was it more of a competition between you two?"

"Kill Finnegan?" Trevor threw himself back in horror, only managing to bash his wrapped wound against the headboard. He cried out in pain, threw a hand back there, but didn't stop. "I didn't kill Finnegan. He was... my friend... kinda. I didn't kill him. I don't know who did. I don't understand it."

I thought I believed him, that he didn't know—if I was reading him correctly, some of the fear wasn't just about being caught, but that whoever had killed Finnegan might come after him. "One more time, Trevor. Why don't you tell us everything you *do* know, and this time don't leave anything out."

When the dam broke, Trevor's words came quick, so fast they nearly fell over one another. "Fine. Yes. I am behind the elves, fruitcake, and coal. Me and Finnegan. That was us. That was never the original plan when I agreed to be in Santa's Cause. It was just supposed to be more exposure. And Mr. Clark made it really easy and appealing by giving me free lodging if I'd be a roommate with his nephew. I think he was really impressed with my motivation and drive and thought it might inspire Finnegan."

He sank back exhausted, this time careful not to hit his head on anything. "It was Finnegan's idea, the whole Santa delivery thing. The two of us actually got along pretty well, and I told him..."

When he just shook his head, Susan leaned forward, resting her weight on the side of the bed, making it creak. "Told him what, Mr. Donovan?"

"That the elves weren't doing well." He sighed, shame washing over him. "I've been middle-of-the-road for a long time, there's a ton of others that look similar to what I produce, and the high-quality materials simply weren't paying off. I went the exclusive route with all the resorts, trying to make the elves high-budget items, and it worked for a little bit, but not enough. The other option, and maybe the smarter option, is to mass-produce them, sell them at all the big-name chains like Target, Walmart, all that stuff. But... I hadn't wanted to do that, and, again, there're already ones there that are too similar. It felt like selling out. Estes was my last attempt before throwing in the towel. Then... Finnegan came up with an idea."

So, it had been what it felt like to me the whole time. "Get a lot of hype for your elves by pulling the Santa routine with fruitcake and coal?"

He nodded. "It was working too. The elves were

getting in the news way outside of Estes Park and Colorado. Some of the photos even went viral on social media. I was actually juggling where I was going to go next year, I had so many offers. And people were already putting in orders for next season's collection, at three times the price I'd ever asked before."

"Then you got greedy. Pushed it too far. Ruined a good thing." Susan tsked like it was the oldest story in the book. "You should've stopped while you were ahead. Things changed when you vandalized the pet shop and assaulted Paulie. That wasn't a line you should have crossed."

"*I* didn't!" For the first time, when Trevor straightened, anger flashed in his eyes. "I about lost my mind when I heard what Finnegan did to Paulie. Number one, I don't want to hurt anyone. That was never my intent. And two, *that* wasn't going to help the elves sell. They're supposed to be charming and fun. High-quality, exclusive, high-priced luxury fun. Sure, breaking into places is against the law, technically, but we weren't harming anything. Just leaving cute little elves and either a fruitcake or a piece of coal. I mean, really, what gets more Christmassy than that?"

Susan studied him wordlessly for a second, but I

could tell she was on the same page as me, and I believed him. "Finnegan did that to Paulie?"

Trevor nodded.

"Finnegan was the one who ruined the bakery and wrote all those horrible things on the marble about Katie?"

"Yeah." Shame joined the anger over his features, and he nodded, slumping somewhat again. "He was starting to get carried away. And maybe I shouldn't be surprised, since *I* was supposed to be a good influence, or whatever. But it was me who was talked into breaking and entering on a nightly basis. But the more we hung out with..." Trevor shook his head and skipped that entirely. "Anyway, Finnegan kept getting darker and darker, and even when I confronted him about what he was doing, not only that it was wrong, but that it was hurting me and what I'd hoped for the elves... he didn't care."

I softened my tone. "You were going to say the more you hung out with Jake Jazz, weren't you?"

He nodded again at me but didn't say anything.

There was no softness as Susan spoke. "So, the three of you were running around town breaking and entering, and ultimately engaging in murder."

Trevor shook his head at Susan, clearly desperate. "I was not engaged in murder. I didn't do that.

And no, it wasn't the three of us. Jake was never involved. We didn't tell him that we were behind the elves."

Susan and I both flinched, looking at each other, but I spoke up first. "You three were together quite a bit, yet you and Finnegan didn't let him in on the secret?"

"Maybe Finnegan did, I don't know." A tear made its way down his cheek. "It wasn't supposed to go like this. None of it."

"I'm afraid that's true, Mr. Donovan. Murder is a whole different ball game." Susan stood. "The good news is, you won't have to stay here for observation. Since you'll be spending the night in jail, there'll be plenty of us who can keep an eye on you."

"What?" Trevor's panic rose again. "I just told you, I didn't even do that stuff to the pet shop or the bakery. Let alone kill Finnegan."

"You said yourself you confronted Finnegan about it. That you nearly lost your mind over it." Susan took on a tone as if she was speaking to a child, or Officer Cabot. "Finnegan's plan was supposed to be helping your career, and now he was quite literally flushing it all down the toilet. It doesn't make it right, but I think anyone can understand how in the heat of that moment, during the middle of a confrontation, you might grab the fire poker and swing it at the man responsible for destroying your dreams. Then you cleaned up the mess, and since your elves were on their way out anyway, gave a final show at Santa's Cause. I can't even blame you for that, not really. For taking a jab at Marty Clark. If it hadn't been for him setting you up as a roommate with his no-account nephew, you wouldn't have been led down this path in the first place. So you quite literally laid it all at his feet."

Trevor shook his head the entire time Susan was talking. And though I could see how she'd arrived at that, it didn't feel right, and one of the reasons hit me just as Trevor had spoken out loud. "None of that happened. Not like that. I don't know who killed Finnegan. We went back and forth being Santa, that way one or both of us would always have an alibi. That night, it was my turn. I broke into the newspaper, left the elf and coal, and came back home. Finnegan wasn't there, didn't come back the rest of the night. I didn't think too much of it. He was bored hearing about my nights as Santa, since I didn't do anything more than what we'd done at the beginning, and I figured he was either just hanging out with Jake or one of the girls he was seeing. I didn't know he'd been..." Another tear made its way. "I didn't find

out about Finnegan until I arrived at work. I heard
Mr. Clark sobbing inside and got the story from the
crowd on the sidewalk. I... panicked, went back
home, and tried to figure out what to do. I decided if
I was Santa's next victim, then I clearly wasn't—" He
finished with a pathetic gesture around the hospital
room, as if he had clearly chosen the wrong path.

I believed him. Susan, however, wasn't
convinced. "This hasn't been completely confirmed
yet, but the fireplace poker from your house is missing, and there's blood in the snow outside your front
door. I'm willing to bet that blood is going to come
back as a positive match for your roommate. So,
you're going to tell me that you came home to a place
where it looked like someone was murdered and you
didn't notice anything?"

"No." More tears fell, though they seemed more
out of fear than anything else. "I really didn't. I
swear. I wasn't worried about him at all. I figured he
was with Jake or a girl or somebody. Nothing was out
of place in the cabin." One of his shoulders shrugged.
"If you say there's an iron poker missing, then I guess
you're right, but I never noticed."

Letting out a huff, Watson finally collapsed to
the floor and curled on top of my boots under my
skirt, apparently figuring donut time was over. I

believed that too, and I leaned forward, trying to sound sympathetic, and maybe in truth, I was a little bit. "Who do *you* think killed Finnegan?"

He sniffed, then ran his forearm under his nose. "I don't know." He shrugged again, this time with both shoulders. "It seemed like every day there was another person Finnegan and Jake had made angry or tormented. I imagine that list of people wanting to hurt them is pretty long."

I thought back to Susan's and my conversation in the waiting room. "Jake is just fine. No one has broken into his house. There's been no elves for him, nothing." When I noticed his gaze flick up at me and dart away quickly, I knew what else he'd been considering. "You said there was conflict between you and Finnegan lately. Is that true for him and Jake as well?"

He was silent for a long time, then finally nodded. "That's not really new, I don't suppose. They'd fight about lots of things. Jake's got a temper, and so had Finnegan, not that I recognized it at first. But... sure... they'd fight." He cleared his throat. "But... Jake was with... um... some girl..."

"Tiffany?" Campbell, nearly forgotten, piped up from the end of the bed.

"Yeah." Still Trevor nodded, but he didn't look at anyone. "I think he was with Tiffany that night."

I laid a hand over his, going the compassionate route. "Doesn't sound like that overly convinces you of his innocence."

Another shrug, and instead of addressing me, he looked to Susan. "Would you be okay to either keep me here for observation or... even down at the station for a night... or two."

Her pale blue eyes widened at his abrupt switch. "Has Jake Jazz threatened you, Mr. Donovan?"

"No." Trevor didn't say anything else, and clearly wasn't going to get more explicit than that, but at his request and expression, he didn't need to spell out he was afraid of the other member of their threesome.

Elves wielding fireplace pokers danced around the Christmas tree in my living room in frantic glee. With the shadows scattered around from the flickering of the fireplace, it was like a demented holiday version of *Lord of the Flies*. The tips of each poker skewered a loaf of fruitcake and a burning chunk of coal. The fever pitch of their chanting grew, making my ears hurt. Even as I covered them with my hands, the elves' words broke through, and I realized they were screaming the lyrics to "Rocking Around the Christmas Tree."

Watson barked and snarled, trying to lower his head and dart out quickly enough to snag their tiny felt feet, but each time, an iron poker with the fiery piece of coal swung down toward his head and he had to scamper away.

Unable to do anything, I watched in horror as the

elves, as if in a synchronized dance, held their heavily laden pokers skyward and then, as one, plunged them into my Christmas tree, which instantly ignited into flames. Watson's barking went wild, and on the roof, Santa's reindeer clomped their hooves in fury. Just when my body was finally able to move and I started to rush in Watson's direction, a swooshing sound filled the cabin, and a cloud of dust exploded from the fireplace. The burning logs scattered over my hardwood floor, and Santa stood up from the hearth and smiled at me. Between us, bits of the ceiling cascaded down under the pressure of the reindeers' chaotic glee.

Choking, I sat up, trying to wipe the soot from my eyes and clear the smoke from my lungs. I squinted in the sudden brightness bursting through the window, then blinked.

Sunshine, the brightness of sunshine. And I was in my bed. There were no elves. No fire, no Santa.

A pounding came, and ridiculously, I looked up, expecting to see more bits of the ceiling crumbling under the reindeers' weight. Then as Watson barked in the other room, I realized someone was knocking at the door.

Still trying to get my bearings, I slid out of bed, grabbed my robe, and stumbled across the room.

Sure enough, the real-life Watson was sitting in front of the door, barking. Now that I was awake, I was better able to judge his tone. Watson didn't sound like he was in danger, or that he was warning me not to answer the door. It was more along the lines of simply demanding I get up and do my job. Even so, after another knock came, instead of trusting his or my instincts, I looked through the peephole.

Katie stood on the other side, a blue knitted hippo hat stuffed over her brown curls. She rubbed her arms together over a puffy pink jacket, then reached out to knock again.

I threw open the door. "Hey, are you okay?"

"Other than quite literally turning into an icicle on your doorstep, yes." She hurried inside, not waiting for an invitation, though she never needed one. "The question is, are *you* okay? I've been calling and calling."

"I was up late. Susan and I were... and Officer Cabot and Watson, too, I suppose... we were all getting Trevor Donovan's explanation of events." That had been late enough, but I'd not been able to fall asleep for a couple of hours after we'd gotten home. Though whether it was because of my mind spinning with all the possibilities, or due to the fact that I'd broken my own rule and had caffeine much too late, who could say? After closing the door behind Katie, I rubbed my eyes. "I didn't hear the phone ring at all. What time is it?"

"Nearly one in the afternoon." Katie reached down and patted Watson on the head as she passed by on her way to the living room. "Sorry to wake you up. But it was either talk to you or Susan. I'd rather talk to you."

I finally picked up on the note of panic in her tone, and it brought me nearly as awake as the break-fast dirty chai. Pulling my robe tighter, I hurried over and sat beside her.

Watson followed, plopped down between us, and with a whimper looked over the couch toward the doorway that led into the kitchen.

"We'll get breakfast later, buddy." I rubbed the white line between his eyes, but quickly refocused on Katie. "You said you're okay, but you're not. What's wrong?"

"Nothing's wrong. I'm sure I'm jumping to conclusions." She snorted out a sardonic sound and looked at me. "Or I just have trust issues, you know my past."

"It's okay." Reaching out, I took her hand. "Katie,

you don't have to give disclaimers, just tell me what's going on."

"This is not how I wanted to have this conversation with you. Not that I'd even figured out if I needed to have this conversation with you. I honestly hadn't even figured out if I wanted to have this conversation with *myself*." Her brown gaze lifted. "I think I do. And I think I probably would've sooner rather than later, but now I have to have it now. It's probably smarter to have it with Susan, but I just can't talk to her first. I can't have her know before you know. But this still isn't how I want you to know." Katie could slip into fast-talking from time to time, but I'd never seen her reach this level of speed, or incoherence.

"Sweetie, how much caffeine have you had?" I gave her hand a squeeze. "I think I caught all the words, and there were a lot of them, but I'm not really sure what they mean."

She looked at me pitifully.

Before Katie could explain, it clicked. It was obvious enough that I could only blame exhaustion and having just been woken up from the weirdest bad dream I'd ever had. "Joe."

Katie sucked in a little breath, looking at me in surprise, and then slumped. "You do know."

Couldn't help but chuckle. "As you pointed out often in regard to Leo's feelings about me, I can be a little dense on the romantic clues, but even I started to pick up there was something going on between you and Joe."

"That's just it. There isn't anything going on between me and Joe." She slumped and fell dramatically back to the arm of the sofa and kicked her feet out, plopping them on the coffee table, her shoes almost colliding with the side of Watson's face in the process. "Oh, sorry, buddy."

Watson chuffed his annoyance, headed toward the hearth, then changed his mind in an abrupt turn before sauntering with his nose in the air. He took the long way around the couch before making his way through the kitchen door and disappearing.

Katie watched him go and continued staring into the kitchen long after Watson was out of view. Finally, I prodded her. "Are you sure there's nothing going on with you and Joe?"

"No." Still keeping her gaze fixed, Katie shook her head and then kind of laughed. "I don't know if that's a *No, there isn't anything going on between me and Joe*, or if it's a *No, I'm* not sure *that there's something going on between me and Joe*."

I forced out a laugh of my own. "Katie, I love you

dearly, and sometimes you rattle off trivia so fast that it feels like riddles, but I'm not even entirely sure you're speaking English right now."

Katie finally refocused on me, took a deep breath, sighed, and then began again, slower. "I... *think* something has been building between Joe and me. And I *think* I actually want there to be. And I thought you and Leo might've been aware of it the other day." A little smile, unlike any I'd ever seen on Katie before, played over her lips. A heated blush rose to her cheeks. "It sounds bad, but I'm not used to talking about this kind of stuff, even with you. Although... I've wanted to. Until... well, I've wanted to."

"It's funny, because I've been thinking the exact same thing." I could feel the boxed-up secrets calling from the bedroom closet, but I refused to look their way. "There's been some... relationship stuff that I should've been talking to you about instead of allowing my head to rattle around alone with the issues getting bigger and bigger. I just—" I shrugged. "—haven't."

Katie looked at me in concern, and maybe in a bit of relief about having the focus off herself. "Are you and Leo okay?"

"Yes, we are. It's just that—" What was I doing? I

shook my head, started again. "We are. And you and I can talk about stuff when there's time. But right now, let's talk about you. You and Joe. You mentioned you felt like you either need to talk to me or Susan. Why Susan?"

Katie opened and closed her mouth several times, each gesture appearing like she was about to dart down a different bunny trail or conversation starter. Finally she picked one, her voice determined, and she met my gaze unflinchingly. "Answer me this, and please be honest. As you've been looking into this whole elf debacle, have there been any arrows pointing toward Joe? Has he been on your radar even at all?" She waved her hand between us. "As a suspect or somehow connected?"

I so wanted to lie, not wanting to be responsible for even an ounce of worry or pain for my best friend. Instead I just gave a solitary nod. "Yes."

"I also thought I noticed you and Leo thinking that the other day as well, but I wouldn't let myself dwell on it too much." She slumped again, and though clearly it wasn't what she'd wanted to hear, there was a little relief as well. "At least, then, I know I'm not being paranoid and it's not simply my trust issues from the past making me crazy."

I momentarily debated which approach would

be better, to have Katie go through all the events and ins and outs of her time with Joe and what she'd noticed, without any prompting from me—like I would with any other person I was trying to get information from. But this was Katie, my best friend and business partner, so I shoved aside what I should do and made it quicker, easier for her. "There's nothing huge connecting Joe to the break-ins or the murder, but there are a couple of large, concerning aspects. You, being the main one."

Katie winced but didn't act surprised. "Because of how Jake and Finnegan spoke to me the other night, in front of Joe."

"Yeah," I answered, even though she hadn't really asked a question.

"And the size of the bruises on his body you mentioned at the bookshop."

I nodded again. "Clearly, you've been thinking all of this as well, and aware of it, so... what happened this morning, why now? Why did you have to debate between talking to me or Susan?"

She finally closed her eyes again and kept them that way, even as she started talking slowly. "I was with Joe this morning, after meeting with the construction crew at the bakery. He came down and brought me some coffee and pastries from the Koffee

Kiln." She brightened. "Carla's new providers on her baked goods are much better than she had before. I mean, they're not Cozy Corgi bakery level, but—"

I touched her again.

It was all she needed to get back on track. And she did so after another sigh. "Anyway, Joe and I were just chatting, coming up with more T-shirt ideas, different bakery possibilities, and all sorts of things... and... I guess, I've just been letting my suspicions build up, and my fears exploded. I should have asked him about them before instead of going crazy. And I didn't really explode, but the question just burst from me. I hadn't even been aware I was about to ask it."

Katie started that fast-talking thing again, so I interjected. "What did you say to him, Katie?"

"I asked him point-blank if he had anything to do with Finnegan's death." Katie winced as if even the memory of it was painful. "That's such a horrible thing to ask someone you think you might have feelings for—if they're a murderer."

"Well"—I tried to keep my tone soothing—"what did he say? Clearly something a little concerning, if you're here and are considering telling Susan."

Katie didn't beat around the bush anymore. "He promised me he didn't. He said, however, that he did confront Finnegan about how he treated me the night Finnegan died." Katie rubbed her hands together. "I didn't mention the bruising on Finnegan's ribs, but I asked if during that confrontation, if it had gotten physical. He said it didn't."

I wasn't sure whether to ask the next question or not, but I did. "You felt like he was being honest with you?"

Katie hesitated, then nodded. "I did. I... I do, but that doesn't mean I'm right. He had some sort of hostile altercation with Finnegan just before Finnegan was killed. If I simply take Joe at his word, it kind of makes me a fool, doesn't it?"

"To a point, I think that's what you do when you love someone. At least until the cold-hard facts in front of you prove otherwise." And again, that stupid envelope tried to flap through the back of my mind. I bashed it away.

"I don't know if I love Joe. And I sure don't know if I want a relationship. I haven't wanted one. I've been completely happy. I'm living my dream life. Even with the bakery torn up, I'm still living my dream life. Why would I want a man or some relationship to come get in the way of all of that?"

"And who does *that* remind you of?" I laughed.

Katie joined in, and then we were both laughing,

a touch hysterical, which proved it was more out of nerves than actual humor.

At our cackling, Watson trotted back into the living room, looked at us both in concern, appeared to determine we were insane, then trotted off once more, this time into the bedroom.

We just laughed harder, until Katie was able to catch her breath. "Yes, there's a reason we're best friends. Even though you have horrible fashion taste, we might just be a touch similar on the romance front. As evidenced, having such a hard time talking about all of this with you at all." She sobered. "It makes it so much worse to think that if Joe did this, that it would be because of me. Because he was defending my name."

"Even if that's true, it *isn't* your fault."

"Maybe not technically, but it would still be because of me. And I'm sure it would bring up everything that happened with his wife, all the pain Joe experienced around her betrayal and... well... all that happened."

"And again, even if all that is true, it still isn't your fault." I waited until her gaze finally met mine, then simply had to give her some form of relief. "Even if Joe's involved, it may not be entirely because of how Jake and Finnegan were speaking to you."

Katie's eyes widened hopefully.

"One of the theories I was playing around with was that the whole elf thing was either a marketing scheme between Marty and Gentry, a fake feud, if you will. Or a revenge tactic from Gentry against Marty, and he might've been using his friends, Joe, Jared, and Pete to..." I broke off abruptly and rubbed my forehead. "Oh, good Lord, I need caffeine. Never mind, none of that is still an option. Trevor confessed that he and Finnegan were behind the break-ins and the elves. It was all a marketing scheme, but between those two, not the Christmas shop owners."

"Obviously." Katie scowled. "Wait a minute, Finnegan and Trevor only? *Not* Jake?"

"According to Trevor, yes. He claims Jake didn't even know that the two of them were behind the elf scheme."

Katie scoffed. "That doesn't make any sense. Those words on my marble were exactly what Jake called me the previous night."

"I'd brought that up directly, but Trevor sort of explained that as well. He said the longer the three of them were together, the worse Finnegan became. Like Jake's influence was a license to do worse and worse things. So it's possible, maybe even probable, if what Trevor says is true, that Finnegan copied the things Jake said to you. Apparently, Finnegan's tendency to mimic everything Jake did was causing conflict between them. With all of them. Trevor was irritated that Finnegan kept going out of the boundaries of what the two of them had planned, and Jake was starting to get annoyed having a mini-me. *That's* causing Susan to lean toward Trevor being Finnegan's murderer, especially since he faked the break-in at his own house." I filled Katie in on the rest of our conversation with Trevor and then we both sat there, considering.

"It's hard for me to believe that Jake has nothing to do with this. He's simply horrible." Katie cocked her head, clearly having just had a derailing thought, and grinned. "This shows that I've been too worked up and too close to it to think clearly. How have I not realized this before? If Joe was doing this because of how I was treated, he would've killed Jake, not Finnegan." Her brightness dimmed instantly. "Unless he hasn't gotten around to Jake yet."

"That's a possibility. But..." I shrugged. "I've considered it, kind of, but it seems far-fetched."

"What does your gut say, about Joe?" Katie leaned forward, hope burning.

"Katie..." I latched onto her hand yet again, not wanting to give her false hope. "My gut isn't infallible. I've been wrong plenty of times. There's nothing magical or some true north about my instincts."

"That's not what your mom would say."

I barked out a laugh. "Well, if what my mother says is the moniker for truth, then why aren't we dripping in healing crystals right now?"

Katie tapped the exposed part of my sternum where I typically wore a necklace of celestine and tourmaline and labradorite crystals my mother and stepsisters made me, one that was supposed to help with protection and a host of other issues.

"Touché." Chuckling, I gave in. "Okay, as long as you keep in mind that it doesn't really mean anything, my gut tells me it *isn't* Joe."

Katie sank back, obvious relief flooding over her. "Really?"

I nodded.

"And you're not just saying that because... well, because I'm me?"

"No." I shook my head and smiled. "It's actually harder for me to say because it is you. I can tell it's giving you hope, and the last thing I want is to be wrong and hurt you."

"I don't think you are. I trust your gut. Mine says

the same. I was just afraid it was hope or something." She gave an affirmative nod as if the decision had been made. "The idea of Joe being behind it simply doesn't make sense, either with the details you've gathered so far, or the man I'm learning him to be. In fact..." Her eyes narrowed and a grin covered her face. "If I make you breakfast and get some coffee in you, what do you say we wander downtown, together, and talk to the missing puzzle piece of this whole thing?"

"I don't know if there's enough coffee in the world to make me able to handle Jake Jazz this morning." I groaned. "Maybe if we had your espresso machine back and I could get a dirty chai."

"Nope. Coffee will have to do." Katie stood and grinned wickedly. "Plus, it's no longer morning. Now come on, let's get you some food and caffeine so you're in top supersleuth form."

From the bedroom, a clatter of scrambling nails sounded over the wood floor, and Watson rushed in, right on cue. He grinned up at us, eyes bright with the promise of breakfast.

NINETEEN

Although it didn't possess the same magic as dirty chai, the pot of coffee—especially when combined with Katie's french toast covered in tart apples, dried cranberries, and brown sugar—brought me fully to life, and helped my synapses fire on full steam by the time we walked into Madame Delilah's Old Tyme Photography.

Watson, despite having neither coffee nor french toast, after his breakfast of eggs and shredded chicken, was practically chipper. So much so, he looked around the second we walked through the door, as if he were hopeful he'd run into Delilah's three basset hounds.

Katie, on the other hand, was unusually quiet and tense. The change began on our drive into town. Part of me wanted to offer her an out so she wouldn't have to be face-to-face with Jake Jazz again. But we were enough alike that I knew that was neither what she needed nor wanted.

Jake was in the back of the store, rearranging the scene of a Charlie Brown Christmas tree and the false front of a saloon bar behind the camera—obviously having just finished a tourist's photo shoot. As we walked in, he turned, a smile on his lips. "Merry Christmas. Welcome to—" The handsome smile, which surprisingly gave him a kind appearance, faded instantly. Like any aggressor I'd ever met, his gaze went directly to his "victim." "Brought your entourage with you this time?" Jake sauntered around the old-time camera to lean against the counter as he sneered at Katie. "Sending your deformed-looking boyfriend to threaten me the other night wasn't enough?"

Katie bristled, but I could tell it wasn't from the insult but from the accusation of Joe. Apparently he'd confessed about confronting Finnegan but hadn't offered anything about his interaction with Jake. It didn't necessarily mean either of our gut feelings were wrong about Joe, but... it didn't help confirm them either.

"In case you missed me reaming you up and down in the middle of the sidewalk the other night, you might notice that I don't need anyone else to fight my battles for me." Triggering pride for my best friend, Katie barely paused before she strode forward and came to a stop only a yard or so from Jake. Watson trotted along beside her. "*Especially* when dealing with an overgrown schoolyard bully like you."

He smirked. "I don't think you're in the position to call anyone overgrown."

It took everything in my power not to give in to a name-calling exchange. Katie was right—he was nothing more than a bully, and it would get us nowhere. Not too long ago, my temper wouldn't have paused long enough for me to think that through. But there were bigger fish to fry. "I'm curious, Mr. Jazz," I stopped beside Katie and waited until Jake's gaze finally deigned to meet mine. "How badly were your feelings hurt when you found out about your little buddies having all the fun every night without you?"

What appeared to be genuine confusion flashed over his expression but cleared instantly and was followed by a laugh. "Oh, Finnegan and Trevor's stupid elves?" He laughed again, and though it was dark and bitter, once more it seemed genuine. "Lady, do I look like someone who wants to dress up like an old fat man and play with dolls every night?"

I didn't respond, couldn't. I hadn't expected that

reaction, and from Katie's frozen position beside me, neither had she.

Jake didn't wait for more prompting, however. He simply smiled, a vicious thing, and leaned forward, clearly enjoying himself. "Let me get this straight. I'm betting, since you like to play detective, you've come up with your main suspect."

From over his shoulder, Delilah walked in from the back, a gorgeous Victorian Christmassy ruby-red gown held in her arms. Though she opened her mouth to interrupt when she saw us, she paused at Jake's tone, clearly debating.

Jake gestured around the photography shop, still grinning. "Is this the part where you and your side-kick..." He cocked his head for a second. "Which one is your sidekick anyway, Red? The fat dog or the fat baker?" He waved me off. "It doesn't matter. Either way, this is the part where you and your sidekick confront the big bad murderer, right? You explain your theory to him—that he found out that his little buddies, as you say, were playing games behind his back, and he went into a fit of rage and got revenge. Is that it? Really? Are you both honestly as dumb as you look?"

The fury over Delilah's face was evident even from a distance, and as she started to take a step forward, I risked a slight shake of my head. To my surprise, she actually stopped where she was.

Katie had drawn Jake's attention away, so he'd not noticed the exchange. "That's not quite the full picture. If you recall, it was *your* words written all over my bakery, and they matched the sentiment you just expressed. You may not be jealous about them playing games without you, but I doubt, especially with your record, you appreciate them implicating your involvement in such a way."

"Trust me"—Jake leaned even nearer to Katie, obviously confident in his ability to intimidate—"I'm hardly the only one to think or say such things about you. Whatever that little sleaze wrote in your bakery was hardly exclusive to me."

It was a rare feeling, but a surge of hatred for the man coursed through me, but instead of giving in to it, I used it for laser focus. "You just called Finnegan, your friend, who was murdered, a sleaze. You don't think that implicates you?" I gestured toward one of his large hands, which was balled-up into a fist on the countertop. "There were massive bruises all over Finnegan's torso, bruises about the size of your balled-up fist there."

Jake flinched just a bit and glanced down at his hand. He unclenched it and shoved it into the pocket of his jeans. When he met my gaze, just a touch of the bravado had disappeared, but not much. "It might be against your pretentious sensibilities, but *real* men fight every once in a while. It happens. Especially when they have it coming. But a few punches here and there don't have anything to do with murder."

"So, you admit you beat up Finnegan?" I hadn't expected a confession to be so easy.

"I..." The other hand mimicked the first and slid into the other pocket. "I'm not admitting to anything. But yeah, Finnegan turned out to be a sleaze, not that I'm too surprised. He was getting more annoying by the day. Following me around like a little lost puppy. It was pathetic. Like he wanted to be me."

"And yet he was doing bigger and better things than you, wasn't he?" Katie's voice held a taunt of her own. "Breaking into different stores and houses every night, making national news. Causing quite the scene."

Watson had been standing between the two of us, but at Katie's tone, he shifted slightly in front of her, preemptively taking a protective stance.

Jake barely spared Watson a glance before mocking Katie once more. "You've even got fluff between your ears, don't you? Didn't I already say that I am not the type of loser that dresses up and plays with dolls? It was bad enough hanging out with the guy who made those prissy little elves. That precious little snowflake actually complained about how Finnegan and I talked about women." Laughing, he jabbed a finger at Katie's face. "About you, actually. His poor little artist's soul might as well be a talking point for the politically correct crowd."

Delilah stepped forward, having heard enough, but I drew Jake's attention, feeling like I'd been missing the forest for the trees. "Tiffany."

Jake shot a look back at me, eyes surprised. "What?"

"Tiffany." As I repeated the Koffee Kiln barista's name, my surety increased. "You've been having a fling, affair, or whatever you want to call it, with Tiffany. And you just said that Finnegan, more and more every day, was trying to be like you. Would that include trying to... date... the same woman? Maybe you're upset he didn't invite you to play with the elf dolls, maybe you're not. *Maybe* you didn't like it when he played around with something you thought of as yours behind your back?"

The hatred that crossed his face confirmed it. "You think any woman would be tempted by

Finnegan Clark after she's had me?" That time, he stepped forward, leering and leaning into me.

Watson switched position in a heartbeat, wedging himself between us and growling in a way that would have made a wolf proud.

Though I straightened to my full height, not willing to give him an ounce of power, Jake didn't stop. "How'd you come up with this theory, Red? Jealousy? Wishing *you* were Tiffany?" He shrugged, and that smile twisted at the corner of his mouth. "I'll give you a go, if you want. Most of the time I wouldn't lower myself to even look at someone like you. But it's Christmas, right? Good time for charity."

"Get out of my store." Delilah was the exact same height as me, and she stood behind Jake, filling out every inch of it.

Jake's eyes were wide in surprise as he turned, his voice instantly changing tone. "Delilah, listen. I'm sorry. I know how you feel about—"

"I said get out." She tossed the gown over the counter so her hands were free, and the anger in her eyes and voice nearly made *me* tremble in fear. "Do you know how many times I've stood up for you in the past couple of months? How many people I called close-minded and elitist? You asked me for a second chance, to look past your record and see the man who was starting fresh, making things right."

"And I am." Jake's tone was softer, but not pleading. "That's exactly what I am. These two are trying to—"

Delilah whipped a hand across the space, nearly colliding with Jake's chest. "No. I don't need to hear it. I've seen it for myself. I saw it the other day with how you treated them with Detective Green. I told myself to be understanding, given your history with the law. But that was just an excuse. You're not starting fresh. You're not trying to make things right." Her sneer matched the one Jake had offered us only moments before. "And you're *no* sort of man. Not even close."

Everything about Jake shifted in that instant, reverting back to how he'd been speaking to Katie and me, although it took an even darker tone. "You think you're too good for me, Delilah? I've heard what people say about you. And you want to talk about seeing something for yourself? How many men have I seen you wander off with in the short time I've been here?"

Delilah laughed, shook her long red hair, and the triumph over her face made her even more beautiful than I'd ever seen her. "And what does that tell you, little Jake? How many times have you hinted that you'd like to be more than my employee? And how many times have I pretended not to understand or pointed out it wouldn't be appropriate, given that you're my employee? But the truth? You just got it in one. How many *men* have you seen me with? *Men*." She did shove her finger into his chest then, hard enough that Jake had to take a step back. "No *man* ever speaks to a woman the way you have to Katie and Fred just now. You're pathetic and about as far away from a man as I can possibly imagine."

Jake lifted his hand as if he was going to strike her. "You filthy—"

I grabbed it and jerked it back down. Simultaneously, Watson lunged at the back of his legs while Delilah shoved his chest.

With a yell, Jake tripped, stumbled backward and threw out a hand to catch himself on the edge of the counter. He would've succeeded, if Katie hadn't stepped in front of it, so that Jake's hand bounced off her arm. He crashed to the ground in an ungraceful tangle of long arms and legs.

Katie cringed. "Oh, sorry! That happens. Sometimes we fat bakers get in the way." She finished with a shrug of exaggerated helplessness.

Sputtering curses, Jake managed to spring

upward, and doubtlessly would've gone after her, or any of us.

Watson lunged, probably would've attacked if I hadn't managed to grab his leash, and then Katie, Delilah, and I made a wall behind my heroic little corgi.

"Try it." I met Jake's gaze. "Please."

Jake looked like he was going to accept my offer for a few moments, then took a step back. He ignored Katie and Watson entirely, his hate-filled gaze flicking between Delilah and me. "Enjoy yourselves. Feel all empowered or whatever you want right now. I'll let you have this moment." He turned and walked toward the front door, and though pausing as he started to leave, Jake didn't peer over his shoulder as he spoke. "And later, when you pay for this, I'll want to hear if you think this moment was worth it or not."

Then he was gone.

The three of us stood there, still as statues except for our trembling. Or at least my trembling, I didn't check to see if Katie and Delilah were as well. And I wasn't entirely sure how much of my own trembling was from fear or anger or adrenaline. Not that it mattered.

The only sound besides Watson's continual

growl was soft folksy Christmas music playing through the photography shop.

Finally, Delilah let out a long breath.

It was as if her exhale gave us permission to move, and all three of us seemed to deflate, leaning on the counter for support. After a moment, I knelt on the floor and started stroking Watson, as he'd plopped down in front of me, seeking comfort.

"I feel like such a fool." Delilah sounded as if she was speaking more to herself than us. "I believed his story. I really did. And then..." A self-depreciating laugh accompanied the headshake. "I don't know. After seeing him with Susan, I think I just slipped into a stubborn place, didn't want to admit—"

"No." Katie reached out a hand and touched Delilah's arm, though she withdrew it quickly. "We're not doing that. None of us." Her gesture surprised me nearly as much as anything that happened that day. I knew how much Katie despised Delilah Johnson. "I didn't deserve having my bakery destroyed. Fred didn't deserve the horrible things he said about her. And you don't deserve judgment because you were trying to give someone a second chance. We're not going to beat ourselves up, or act like we were the ones who were stupid or deserved any ounce of what just happened. We're not doing it."

Delilah laughed again, this time a little relief and humor in it. "I can't believe I'm saying it, but Katie Pizzolato, you actually would make a wonderful Pink Panther."

Katie laughed as well and shook her head, those brown spirals dancing around her face as they often did. "Not on your life. I hate that stupid group of yours."

Then they both laughed. And maybe if we had just a touch more Hallmark magic, the two of them would've hugged. But it was close enough.

"Well, *that* happened." Pressing a kiss to Watson's forehead, I stood once more. "I'm not even sure what to do with all of it, honestly. But..." I focused on Katie and smiled. "Jake didn't actually admit to beating up Finnegan, but he might as well have. I think we're safe to say *that* question's been answered."

"I agree." She brightened at the thought. "Thank goodness."

Delilah looked quizzical at that response but didn't question it. Instead, turning to me, she asked, "You think Jake's the one responsible for Finnegan's murder and Trevor's attempted murder?"

"No." I forgot Delilah wasn't in on the loop. "We know with certainty that Jake had nothing to do with the break-ins or Trevor's assault."

"He might have still been responsible for killing Finnegan, though." Katie lowered herself to Watson, who'd come to stand in front of her after me.

After a second, Delilah joined Katie on the ground, so Watson was lavished with four hands and offered his own Christmas gifts by spreading a hurricane's worth of corgi fur.

"I truly didn't expect that reaction from him. I figured Jake and Finnegan were genuinely friends. Well, them and Trevor." Katie continued, still stroking Watson, "I think I believed him that he despised their elf scheme. I don't really think that was jealousy talking. But the whole Tiffany thing? That was real. He seemed angry enough to kill Finnegan over it." She stiffened. "Actually, I think we may want to call Susan so she can check in on Tiffany. Make sure she's safe and stays that way."

A shot of cold went through me at that thought. "Yes. We definitely will." I pulled out my phone and got ready to call Susan. As it rang, I couldn't help but speculate. "I could be wrong, but something about that theory doesn't play right. Jake for sure seemed angry enough, and I believe him capable of murder, in a heartbeat at this point. But... why kill Finnegan somewhere and then take his body to the Christmas shop? Especially when the scene was dressed up just like all the others, with an elf and a piece of coal? I could believe all of that of Jake, except for the location. It just doesn't make any—"

"Whose body did you discover this time?" Susan's voice barked from the other end.

TWENTY

"I can't decide if taking a chance on visiting the Koffee Kiln for a dirty chai is worth it or not." I paused outside of Delilah's shop, holding Watson's leash tight as I looked both ways across the street. A long row of cars made their way up Elkhorn Avenue, so Katie, Watson, and I remained where we were. "The caffeine would definitely soothe, but I'm too on edge for any chance of a run-in with Carla."

"Nope." Katie shook her head definitively. "I don't have it in me. Chances are low on a good day, but definitely not right now. And just think, what if Ethel Beaker is in there."

I shuddered and decided my caffeine craving would have to wait. At an opening in the traffic, I started to cross, only to be stopped by a frantic pounding behind us, instantly followed by earsplitting yapping.

As one, all three of us turned around to find Anna Hanson knocking on the inside of Cabin and Hearth's window. Though her words were cut off by the wild, scruffy dog held over her breast, her intent was clear enough.

Katie wobbled in place. "I love Anna, but I don't think I have the strength for her either right now. Any chance we can turn around and pretend we didn't notice?"

"Not on your life." I nudged Katie with my elbow. "And if she's able to read lips right now, you're to blame when we get killed for what you just said."

What had seemed earsplitting from our spot on the sidewalk became nearly migraine-inducing as the three of us walked into the exclusive log-furniture store and Winston's yapping was felt full force.

Anna hurried toward us, not seeming to notice that her dog was gnashing its fangs in our direction. "I'm so glad I caught you. You know it hurts my feelings when you avoid Carl and me, refusing to give us details about the case."

Just when it looked like Winston was going to launch himself for my jugular, Anna lowered him in a sweeping gesture to the floor.

"There you go, my darling." She ruffled his wiry hair. "I know you want your friend."

With his diaper squeaking, Winston lunged, gnawing on Watson's right ear.

Though it took everything in me to remain in place, as he'd done every time before, Watson merely dropped to all fours, looking like a big log, and let the smaller dog tug and yank on his ear with forlorn acceptance.

"Such a sweet boy, no wonder I've always loved you." Anna sighed, and proved just how daring she was by sticking her hand out and scratching Watson's head. "I'm so glad you and Winston are BFFs."

I wouldn't put it like that. It always struck me that Watson had more of a grandfatherly attitude where the little white demon was concerned. I couldn't explain it. There was no other dog in the world Watson would let treat him that way. However, from what I could tell, as aggressive as Winston was, none of it seemed to be done with the intent to hurt Watson. Merely to play.

Carl emerged, saving me from having to figure out what to say. At the sight of him, Katie laughed. "Oh my Lord, Carl, I don't think you've ever looked more adorable."

In response, Carl tilted his head and pulled one of the large fuzzy red earmuffs aside. "Sorry, what was that?"

"Oh, for crying out loud." Anna rolled her eyes, but noticeably didn't swipe at Carl like she normally would have. Instead, she rolled her eyes at us. "Carl's being dramatic. Says that Winston's talking is giving him a headache."

"Well, it is, *if* you can call it *talking*. Don't you hear that? It's like..." Carl paused again, glancing down in surprise as Watson remained motionless under the assault and muffled Winston's noises. "Oh, well, that's much better." He pulled off the earmuffs entirely, letting them hang around his neck. "I'll be right back. I'm going to go get Watson one of his favorite dog bone treats. That's the first time we've had anything close to silence all day."

"You do take on, Carl Hanson." Anna huffed again but grinned after him as he disappeared. "But Watson always deserves a treat, so good call."

"Say that I take on all you want," Carl called back over his shoulder before disappearing through a path that led behind a large log dresser. "There's a reason we've only had two customers today."

Anna grimaced and shocked me by not replying, instead glancing down at Winston as if she didn't

have an argument for that. After a moment, she beck-
oned us to follow her toward the counter. "So, fill
me in."

"You can come too if you want, buddy." I bent
down, getting ready to pat Watson, but had to jerk
my hand back to keep it from getting bitten by
Winston's gnarly fangs.

For the first time, Watson growled, remained
motionless, but showed his own fangs.

Winston hesitated, looking back and forth
between me and the corgi fluffball perch. Though a
low rumble continued in his chest, he quit snarling.

"Careful, Fred," Katie warned as I started to
reach back down.

I hesitated, but pushed onward, testing the
theory. Sure enough, I was able to scratch Watson's
head, and despite the show of sharp little fangs a few
inches from my hand, Winston made no other movement to attack. Pushing my luck, I lowered my other
hand as well so Watson's face was cupped in my
palms. "You do beat all, Watson Page. Just when I
think I have you figured out, you surprise me. I have
no idea why you're putting up with this little—" I
caught myself. "With Winston, but clearly, you're
still the one in charge."

"Here we go!" Carl returned, sounding every bit

like the Santa Claus he resembled. "Treats for everyone! Well, everyone with four legs, that is." He set
the large dog bone purchased from Katie's bakery in
front of Watson, and a smaller version close to where
Winston still roosted on Watson's flank. Before he
could finish depositing the small bone, Winston
lunged, barely missing Carl's fingers.

Watson offered no reprimand.

After making sure all fingers were intact, Carl
cast a quick glance over his shoulder, and finding
Anna out of earshot, turned toward us with a barely
audible whisper. "I don't think I've ever had such
mixed emotions about a living being in my life. On
the one hand, I hate that little devil, but on the other,
he makes Anna so happy I don't know when she's
ever been nicer to me. I swear, she hasn't even
thrown in my face for weeks all the humiliation I put
her through a few months ago."

Chuckling, Katie patted his cheek. "You're a
sweetheart, Carl."

"What are you all doing?" Anna screeched from
farther into the depths of the store. "If you're filling
Carl in on the details of the case, just get ready to
repeat yourself."

With the final check on Watson—who was
chomping lazily away on the dog bone, with Winston

doing the exact same thing from his reclaimed position on Watson's back—I followed Katie and Carl as we joined Anna at the counter.

Despite still being somewhat shaken and angry from the interaction with Jake, I realized I hadn't been in Cabin and Hearth all season—other than glancing in from the windows—and I gaped around the shop. "Guys, this is phenomenal. I feel like I'm on the inside of a gingerbread house." Their shop was bordered in Christmas lights, some of them even wound tightly around bedframes and lampstands. But in addition, pure white streamers interwoven with cellophane lined every plane, making it resemble icing at the seams of gingerbread walls. Apparently they'd gone Christmas decoration shopping with Percival and Gary, as they too had giant candy pieces. Unlike my uncles, Anna and Carl had stayed with only two varieties that they alternated back and forth along the lines of icing—various colored gumdrops, and big swirled peppermints. It was lovely, and a shame their barking dog was scaring away customers.

"That was exactly what I was going for." Anna beamed and laid a hand on her husband's bulging belly. "Carl. It was all Carl. I said, 'Carl, you big bundle of fluff, turn this into a gingerbread house,' and he did." She finished with another pat on his belly.

Carl flushed pink in pleasure.

Anna pulled back her hand, and just like that, the moment was gone. "Okay. Time to fill me in. I just saw you walking out of Delilah's. *Please* tell me she's the one responsible. It would make this town a better place if that hussy was put away for the rest of her life."

"Now, Anna—" Carl started to chastise, but wisely shut his mouth at the glare he received.

"She's not involved at all. In fact, she just stood up to Jake Jazz for me." Katie offered another surprise by coming to Delilah's defense, but she didn't sound reproachful as she addressed Anna. "And don't get me wrong, you and I have always been on the same page about that woman, but..." She shrugged. "Where it counts, I think Delilah may be the real deal."

Anna sniffed. "Easy for you to say. *You* don't have a husband she's constantly trying to steal."

"Anna, sweetheart," Carl cooed. "You know there's no other woman for me but you. I wouldn't look at Delilah Johnson twice." He leaned in, intending to kiss her cheek, but she shooed him away.

Katie and I exchange amused glances. It was true enough that Delilah had a reputation regarding husbands, but it was rather charmingly sweet that Anna thought Carl would ever be in the living pinup's line of sight.

Not wanting to have to go through every single detail, I cut to the chase. "We were at the photography shop to see Jake, not Delilah. He's involved, but we're not sure to what extent. He claims to have not murdered anyone, and at this point we have no choice but to believe that."

Anna raised a warning finger to me. "Maybe so, but mark my words, that man is no good. He's got killer in the eyes if I've ever seen it." Beside her, Carl nodded, though who knew if he truly thought that or if he was just agreeing out of self-preservation.

"I think you're right." I leaned forward, lowering my voice to a conspiratorial level, knowing that if Anna and Carl felt included in our confidences, which they often were, things would go quicker. "What are your thoughts, both of you?"

"Maybe you two haven't heard," Katie chimed in, matching my tone, "but Trevor Donovan, you know, the artist who made the elves, already confessed that he and Finnegan were the ones behind the break-ins."

"Katie, of course they know." I didn't know if it really counted as manipulation to play Anna and Carl like this, but I didn't feel bad about it. I knew they enjoyed the game of it all. "Anna and Carl are the reigning champs, alongside my uncles, as far as Estes Park gossip."

"Oh please," Anna snapped. "Percival and Gary are talented, I'll give you that. But despite what they may say, they have yet to reach Carl's and my caliber. And *naturally*, we knew about Trevor's confession."

"We did?" Carl blinked in surprise.

Anna wheeled on him with a hiss. "Of course we did."

"Oh, well, you didn't tell me." Carl sounded thoroughly hurt.

Anna didn't reply, refocusing on Katie and me. "I must say, I'm still a little miffed that Cabin and Hearth didn't earn a fruitcake with that stupid little elf. I can't understand why we got coal, but at least we weren't murdered. That's a plus, I suppose."

"I *still* say it's stupid that people call them elves. They're gnomes, obviously." Carl sighed, leaning his weight on the countertop. "They're nothing more than those great big hats, beards, and shoes. Total gnomes. Even if the hats aren't the typical gnome-red."

Anna looked on the verge of swiping at Carl but didn't. "For the billionth time, Carl. There's no difference. Elves and gnomes are the same thing. Not to mention, they're make-believe, so what does it matter?"

"Actually..." The bright pitch in Katie's tone—resembling the know-it-all schoolgirl in class with her hand raised and shaking for the teacher's attention—revealed she was about to lay some trivia knowledge. "Elves date back to Norse mythology, eons and eons ago, right alongside trolls, if you'd believe it. Gnomes came along much later."

"See?" Carl nudged Anna with his elbow, proving that he might be getting too confident in Anna's less aggressive behavior, especially when Winston wasn't in her arms. "I've been telling you, those things sold at Santa's Cause *aren't* elves. They're gnomes, just without the red hats."

"Exactly..." Katie nodded and then abruptly switched to shaking her head. "Well... I'm not sure about that, if the things Trevor made were elves or gnomes or not, but they're definitely not the same thing. Plus, elves, at least the Christmas variety—which aren't really the same thing as fae at all—are little more than servants to Santa, making toys for him all year round. I have read stats about how many toys elves would have to make in an hour to supply every child on earth with a present... even if there were thousands of elves, it would amount to little more than forced labor." Katie took a quick breath but launched again before anyone could interject. "Gnomes, despite the statues we stick in gardens today, are more along the lines of satyrs and goblins. Living on their own accord and possessing an affinity for nature and such. In fact—"

"Good Lord, woman." Anna gave an all-over body shake as if cleaning herself off. "Breathe. Breathe." At that moment, Watson arrived at my feet, with the snarling Winston nipping at his heels and catching Anna's attention. She smiled down at them, then leveled her steely gaze on me. "Now, you asked for my thoughts on the matter. Well..." Anna took a deep breath, apparently getting ready to launch into a diatribe just as lengthy as Katie's. "I'd say there are lots of people who wouldn't mind killing that Finnegan character, at least judging from the crowd he ran around with. Absolute scum. Scum, I tell you." She banged her hand on the counter but didn't pause. "But my guess is you'll find the answer in who has it in for his uncle, Marty Clark. Otherwise, why leave the body at his store. Now... I ask you... *who* do you think might have it in for someone who just opened a *second* Christmas shop in town?"

"You're suggesting Gentry Farmer." Katie didn't make it sound like much of a question.

"Right. In. One." Anna swiveled her attention from me to Katie, once more lifting a shaking finger. "I can't believe you two didn't think about it. Good thing you came to see us."

"Actually..." Katie took that tone again. "That's one of the possibilities we've been—"

"Hold on." Something Carl said had been nagging me, but I'd only just figured out what it was. I turned to him. "Carl, what did you mean about the elves, or gnomes, whatever you want to call them... what do you mean about their hats?"

"Well." Carl startled for a second, as if surprised at being called upon in the middle of his wife's theory. "In nearly any picture I've ever seen, gnomes have those great big hats, just like the ones Trevor Donovan makes. Not to mention, he gave them those huge beards, which are also gnome-like."

"Haven't you ever seen a Christmas movie, Carl?" Anna whirled to him once more. "Plenty of Santa's elves have beards."

"No, about them being red, I mean." That familiar sensation rose, that told me the answer was there, if I could only touch it. "You said the elves Trevor makes didn't have red hats, which was the only thing making them different from gnomes."

"Right. Gnomes have red hats. Trevor's don't." Carl looked confused. "At least I don't think so. Every picture I've seen from the break-ins, they've all had various shades of blue and green hats. Emerald, teal, chartreuse, cerulean, pine—"

"Good Lord, Carl." Anna stared at him. "When did you learn all the different names for different color shades? You're starting to sound like Percival."

Despite myself, I couldn't help bursting out with a laugh. "That's actually kind of true. And my uncle would be very proud of you." I smiled at Carl. "But some of the hats *have* been red."

Carl shook his head. "No, I don't think so. I noticed, because with all the different shades of blue, they always struck me as a little more Hanukkah colors than Christmas, though the greener shades, not so much, I suppose. Never mind that they're gnomes to begin with and not elves."

"Oh, saints preserve us! Now gnomes are Jewish, Carl?" Anna sounded thoroughly fed up with being on the outside of this conversation. "If what Ms. Smarty-Pants over here says, they're from the Norse mythology, which means they're Catholic."

"Actually..." Katie's voice returned to that star-pupil tone, and despite Anna's groan, she continued. "The Norse were polytheistic, which means they believed in more than one god. Obviously, that doesn't work for Judaism, or Catholicism for that matter."

I was barely listening, wracking my memory. I was certain I'd seen a red-hatted elf. With a gasp, it hit me. "Finnegan!"

They all three looked at me, but it was Katie who spoke. "What about Finnegan?"

"The elf he held, it had on a bright red hat." I refocused on Carl. "Are you sure all the other elves' hats were in blues and greens?"

He started to speak, but Katie beat him to it as she pulled out her cell. "That's easy enough to check. The newspaper had a picture of the elf in every single break-in, except for Paulie's and Santa's Cause, and the photos are in color online."

Within a few minutes, all of us were gaping at Carl, when his memory was proved true. Anna finally swiped at him, slapping his shoulder hard. "Well, Carl Hanson, look at you. You cracked the case! I don't think I've ever been prouder."

Carl rubbed his shoulder but grinned in pleasure. "Thank you, my dear!" Smile waffling, he angled toward me. "*How* did I solve the case exactly?"

Instead of answering, I turned to Katie. "Can you go to the Santa's Elves website? Are there any with red hats?"

It was only another couple of minutes before we had our answer. She held the phone up to Carl. "A ton of them. This year's entire collection was nothing but red hats."

Disappointment settled in. Even though I couldn't explain, it had felt like a breakthrough. I peered over her shoulder, hoping Katie was wrong. She wasn't, of course. A photo of twenty-five elves, all little more than big red felt boots, ridiculously fluffy white beards, noses in a variety of skin tones, and on top of every single one was a bright red hat. "Wait a second." I pointed to the label above the photo. "It does say this year's collection, but it says Part B."

"Oh, good eye." Katie hummed appreciatively and hit the menu bar. "Let's see what else we can find." Without even having to scroll, she came across the *Collections* tab. The screen was filled with photos of different years' collections, each one having the standard twenty-five elves. And each one had a different theme. Three years ago, all the hats and boots were in various colors, but all of them had the same pattern of white snowflakes as the prominent feature. Two years ago, they'd all been done in shades of pink. The year before, once again in a variety of colors, but all in stripes.

And finally, we found another picture from the current year's collection, this one labeled Part A.

There they were, twenty-five elves, all wearing hats and boots of varying shades of blues and greens.

"That's them." Carl pointed at the phone. "Those are the ones all over town."

"You're right. But I'm certain the elf found with Finnegan's body had a red hat. And I know I've seen more than one of those." I closed my eyes, and without thinking knelt to stroke Watson.

He gave a warning snarl, and there was no Winston-sized bite on my hand.

As I patted him, the vision came back, as did part of my dream from the night before. "Rocking Around the Christmas Tree" played in my memory as the multicolored trees filling Santa's Cause spread out before me. And near the back, in a large glass case on the counter, was a collection of elves all wearing red hats and boots. Superimposing the memory of discovering Finnegan with the dream, it all lined up.

The case of elves.

The elf in Finnegan's grip, its red hat lying over his chest, the tip nearly pointing to his face.

Finnegan's swept-back red hair, causing him to look more put together in death than I'd ever seen him in life.

Gasping, I looked up and met Katie's eyes.

"I know that expression." She grinned. "You just figured out who killed Finnegan, didn't you?"

I nodded. "Yeah, I think so."

"Who?" Carl and Anna said it together, practically shouting it.

I didn't break Katie's gaze. "Marty Clark."

She flinched. "Finnegan's uncle? Why?"

"Don't know." With a final pat on Watson's head I stood, though my own smile grew as I addressed Katie. "Want to go see if we can get him to tell us?"

Considering it took less than seven minutes to walk from Cabin and Hearth to Santa's Cause, the plan Katie and I concocted barely qualified as a plan at all. However, I didn't think we'd require much of one. Even if we only got a few more details, it might be enough to turn over to Susan so the police could handle combining what we gathered with the forensic evidence of different crime scenes. And if, for some reason, Marty Clark got triggered and hostile, Katie and I were together, not to mention the slew of afternoon Christmas tourists milling about.

As the three of us stepped into Santa's Cause and the colorful forest of Christmas trees, Katie and I both stopped dead in our tracks and stared at each other. The music playing through the shop was from the old stop-motion Christmas movie, *Rudolph the*

Red-Nosed Reindeer, and frantic little voices sang the Burl Ives's song, "We Are Santa's Elves."

"Okay, that's just creepy." Katie shuddered. "Like, in every imaginable way."

"I don't disagree." Even without the elfings in Estes over the month of December, the song would've been a little creepy, but as I looked back toward the counter to where we had found Finnegan's body, and lasered in on the case containing the remaining red-hatted and booted elves, a shiver ran down my spine.

The only one unperturbed was Watson, who put his nose to the ground and snuffled here and there looking for crumbs, as far as the leash would allow.

The song was short enough, that by the time we reached the elf display, it switched to the Jackson 5's "I Saw Mommy Kissing Santa Claus." Still, the damage had been done, and if there was any chance of me ever finding elves, gnomes, or whatever they were, cute again, the chance had passed.

Marty Clark rounded the corner, appearing from behind a silvery tree decorated all in teal, with a customer by his side. His gaze met mine, and he halted. There hadn't been much doubt left in my mind, even if I hadn't had definitive proof, but what remained evaporated. He'd aged an astonishing number of years in the few days since I'd seen him last. His eyes were tired, and empty-looking. It could be easily mistaken as grief, but to me it screamed so much more. Pain, yes. But also shame. Guilt from an uncle who had taken the time to lovingly sweep back the long, unruly bangs of the nephew he'd killed.

Marty sighed then gave the customer a gentle smile before waving over one of his employees.

As he walked away, my adrenaline spiked. At his appearance, I wasn't sure if the plan Katie and I had come up with was the right way to go anymore. Marty offered another attempt at a smile and gave a little wave down toward Watson. "Nice to see you again, Mr. Corgi."

Watson looked up, panting, his nub of a tail wagging. Then he whimpered.

With the tiniest bit of the most tired laugh I'd ever heard, Marty gestured over his shoulder to another part of the store out of view. "We've got a station of hot apple cider and bacon-wrapped chestnuts. From the way your dog is drooling, I think he's requesting one."

Leaning forward slightly, I glanced down at Watson again. I hadn't noticed the drooling aspect. "Sorry about that. I didn't realize Watson was having that reaction. I imagine it's a little bit more about the bacon than the chestnuts."

Another motion over his shoulder. "Would you like me to get him some?" Marty winced a greeting toward Katie, including her for the first time. "Or either of you? Not just bacon. You're welcome to the entire appetizers and the mulled cider." Another attempt at a laugh.

"No, thank you." Katie sounded as nervous as I suddenly felt. "But I appreciate it."

"None for me, either, but thank you." Marty's reaction threw me off. The way he scrutinized us, like he knew why we were here, and yet he was offering us holiday hors d'oeuvres?

"Okay then." He smiled again, then walked behind the counter, putting a little space between us before letting out another sigh, one that, unless I was projecting, sounded like defeat. "What can I do for you?"

I struggled not to glance at Katie, trying to determine if she was picking up on the same sense I was. Given that the whole situation was throwing me off, I decided to fall back to our plan, as much as I wanted to ask point-blank if he'd killed his nephew. "If you have a few minutes, I was wondering if I could get a record of all the people who've purchased some of your collection of elves." I gestured toward the case and felt more at ease as I settled into our ploy. "While we were going through the details of the case with Detective Green, we noticed that all the elves left at the break-ins were from the collection that was stolen from you in November."

As I spoke, Marty's eyes widened, just a touch, and he spared a quick glance toward the case. When his gaze returned to me, the defeat I noticed before had been quadrupled, as did my surety.

Even so, I kept going with the ruse. "As I'm sure you heard, Trevor has already confessed that he and Finnegan were behind that break-in to your shop in November and then used that collection in the following break-ins that happened all of this month. But..." I let the pause linger, waiting to see if Marty's gaze would flick to mine again. It didn't, nor did it return to the case of elves. He stared, frozen, gazing at the top of the counter, maybe seeing Finnegan's dead body. "We realized that the elf Finnegan held when he was left here was from *this* collection. So, if we can get a record of who's purchased the ones that aren't here, then we can narrow our suspect list. Unless the elf in Finnegan's hands hadn't been sold yet, and the killer grabbed it out of this case at the time." I hurried on, trying to make it sound as professional as possible. "Of course, I'm not official. If you want Detective Green to get a warrant—"

"How do you know?"

Marty hadn't moved, but for a second I thought he was getting ready to confess. "Excuse me?"

He finally looked up at me again, and had aged another decade in those few seconds. "How do you know the elf came from this collection and not the one stolen before?"

Oh, not a confession. "As I'm sure you've noticed, Mr. Donovan's elf collections have a different color theme every year. The ones that were stolen and left all over town are in shades of blues and greens." I pointed to the case once more. "These, his replacement collection for you, were all done in red."

Marty's shoulders slumped. "And the elf Finnegan held was red." He sighed again, and a tear left his tired eyes.

I nodded, unable to determine just how direct to be.

Katie made the decision for me. Demonstrating both her intuition and compassion, she stretched out her hand and laid it over Marty's forearm. "Mr. Clark?"

He didn't look at her, but Marty shifted his gaze

from where he'd returned to staring at the countertop to Katie's hand on his skin.

Without waiting for any more of a reply, Katie continued, her tone tender. "Why did you kill your nephew? Was it an accident?"

It took all my power to refrain from interjecting, not wanting to give Marty an out.

He continued staring at Katie's hand, more tears fell, and then shuddering, he stared at the elves once more and remained fixated on them as he spoke. "It was kind of an accident. I'd never hurt Finnegan. I loved him. But... yes. I killed him."

"Oh." Katie's hand jerked over his arm, breaking the spell, and he looked toward us.

In his confession, I prepared for him to turn and dart away. He didn't. Instead, his gaze lifted to mine, and his trembling voice spoke softly. "I'd had my suspicions, but I didn't really let them go any further than the back of my mind. But that day when you came in... how Finnegan spoke to you..." He wiped his tears away. "I knew. I didn't want to believe it, but I knew."

Following Katie's lead, I tried to make my tone sound sympathetic. In a way, in the face of his clear pain, it wasn't that hard. "You want to tell us what happened?"

"No." He shook his head, another tear fell, and he wiped it away. "I went to Finnegan's house that night." He choked out a little laugh. "The house I'm paying for, for him and Trevor. When I confronted him, he denied the whole thing. Adamantly." Marty straightened, and for the first time when he looked at us, there was a flash of anger in his eyes. "I went into his bedroom and found that Santa outfit in his closet, not even an attempt to hide it. When I showed it to him, Finnegan just laughed, but still said it wasn't his. I begged and pleaded. Swore that I'd understand and love him no matter what."

As more anger seeped into his tone, Katie finally pulled her hand away.

"Finnegan had a good soul. I swear he did." Marty's lips pulled into snarl as he spoke. "He had too much of my worthless brother, Finnegan's father, running through his veins, though. When he got out of jail, Finnegan wanted a fresh start, away from the rest of the family, away from his father. I'd been planning on moving here and opening a Christmas shop anyway, so I thought it was the perfect chance. Then the opportunity to host Trevor Donovan's elves came along, and it seemed like kismet. Good for the store, and even better for Finnegan. He'd never had much of a chance, no good influence other than me. I thought... seeing Trevor's success, how he conducted himself..."

When his words faded away, I pushed, just a little bit. "You said that Finnegan denied it even when you found the Santa suit?"

"Called me crazy, paranoid. That I was just like everyone else, only thinking the worst of him." Marty's nostrils flared. "He laughed. Finnegan *laughed* at me, then turned around and walked out. He was just going to leave me standing there in the living room. Even left the door open, letting the snow blow in... All the snow was blowing in."

After another pause, Katie prompted the next time. "Is that when you picked up the fireplace poker?"

Marty nodded. "He was halfway down the porch steps. I don't know what came over me. I just grabbed it, ran after him, and... and..." The anger faded and the tears returned.

He didn't need to say any more, we all knew what happened next. "And you put him here, in your shop, so it would look like just another Santa break-in gone bad?"

He nodded.

I got the impression he'd not expected it to work. Not really. "And you smoothed his hair back, didn't you?" I barely whispered the words. "Like you would putting an innocent child to bed."

He choked out a sob, and as tears fell, he nodded again. "Finnegan was such a handsome little boy, and I could still see it there, in him. If he'd only had more of a chance. If only... I'd given him more time."

"Mr. Clark?" When Katie spoke, she sounded like that schoolgirl again, but not the one with all the answers, the tentative one worried about what her teacher might say. "Would you like us to call Detective Green? If you'd rather, we can tell her what you told us so you don't have to go through it again."

I knew that last part wasn't true. Who knew how many more times Marty Clark would have to go over the details of how and why he killed his nephew.

Marty returned to silence once more, and just nodded again.

As I picked up my cell and tapped Susan's name, Elvis Presley began crooning "Blue Christmas" through the shop, and Marty Clark started to cry harder.

TWENTY
TWO

Katie paused in the doorway, her arms laden with all of her hippo Christmas ornaments, looking back at me. "You sure you don't mind being in charge of bringing the desserts to your folks' tomorrow?"

"Of course not. I can't thank you enough for making them. It was fun to do it together, though I'm sorry I burnt one of the trays of lemon bars."

Leo chuckled and pulled the arm he had at my waist tighter. "We'll just call those caramelized."

"Now you're talking like a baker, though *not* one at the Cozy Corgi, I promise you." Katie turned and made it to the end of the porch and gazed out at the starlit forest and mountaintops. "Wow, the snow is really coming down. It's a perfect Christmas Eve."

Watson pushed between Leo's and my legs, trotting onto the porch, followed Katie's example of checking out the weather, then chuffed and hurried right back inside.

He had a point. "You can stay here tonight. I don't want you to take any chances on the road."

Leo's hand flinched at my side, at least I thought it did. "Are you kidding? Katie might claim she's going home, but I've got my money on her swinging by a certain T-shirt maker's place."

Katie glowered. "No, I'm not, but don't worry, Smokey Bear, I'm not going to intrude any further on your first official Christmas Eve together." She winked at me. "And the roads aren't bad, nothing my little car can't manage."

When Leo and I shut the door, we found Watson warming himself by the fire as if he'd been trapped in a blizzard for hours. Sighing, I crossed the room, knelt, and ruffled his fur. "You'll literally tunnel through the snow like a gopher and act like it's a day at the beach, yet *that* was too much for you?"

"Well, you weren't prepared, were you, buddy?" Leo joined in the petting, completing Watson's perfect Christmas Eve plans. "A guy needs a little warning."

"And speaking of not being subtle"—I offered

Leo the side-eye—"someone was pretty obvious about wanting the rest of the night to ourselves."

"I was, wasn't I?" He simply grinned, then stood and offered his hand to me. "I've got big plans for us on our first official Christmas Eve, as Katie said."

I stared at his hand, a flicker of panic rising. "I thought we agreed no actual presents." *I knew I should've bought him something and kept it tucked away in case he did something like this.*

Leo chuckled. "Breathe, sweetheart. There's no present. I wouldn't do that to you and make you feel bad for not having one for me." He gave his hand a small shake. "Now, come on."

Somewhat mollified, I took his hand and stood.

He led me across the room, back toward the front door, but paused to slide his cell phone out of his pocket. He hit a couple of buttons and then sat it on the windowsill by the Christmas tree. The way he angled the speakers, the music amplified over the glass, and Dean Martin singing "I've Got My Love to Keep Me Warm" filled the room. Leo refocused on me. "May I have this dance?"

Despite having been together for nearly a year and friends for over two, I felt my cheeks heat, like we had an audience, other than Watson. "I'm not a great dancer."

Leo shrugged a shoulder and pulled me closer. "That's okay. I've got a whole playlist of romantic Christmas music—which is shockingly hard to pull off, by the way—so you'll get plenty of practice."

Before Dean finished the first verse, I was swaying with Leo by the tree. The living room had already been dimmed and the kitchen lights were off, so only the tree and the fireplace glowed, and with the snow falling on the other side of the window, I couldn't think of a single way it could be any more beautiful.

And then, with his cheek pressed to mine, Leo began to softly sing along.

I reared back instantly, meeting his gaze. "You can sing?"

He shrugged. "In the shower."

I laughed. "We're not in the shower."

"Oh." Another shrug. "Well, I can sing."

"You've been holding out. All the times I have music playing in the car while we—"

Leo stole my words as he kissed me. Even the swaying stopped, and he pulled me tight against him, his lips on mine, one hand at the small of my back, the other slipping into my hair.

In that moment, I knew what I'd known all along. I was safe with Leo, and I loved him. It didn't matter what truths or lies were in the envelope. I was safe with Leo, and he was kind and good. So very, very good.

The next chance I got, I'd throw the thing in the fire.

Leo paused, breaking the kiss and holding my gaze, concern in his low, warm voice. "You okay?"

"Yes." I little more than breathed out the words, like they were a relief. Finally. "More than okay." I searched his eyes in the twinkling lights of the tree and let him search mine. "And I love you."

"I love you." Leo smiled, kissed me sweetly, then began to sway once more.

A few heartbeats later, with Leo singing softly by my ear, Watson began to snore, and I didn't think I'd ever been happier.

Watson growled, his upper lip curling back, revealing wolf-like fangs most people wouldn't attribute to a corgi. After the warning was ignored, he barked, then lunged.

"When he tears half your face off, you've only got yourself to blame." Gary didn't make a move to get up from where he was sprawled in a near turkey-induced coma, over Mom and Barry's sofa.

"Oh, Watson loves it!" Laughing, Percival reared his head back dramatically and then lunged forward again so the mistletoe at the end of a spring attached to the headband he wore nearly bopped Watson on the nose.

Watson sprang again, getting close enough that time that one of his teeth nicked the plastic mistletoe and caused it to bounce back and hit Percival's nose instead.

"Clearly. Watson's obviously having the time of his life." Gary let out a nearly silent belch, then looked to where I sat with Leo on the love seat. "I should've thrown the thing away. But with where I hid it, I would've sworn it was as good as gone. Percival never pays the bills."

"Which proves why I'm a better chess player than you." Percival pointed at his husband, then tapped the headband close to his temple. "You gotta think like your opponent, predict moves, always be a couple of steps ahead. Under the bill pile was *obvious*."

"Even if it did take you weeks."

After snorting at Gary, Percival refocused on Watson and flicked the mistletoe once more.

That time, Watson didn't miss. Snagging the spring between his teeth, he jerked it off Percival's head, then froze in place, looking nearly as surprised as my uncle at his success.

It was Percival's turn to growl. "Now you listen here, pup. That is not to play with. Give it back."

"Run, Watson, run!" Barry called from where he was helping Mom and both sets of twins clear the table from dinner.

Watson did, but instead of running away, he tore straight at Barry, in a mix of panic and pleasure.

Barry was thrown off-balance as Watson's weight crashed into him, and together they rolled onto Barry's back.

"Hand it over!" Percival rushed toward them. "Before it gets broken. That thing is practically an antique"

"*You're* an antique," Barry retorted and pulled the headband out of Watson's grip, which Watson released instantly, and then tossed it across the room. "Okay kids, keep this from your overly dramatic great-uncle who refused, yet again, to try the Tofurky."

The headband landed at my nephews' and nieces' feet, where all four of them sat playing on their cell phones. Christina, the youngest of my nieces, gave it a passing glance, then returned to her screen.

Still laughing, Barry sweetened the deal. "Did I mention there's a hundred dollars in it if you can manage to keep it away for half an hour?"

As one, Ocean, Leaf, Britney, and Christina flung their phones aside and lunged for the headband. Leaf snagged it and took off, followed close behind by his brother, cousins, and lastly Great-Uncle Percival himself, who paused only to shoot daggers from his eyes at Barry and Watson.

"Don't knock over the tree!" Mom called out from the kitchen doorway as the riotous herd tore through the living room. "And Katie almost has dessert ready, so don't be too long."

Somewhere out of sight, a door slammed, and a few seconds later, Percival reentered the living room, wheezing. "I'm too old for this. And I'm not about to go chase those whippersnappers outside. Not in this bitter cold. And not even for that headband."

"Good Lord." Gary shifted on the sofa to bug his eyes out at Percival. "Barry's right—my husband is an antique! When did you start using the term whippersnappers?"

"I know I've said this before, but I love being part of your family." Beside me, Leo chuckled, slipped an arm around my shoulders, and pulled me close. "I mean, don't get me wrong, they're absolutely bonkers, but I wouldn't have it any other way."

Reaching across my chest, I squeezed his hand, tightening his embrace. "Me neither."

I watched Barry continue his love fest with Watson in the middle of the floor, Percival come over to the couch and shove Gary's feet out of the way before plopping down, and my sisters and their husbands returned from the kitchen and gathered around the fire while Mom and Katie finished dessert. There was just a flash as my nephews and nieces raced past the window, the fight over the headband now among themselves, and leaving a billowing swirl of snow in their wake. I vaguely remembered these Christmases—all the holidays, really—used to feel claustrophobic and chaotic. So very different than what I was used to when it had been just Dad, Mom, and me. I would never stop treasuring the time the three of us had together. However, it struck me how unbelievably lucky I was that I got to experience both types of joy. And this loud, chaotic version was pretty wonderful. Especially when I knew at the end of the day, my own quiet little cabin would be waiting with just Watson and Leo at my side.

"Dessert!" Katie called out, making me jump and realize I'd started to nod off.

"I can't do it. I just can't. I'll explode." Gary groaned, rubbing his stomach, then springing off the sofa as if his football days had ended only the week before. "Well, if you insist."

"Please tell me you have the sweet potato pie you made last Christmas." Zelda got up from her place by the fire. "I haven't been able to quit thinking about it all year."

"Or your lemon bars." Verona joined her twin as they left their husbands behind. "I know we can get them at the bakery any day, but there's just something about them on Christmas Day."

"Nope." Leo stood, then extended his hand to me, sweetly helping me up. "With the bakery closed, Katie came over to Fred's, and the three of us spent last night making a whole bunch of fruitcakes."

The room went silent, save for Watson's happy panting as he continued to lick Barry's face.

As one, everyone turned to Katie, who was still standing in the doorway next to my mother. She laughed. "It's true. Lots of fruitcake. Fruitcake roll, fruitcake loaf, fruitcake Bundt, fruitcake cake."

"Oh, well..." Verona gave a forced smile.

Zelda attempted the same, and for once their

faces weren't identical. "I'm sure they will be delicious."

"Are you all nuts?" Percival gaped at the twins, then pivoted toward Katie. "Darling, I love you. And you are a strong, independent, talented woman. But fruitcake?" He sniffed. "I've been called a fruitcake more than once, and while it's meant as an insult, I'd still rather be called that again than have to eat one."

"Hush." Gary swiped at him, reminding me of Anna. "You haven't had Katie's version. She could make coal taste good."

Katie laughed. "I don't know about that, and if I never see coal again it'll be too soon." She went to Percival. "And I didn't say I *only* had a fruitcake. We also may have sweet potato pie, lemon bars, cherry pie, and a chocolate torte. But—" She lifted her finger at Percival, mocking him with his own gesture. "—you're not allowed to have any of them until you've at least tasted my fruitcake. I wouldn't be surprised at all if you forget the others even exist."

He scowled as he muttered, "Some Christmas this is. Bested by a corgi *and* Little Miss Perfect over here."

Proving she'd fully and completely ingrained herself into our family, Katie squeezed both his arms to give herself leverage and hopped up to press a kiss to his cheek. "And don't you forget it."

When the kids had come back inside and we were all once again gathered around the dessert-laden table, Percival declared that the fruitcake was passable, though I occasionally noticed him snagging morsels of it off Gary's plate.

"How are the plans going at the bakery, dear?" Mom looked over at Katie as she sent the platter of lemon bars on their second journey around the table. "Fred told me you've picked out a lovely marble for the countertop."

Katie clasped her hands at her heart in a declaration of true love. "Leathered Bianco Velluto. It's so beautiful that I almost want to send Finnegan a thank-you note for making me..." Her eyes widened, clearly remembering Finnegan's comeuppance. "Um, thank Santa and his elves for an unexpected beautiful outcome at the end of all of this. Really, the whole thing, not just the marble."

Leo hummed his agreement through a mouthful of sweet potato pie. "I'm afraid we might lose our baker to a love of decorating. She designs, she redesigns, and then redesigns again."

Katie blushed. "I may be going a little overboard with the plans. It's true." She laughed. "Nick and Ben aren't helping me in that arena, as they're just as full of ideas as me. But the insurance is covering the total loss of everything, so J—" Her cheeks went even more crimson as she caught herself from finishing Joe's name. "So, we'll get reimbursed, and I figure, there were some ideas that I had at the beginning I held back on. We weren't sure if the bakery was going to be a success or not. Now that it is, well..." She shrugged.

"We're going to splurge," I chimed in. "Honestly, I thought it was perfect before, but I think it truly will be now."

Barry looked at me in surprise. "You're redoing part of the bookshop too?"

"No." I shook my head, tearing off a bit of the back end of crust and passing it down to Watson, who snagged it delicately from my fingers. "I thought about it since the renovations of the bakery are going to be big enough we need to close down for a couple of weeks. But I love the bookshop how it is."

"Oh?" Mom swiveled toward me. "You didn't mention the bookshop was going to be closed for that long. Although it's really the perfect time. There's some New Year's Eve tourism, but nothing like summer or Christmas."

"That's what we were thinking. So, Leo and I decided we'd take advantage of the extra time off." I smiled at Leo as he slipped his hand over mine on the table.

Verona and Zelda screamed in unison, "You're getting married!"

"What? No!" I flinched so hard, I accidentally yanked my hand from under Leo's. "We're taking a trip."

In that split second, Percival had gone pale, but issued a relieved breath. "Oh, thank the Lord. I wouldn't put it past you to try to plan a wedding in a week's time. Knowing you, you'd put all your brides-maids in broomstick skirts, and call it good." He started to take a bite of cherry pie and then looked back up at me, glaring as if I'd done something wrong. "In fact, you'd probably still be wearing a broomstick skirt. You'd find some white thing and pretend it was a wedding dress."

Leo chuckled. "No wedding. If you'll remember, for Fred's birthday I gave her a certificate from Snowy Peaks Travel Agency. We decided to cash it in."

"And we *upgraded* it." I didn't even try to hold

back my excitement. "Between Leo being busy with the uptick in the holiday traffic at the national park, and me with the whole elf debacle, we didn't have time to think about Christmas gifts for each other, so we decided to combine resources and get an even better trip."

"Oh! That's wonderful!" Mom clapped her hands. "Where you going? And for how long?"

"Watson can stay with us." Barry leaned down, wiggled his fingers, and Watson scrambled from his place beside me to receive his affection.

"New York. We thought maybe it would be fine, although intense, to spend New Year's Eve in New York City. Watch the ball drop. Go to a couple of shows on Broadway, see Athena's granddaughter perform." A little tingle of guilt shot through me, but I pushed it aside. "And I'll take you up on the babysitting offer. I feel horrible leaving Watson, but I think he'll be just as happy with you as he would be in New York."

Again, Leo's hand closed over mine, knowing that one complication had nearly made me take a different route. "It's all been really sudden. Just in the past couple of days. I'm honestly surprised they were able to find us decent accommodations so last-minute."

Ridiculously, though I smiled, I couldn't bring myself to say anything more. I truly was excited—to get away with Leo, to see New York City still awash in Christmas lights and snow. Broadway, the bookshops, the bakeries, the winter fairyland that Central Park must be. But... there was a literal ache at the idea of being away from Watson. Since he'd walked into my life, we'd not been apart more than a couple of hours at a time, and even those occasions were rare.

"He'll have the time of his life." Barry smiled gently at me, reading my mind. "I'll even invite Ben over. Watson will be in heaven."

Mom smiled reassuringly at me, and also proving just how well she knew her daughter and that I was getting uncomfortable with all the attention my way, she refocused on Katie, her tone bright and chipper. "Speaking of news, rumor has it, there might be a tall certain someone *you'll* be taking trips with soon enough."

Barry waggled his eyebrows. "Maybe bring him here with you next year."

Once more, Katie became nothing but a bright red blush, and she looked toward me, hair whipping around her face with her speed. "Winifred Page!"

I just shrugged. "Sorry. Mom and I were chatting, and... well... I'm happy for you. That's all."

"We all are, dear." Mom spoke up again, the genuine pleasure in her voice clear. "Joe's a good man. And after all the heartbreak he's been through, he deserves someone as wonderful as you."

Katie cleared her throat, and I knew she was refusing to let tears form. "That's very kind. But it's all a little bit of the cart before the horse, or reindeer before the sleigh, in this case. We haven't had our first date, or even talked about a first date. For all I know, Joe probably just thinks of me as a—"

"Oh, come now." Leo stopped her with a soft chuckle. "How many hours have you two been together designing T-shirts? Fred and I never really had any dates before we—"

"Took forever and a day to get together? Yeah, we noticed," Percival piped up once more, then spun to Katie. "We are happy for you, enough so that I'll admit this fruitcake doesn't make me want to die. But then again, anything with rum inside of it..."

"No joke!" Gary leaned forward, cutting off a huge slice of fruitcake and plopping it on his plate in front of him. "By the time Christmas is over, I'm going to be the size of a hippo!"

Katie gasped and pulled out her phone. "Oh,

speaking of, you have to see these. Fred gave them to me last night while the pies were baking. It's a whole collection of hippopotamus Christmas ornaments. They're the most beautiful things I've ever seen."

I'd planned on spreading them out, but the notion of giving them to her all at once hit me the night before, and it just felt right. And watching her smiling, beaming face as she swiped through picture after picture, describing each hippo in minute detail as if they all couldn't see for themselves, I didn't regret a single bit of it.

With Barry distracted, leaning up on the table to get a better view of the hippo collection, Watson plodded back over, plopped down by my chair, and nudged my elbow with his nose—demanding, rather than requesting affection, in his normal way.

Keeping one hand in Leo's on the table, I lowered my other and stroked his face. As ever, my heart melted as his chocolate eyes beamed up at me in so much adoration it was humbling. I leaned nearer so I could whisper only to him, "Merry Christmas, my sweet, darling boy."

Katie's Fruitcake recipe provided by:

2716 Welton St Denver, CO 80205
(720) 708-3026

Click the links for more Rolling Pin deliciousness:

RollingPinBakeshop.com

Rolling Pin Facebook Page

KATIE'S FRUITCAKE RECIPE

Ingredients:

Fruit:

    1 1/2 C dates, chopped

    1 1/2 C candied fruit

    1 C   candied red and green cherries

    1 1/2 C golden raisins

    3/4 C   brandy or rum

Batter:

    1 C   butter, unsalted

    1 C   dark brown sugar

    1 C   light brown sugar

    3 C   flour, all purpose

    1 t   salt

3/4 t   baking powder

2 t   pumpkin pie spice

4   eggs, large

1/2 C   apple juice

1/4 C   corn syrup, dark

2 C   nuts, pecans and walnuts, toasted

Directions:

1. Combine all fruit with brandy or rum and let sit overnight in glass bowl.

2. Preheat oven to 300 degrees. Lightly grease 2 9X5 loaf pans.

3. Sift together flour, salt, baking powder, pumpkin pie spice and set aside.

4. Cream together butter and sugars until light and fluffy.

5. Add eggs one at a time, scraping bowl well between each addition.

6. Add dry ingredients, juice and corn syrup and mix until combined.

7. Add fruit mixture and nuts to bowl and stir until combined.

8. Bake for approximately 2 hours to 2 ¼ hours (until toothpick stuck in center of the cake comes out clean.

9. Let cool for about 5 minutes, remove from pan.

10. Brush with simple syrup (1/4 C sugar + 1/4 C boiling water) mixed with a small amount of brandy or rum.

AUTHOR NOTE

Dear Reader:

Thank you so much for reading *Evil Elves*. If you enjoyed Fred and Watson's Christmas adventure, I would greatly appreciate a review on Amazon and Goodreads—reviews make a huge difference in helping the Cozy Corgi series continue. Feel free to drop me a note on Facebook or on my website (MildredAbbott.com) whenever you'd like. I'd love to hear from you. If you're interested in receiving advanced reader copies of upcoming installments, please join Mildred Abbott's Cozy Mystery Club on Facebook.

I also wanted to mention the elephant in the

room... or the over-sugared corgi, as it were. Watson's personality is based around one of my own corgis, Alastair. He's the sweetest little guy in the world, and like Watson, is a bit of a grump. Also, like Watson (and every other corgi to grace the world with their presence), he lives for food. In the Cozy Corgi series, I'm giving Alastair the life of his dreams through Watson. Just like I don't spend my weekends solving murders, neither does he spend his days snacking on scones and unending dog treats. But in the books? Well, we both get to live out our fantasies. If you are a corgi parent, you already know your little angel shouldn't truly have free rein of the pastry case, but you can read them snippets of Watson's life for a pleasant bedtime fantasy.

Book Sixteen, Phony Photos, will arrive by the end of March 2020. Thanks to some health issues and life changes, there will be a larger time between books, but Fred and Watson aren't done. Not even close! In the meantime, again, please continue to share your love of the series with friends and write reviews for each installment. Spreading the word about the series will help it continue. Thank you!!!

Much love, Mildred

PS: I'd also love it if you signed up for my newsletter.

That way you'll never miss a new release. You won't hear from me more than once a month, nobody needs that many newsletters!

Newsletter link: Mildred Abbott Newsletter Signup

ACKNOWLEDGMENTS

A special thanks to Agatha Frost, who gave her
blessing and her wisdom. If you haven't already, you
simply MUST read Agatha's Peridale Cafe Cozy
Mystery series. They are absolute perfection.

The biggest and most heartfelt gratitude to Katie
Pizzolato, for her belief in my writing career and
being the inspiration for the character of the same
name in this series. Thanks to you, Katie, our beloved
baker, has completely stolen both mine and Fred's
heart!

Desi, I couldn't imagine an adventure without
you by my side. A.J. Corza, you have given me the
corgi covers of my dreams.

To the Rolling Pin Bakeshop and Jay Thomas,
thank you for providing Katie's recipes from the very

beginning of the series. You and your creations have been priceless. The Cozy Corgi will miss you, and Denver will be a little less delicious without your charming bakery. Katie wishes you all the best in your new adventures!

To the members of Mildred Abbott's Cozy Mystery Club on Facebook, thank you for all your help and feedback. *Especially*, Debby Moran for naming Santa's Cause, and Margie Frentress for naming the Christmas Cottage. Also, Melanie Logan Groover for helping name Drunkin' Donuts and the proprietor, Jed Logan. Samantha Koenig, thank you for making the fruitcake recipe and taking the perfect photo.

A huge, huge thank you to all of the lovely souls who proofread the ARC versions and help me look somewhat literate (in completely random order): Melissa Brus, Cinnamon, Ron Perry, Rob Andresen-Tenace, Anita Ford, Victoria Smiser, Lucy Campbell, Sue Paulsen, Cecelia Stroessner Clark, and Mary Parker Amolsch,. Thank you all, so very, very much!

A further and special thanks to some of my dear readers and friends who support my passion: Andrea Johnson, Fiona Wilson, Katie Pizzolato, Maggie Johnson, Marcia Gleason, Rob Andresen-Tenace,

Robert Winter, Jason R., Victoria Smiser, Kristi Browning, and those of you who wanted to remain anonymous. You make a huge, huge difference in my life and in my ability to continue to write. I'm humbled and grateful beyond belief! So much love to you all!

-the Cozy Corgi Cozy Mystery Series-

Cruel Candy

Traitorous Toys

Bickering Birds

Savage Sourdough

Scornful Scones

Chaotic Corgis

Quarrelsome Quartz

Wicked Wildlife

Malevolent Magic

Killer Keys

Perilous Pottery

Ghastly Gadgets

Meddlesome Money

Precarious Pasta

Evil Elves

Phony Photos (Coming Soon)

(Books 1-8 are also available in audiobook format)